W9-DDJ-125

A *Secret*

IN THE

Shadows

WELLES BRANDRIFF

Copyright © 2013 Welles Brandriff
All rights reserved.
ISBN: 1481805002
ISBN 13: 9781481805001

DEDICATION

For Maria, as always

And for my two daughters, Lisa and Leigh, whose roots are in Okinawa

I

Christie Atherton leaned back in the seat and closed her eyes. The last of the passengers had disembarked from the plane and for the first time in fifteen hours she was alone. The silence washed over her and she basked in its recuperative arms. As was so often the case, the shutting down of one sensory source sharpened the acuteness of the others. She was conscious of the distant sounds of the airport and the low voices of the flight crew as they collected their gear and discussed various dinner options. Familiar sounds. The scents that wafted in through the open door were a mixture of the familiar and unfamiliar. Jet fuel mixed with the heat-scorched smell of the creosote on the tarmac. Laced with those acrid odors were other more pleasant but subtle scents which she couldn't readily identify. With the exception of one. The smell of salt air managed to push through all those sharper scents and titillate her senses. She knew the smell of the salt air on the Northern California coast, on the Cape Cod beaches, and the Florida Keys. Yet this was different from each of the others. It fascinated her how the ocean could have so many different scents.

"Are you feeling all right, miss?"

Christie opened her eyes and looked up at a tall man in uniform standing over her. It was the copilot; she could tell by the three stripes on his sleeves. His voice was a proper blend of professional concern and male solicitude.

"Yes. Thank you. I just thought it would be easier to wait until everyone else got off the plane. Especially the women with young children." Of course, that was only a partial truth. The real reasons were more personal and complex. Christie was conscious of wanting to be alone for a short while so she could savor the moment before she stepped out of the plane and into a new phase of her life. Several minutes later she picked up her carry-on bag, slipped the purse strap over her shoulder and walked quickly to the exit door.

As she stepped off the air stairs onto the tarmac and began walking towards the terminal, the heat enveloped her like some elemental force. Heat unlike any that she had ever experienced before. The sun was low on the horizon over the East China Sea, but she could still feel it burning into her back. Beads of perspiration appeared on her forehead and she could feel others trickling down the small of her back and flowing out along her bra strap. Christie had never felt quite so dirty before. It was bad enough that she had to sit in the same clothes for over fifteen hours without being able to shower and change. Of course she had tried to freshen up in the washroom just before they landed, but now she felt sticky and dirty again—even worse than before. She just had to get into the ladies room and do whatever she could before meeting Sally Rehnquist. Christie hoped she would be late. It would be mortifying to meet her sponsor in her present condition.

Hurrying into the terminal, Christie looked around for the sign to the ladies room while scanning the room quickly to see if she could spot anyone who looked as though they were waiting for her. Good. There was no sign of anyone yet. What might have been a source of irritation on another day was a blessing at this time. Pushing through the door to the ladies room, she found to her relief that it was designed for a single occupant with only one stall and wash basin. An air conditioner of uncertain vintage rumbled away in a small upper window. She noted with a sense of resignation that the air inside the room was only marginally cooler than that outside. But at least there was some movement to it which gave one the sense of a cooling effect.

Taking a washcloth out of her travel bag, Christie dampened it and held it against her forehead before applying it to the nape of her neck. It was a balm to her spirits and she luxuriated in the small pleasure. Reaching beneath the neckline of the dress, she patted as much of her skin as she could comfortably reach with the cool cloth. The idea of slipping out of her dress crossed her mind but she resisted the temptation. Sally might have arrived and be looking around for her; besides it wasn't fair to tie up the only ladies room for any longer.

Pulling out her hairbrush, Christie tilted her head to one side and brushed her hair vigorously for a minute. After applying a fresh layer of lipstick, she stopped in front of the full length mirror before reaching for the door knob. Christie wasn't exactly thrilled with the image that looked back at her. A woman of medium height with a lush full figure. She wrinkled her nose in annoyance at that thought. Lush indeed! More like heavy, or chunk-style as her stepbrother used to teasingly refer to her.

But there were some positive things. Tanned shapely legs that had no need for a pair of stockings. Perfect teeth and of course the shoulder-length, honey blonde hair which was arguably her best feature. The tan sleeveless dress with its narrow vertical black stripes was a favorite because it made her appear taller than she actually was. Christie shrugged as she turned the doorknob and stepped back out into the terminal, reminding herself for the hundredth time that the main reason for her journey to Okinawa was to search for information about her father, not impress all the men on the island.

A young mother with two small children pushed by her before Christie was halfway out the door. Feeling a little guilty, Christie mumbled an apology and took three quick strides towards the side entrance when a resonant male voice directly behind her called out:

"Christie ?"

Before she even turned around Christie recognized Quint Brewster's voice. *What the hell was he doing here?*

"What are you doing here? Where's Sally Rehnquist?"

"She's tied up in a meeting."

"She sent you to pick me up?"

"Yeah."

"How do you happen to know her?"

"She spends a lot of time at the Officer's Cub."

"Which means you must also."

"Not necessarily."

Taking her travel bag in one hand and suitcase in the other, Quint directed Christie to the door to the parking lot, then guided her towards a nondescript-looking, late fifties Chevy. Behind it was a dense bank of flowering shrubs including the ubiquitous bougainvillea, a reminder that Christie was far removed from northern New England. As she bent down to slide into the seat, her dress slid up, partially revealing a shapely golden thigh. Out of the corner of her eye she saw Quint's appreciative glance at something which had been revealed for only a fleeting moment.

A pair of phantom jets flashed overhead with a deafening roar just as Quint reached for the door handle on the driver's side. Pausing by the open door, he watched them until they faded into the distance. When he stooped down to squeeze his large frame into the car Christie was struck

4

by the power he exuded. As Quint backed the car out of its parking space and started towards the main gate, his expression made it clear that he was determined to avoid any conversation with her. That was fine with Christie. If he was going to continue to be pigheaded, she'd use the opportunity to acquire some first impressions of her new home.

The military presence was a ubiquitous feature of the landscape—that was obvious—at least in this part of the island.

Christie noticed a large, multi-level white building sitting on the side of a steep hill and decided to take a chance and ask Quint about it. Big mistake.

"What's that? The commanding general's headquarters?"

"No."

"No? What is it then?"

"An officer's club."

"The one where Sally hangs out?"

"No."

She wondered if monosyllabic answers were his MO with everyone or just with women who spoke their mind.

"So where do the Okinawans live? The only thing I've seen so far are military buildings, warehouses and long stretches of cyclone fences with KEEP OUT signs."

"They're around."

"Where?"

"Everywhere."

"Where is everywhere?" she snapped.

"All over the island. There's no one particular location where you'll find them."

"Do you know any of them?"

"Sure. One of the local women cleans my house, does my laundry, and makes an occasional meal for me."

"And that's it?"

"Yes."

"Does she speak English?"

"A little."

"Do many Okinawans speak English?"

"No."

"Did you ever consider taking any Okinawan language lessons?"

"Oh sure," Quint said, rolling his eyes, "I was thinking about playing a recording of Okinawan phrases while I sleep. That way I can learn by osmosis. A nice painless way to go about it don't you think?"

Damn this man and his chauvinistic attitude. Burdick and Lederer could have used Quint for a role model when they wrote their book *The Ugly American.*

Still, as annoyed as she was with Quint, there was a remote corner of her mind where Christie still held memories of the mesmerizing effect that his presence had on her. And buried among those memories there flickered a small flame of interest that had never been fully extinguished. Not yet, anyway.

Quint cursed under his breath as a small Okinawan cab cut in front of them and darted down a narrow gravel side road. "Look, Christie I don't mean to sound callous, but the typical American simply doesn't spend much time thinking about the Okinawans. Like I said, they clean our homes, do our laundry, fix our cars, and wait on our tables. So you could say that they're a part of our lives but not a part of our lives, if you know what I mean."

"That sounds pretty damn callous to me," was Christie's response. "Do all our dirty work and menial labor but don't expect us to acknowledge your existence in any other setting!"

Quint shrugged, refusing to be drawn into another argument with her. He was still feeling guilty over the way he'd treated Christie at his sister's apartment back in July. Besides, he grudgingly admitted to himself that there was something refreshing about her concern for others. It was yet another unneeded reminder of how little interest Cally Lameroux displayed in anyone or anything outside of her own field of interest.

"People don't have to socialize in order to have a satisfactory relationship." Quint countered. "As a matter of fact, Americans and Okinawans are connected in a number of ways. A lot of them have jobs with the U.S. military. Not surprisingly, the Okinawan economy is heavily dependent on the continued presence of U.S. troops."

"But that dependence can be a source of deep resentment, Quint. Don't you remember from your high school history classes how the colonists in Boston and Philadelphia felt when the British soldiers were quartered there?"

"Yeah, but the Brits were the enemy. We're here to help the Okinawans."

"Even so, people who are in such a position don't normally have feelings of gratitude towards the country they're dependent on, even if it does benefit them."

"Well, they should. They're a lot better off economically. And despite all the help we give them we're hemmed in by all kinds of restrictions that are designed to benefit the Okinawans at the expense of the Americans.

"Do you know, for instance, that I'm not even allowed to own the land that my house sits on, because I'm a foreigner? And I pay an exorbitant amount to the Okinawans for electricity each month in spite of the fact that the electricity is generated with U.S. government equipment and maintained by our military technicians."

Quint's frustration was building towards a crescendo as he jabbed at the steering wheel to emphasize each point. "I could cite a dozen more instances: for instance, if you're not an Okinawan the typical wait for a phone to be installed is a year—one year, mind you—and then it takes about a half an hour to make a simple local call. Here's another example:

there are certain times of the day when American cars are not even allowed on the main highway because it might interfere with Okinawan traffic. It's the Americans who are subjected to endless restrictions and aggravations!"

Christie refused to be mollified. "Why shouldn't Americans be subject to restrictions? This isn't our country even though we act like we own it. The Okinawans should be free to live their lives and shape their own destiny without having someone standing over them making decisions for them."

Quint stared fixedly at the road ahead as he tried to rein in his anger.

Christie suddenly grew very quiet, as if dealing with some painful memory that had abruptly surfaced in her mind. "I wonder what it was like here? During the war, I mean."

Quint wasn't sure whether she was talking to him or just thinking out loud.

"Haven't you ever read anything about the battle that took place here? Wasn't that part of your required reading before you came here?"

Christie shook her head. "I find violence repulsive. I don't even like to think about it. It's just horrible—the way people, countries treat other."

When Quint spoke again, his tone was less strident. "Yeah, it must have been a living hell all right—for everyone caught up in the battle. To this day, the Okinawans refer to it as the typhoon of steel."

"Typhoon of steel?"

He nodded. "The naval gunfire and aerial bombing were so intense that even the topography of the place was changed. Especially from Kadena south where the heaviest fighting took place. The Americans and Japanese all suffered heavy casualties, but I have to admit that the Okinawans suffered the worst. More than a hundred thousand of them were killed."

Christie's innate compassion for others less fortunate momentarily dampened her spirits as she tried to picture what it must have been like for someone, anyone— but especially a young child—to be caught up in that horror. Her sensitive imagination etched such strong images on the photographic plate of her mind, that her eyes began watering. She found herself identifying with the terrors of being a child in an alien and uncaring adult world.

Quint glanced over at her and noticed that she had clasped her hands on her lap and was staring unseeing at them. He would come to realize in time that was a sign she had been deeply moved by something and was momentarily swept away in a cascade of emotions.

He would also come to understand that one of the most beautiful qualities about Christie was her ability to empathize with others—to the point where she made their hurt, her hurt.

The traffic had slowed to a crawl as the two southbound lanes converged into a single lane through the construction area. It finally came to a complete halt while some heavy equipment was being off-loaded from several large flatbeds. Quint turned off the engine and rolled down the window.

"Sorry about the loss of the air conditioner, but the engine will overheat if I keep it running."

Christie glanced over at him. "That's all right. I've been hot and uncomfortable for much of the past twenty-four hours. Another few minutes won't make any difference." But it wasn't just the heat. There was also the dust. And now this terrible stench, she thought, wrinkling her nose in disgust.

Quint chuckled at her expression. "Welcome to the real Okinawa!"

"What is that!"

"That's the smell of the binjo ditches."

"Binjo ditches?"

"The local sewer system," Quint responded, dismissing it with a shrug of the shoulders.

"Do you smell this everywhere on the island?"

He shook his head. "No. And mainly at this time of the year. A good reason for keeping the windows up and the air conditioning on." Leaning forward, he placed both hands on the top of the steering wheel and rubbed his chin on the back of them absentmindedly. After staring at the distant construction activity for a couple of minutes, he abruptly twisted in his seat and said to her:

"Look, I apologize for being short with you. Not that it's an acceptable excuse, but I've had a lot to contend with lately, and the pressure just seems to keep mounting."

"It isn't all your fault, Quint, any more than it was at that luncheon back at Lisa's place."

But it's more than just being short with me, it's your attitude towards the Okinawans. When you went on about them at that luncheon back at Lisa's place I began seeing you in a different light. You know, when you risked your life to pull me out of the lake that day we went skating, all I could see was your genuine compassion for someone who was in trouble. Was that simply because I was a white American?"

No. I'm not like that, Christie."

"Well, what's the problem, then?"

"Okay, I might have come down on them a little too hard. I admit that."

"Is that because you hold them responsible for getting grounded?"

"Well, they are—sort of."

"What do you mean?"

"It's a long story, Christie."

"I'm a good listener."

"I was taking off from a short runway up in the northern part of Okinawa and just as the plane broke ground an Okinawan civilian drove a bulldozer right across our flight path. I was still fairly low to the ground so I hit the dozer a glancing blow and killed the driver, of course. Anyway I managed to fly the plane down to Naha and land it safely but there was hell to pay because the driver turned out to be the brother of one of the top Okinawan politicians."

"So they hold you responsible."

"Yeah."

"Were you?"

"No way. But the investigation is still underway."

"What are they looking for?"

"Evidence to support my contention that the plane was overweight."

"How could that have happened?"

"The marines loaded a six by six with ammunition and didn't inform our loadmaster."

"Six by six?"

"A truck."

"Oh. So that meant you were still low to the ground after you got into the air?"

"Yeah. Now the guy shouldn't have been driving across the flight path but if we hadn't been so heavy we probably would have cleared the bulldozer. It was the marines' fault as far as I'm concerned, but they're trying to cover their butts and shift the blame onto me. It's another example of inter-service squabbling."

"So, what's likely to happen?"

"I don't know. But I've been temporarily grounded until they clear this up."

"So this has become a political hot potato?"

"That's about the size of it."

But if it's only a few Okinawan politicians responsible for your grounding, don't you think it's unfair to take your resentment out on all of them?"

He shrugged. "Maybe.

Christie started to say something further, then thought better of it and decided to change the subject. The traffic had started to move again and the military flavor to the scenery had disappeared. In its place was a stretch of highway jammed with every imaginable kind of business from used car lots, rental stores, and glass factories to restaurants, dairy bars and souvenir stores.

"This stretch of highway looks like it could have been transplanted from somewhere in the states."

Quint nodded. "The Okinawans have developed a taste for just about everything American. So you're just as likely to find them as us in many of these places."

Christie studied him circumspectly while he was preoccupied with the traffic. She had to admit, he was one of the sexiest men she had ever known. But also one of the most chauvinistic.

"Since you're not flying any more, what do you do?"

"I run one of the large maintenance sections in the Wing."

"Does a job like that call mainly for management ability or do you also need technical skills to go along with it?"

Quint was impressed. That was a very good question. He liked that. And he couldn't help thinking that it never would have crossed Cally's mind to ask him such a question. In fact, in the ten months he had known her, she had rarely asked him anything about what he did.

"Most of the maintenance officers have at least a general knowledge of the technical side of the job. That goes along with the training they've had. But they're mainly called upon to make management decisions."

"But your degree is in hydrology, isn't it?"

"Uh huh."

"So how does that make you qualified in the aircraft maintenance field?"

"I went through a tech school program back in the states but my engineering background helps me to understand the technical issues—for the most part, anyway—even though it wasn't an aeronautical engineering program."

"My stepfather's an aeronautical engineer."

Quint had no response to her comment, so Christie assumed he had not heard what she said or didn't care.

He continued, "Actually, the technical issues are usually the least of my problems. Once you fix them they tend to stay fixed. It's the so-called management problems that give me the biggest headache. There's never any easy solution, so they don't tend to go away. The other problem is I've got a number of additional duties that take up a lot of my time.

"By the way," he said, changing the subject as he waved his hand in the general direction of the scene outside the window, "that was the main business district in Naha—such as it is—that we just passed through, and that's Tomarii port coming up on the right."

II

As they passed through the entrance to Naha Air Base, Quint slowed down and held up his I.D. badge for the gate guard to see, while casually returning his salute.

"Is that just for show or do the guards really mean business?"

"No. They take their jobs seriously.

"Even though they're Okinawans?"

"That was a cheap shot. Christie."

She shrugged. "Maybe."

At this point they were passing through a housing area which was at least equal to what one would see in an upper middle-class suburb in the states. Large three, or perhaps four, bedroom ranches with immaculately maintained lawns and shrubbery lined side streets with names such as Wisteria Drive, Mimosa Lane, and Magnolia circle.

"Is there some requirement that the lawns have to be cut at least once every week?" Christie asked light-heartedly, fully intending it to be taken as nothing more than a casual comment.

"Absolutely," Quint responded. "If you let your lawn go you get one warning from the base commander's representative. If you get a second warning it could lead to an Article 15."

"What's an Article 15," Christie said, although she had a pretty good idea even before asking the question.

"It's an administrative punishment. Obviously, nothing like a court martial, but not the kind of thing you would want in your 201 file. "Sorry," he said, "I mean your personnel record."

"The punishment seems a little excessive when you take into consideration the nature of the misdemeanor."

"This is the military," Quint said firmly, "and anyone who joins should expect that the freedom of choice which is appropriate in civilian life simply isn't an option in this environment."

Christie studied him thoughtfully, a trace of a frown on her face. "I'm not sure that I agree with the idea of anyone having so much control over what is obviously a non-military issue."

"But it isn't a non-military issue; that's my point," Quint retorted, the irritation once again present in his voice.

"I can see that I've got a lot to learn about the military."

Quint looked at her curiously. "If you're going to be around the military for a while it would be a good idea." Abruptly changing the subject, he said: "Where do you want to be dropped off?"

"How about the Officer's Club? If Sally spends as much time at the Club as you say then maybe she'll turn up there after her meeting."

"That works out fine for me. I was supposed to meet a friend there for a drink anyway."

Christie gave him a quick look, wondering idly if the friend was male or female. Quint's next comment answered that question. "Rick has been looking forward to meeting you ever since he saw that picture of you that Lisa gave me."

Christie looked at him with a puzzled expression on her face. "What picture are you talking about?"

"The photo of you and Lisa taken last summer up at Acadia."

"Oh. That one. And who is Rick, by the way?"

"My best friend."

Christie looked out the window just as they turned onto a narrow tree-lined drive that overlooked the main runway and the harbor just beyond. The late afternoon sun shimmered with such brilliance on the distant water that she found it painful to look at even with sunglasses on. Up ahead a low two story white structure with a circular drive in front came into view. It looked like a smaller, less pretentious version of the club she had noticed shortly after leaving Kadena.

Quint dropped her off at the front door and told her to wait inside where it was cool while he went and parked the car.

Being inside wasn't a lot more comfortable than being outside in the heat, she immediately decided. The air conditioning actually felt cold compared to what she was used to. The interior was dark and it took her eyes a few minutes to adapt to the change. A casual survey of her surroundings convinced her that there must be some universal design which served as the pattern for places such as this. A few slot machines just inside the entrance, a cigarette machine, a few strategically placed plants and the usual drab decor were all that greeted her eyes. The stale smell of liquor and cigarette smoke permeated the atmosphere, reminding her of how much she disliked such places.

Quint stepped through the door just as she completed her brief inspection. Placing her bags in the cloakroom on a low shelf, he suggested they go downstairs for a drink since it was apparent that neither of the people they were to meet had arrived yet. Christie agreed, but with mixed feelings. On the one hand, she had been looking forward to a nice glass of wine but would have preferred to enjoy it alone.

"What would you like to drink?"

"A glass of white wine please." She glanced idly around the room as he walked over to get their drinks. The lounge consisted of a semi-circular bar at one end of the room, a dozen or so small cocktail tables with matching chairs, and a baby grand piano shoved into one corner of the room. There was a small dance floor of parquet design and a juke box in an adjacent corner. The walls were decorated with a number of flight scenes and what appeared to be a series of photographs of the chain of command starting with the local base commander and ending with the Chief of Staff of the Air Force. A large bulletin board near the entrance was covered with hundreds of small business cards. When Quint returned to the table with the drinks she asked him about the cards.

"Air force protocol requires that each officer have a card to leave when they attend official functions. The idea of going beyond the usual mundane format started with some of the hotshot fighter pilots in Vietnam. Now everyone's into the act, all trying to outdo each other with the cleverness of the design and message on their card. It's sort of become a craze."

"So civilians aren't the only ones who get caught up in such things."

"Of course not. We're not that much different from the rest of the population you know," Quint said, with a touch of whimsy in his voice. Before he could say anything more, she had picked up an earlier thread in their conversation.

"You were saying before that the most aggravating part of the job was the managerial responsibilities. What are some of the typical kinds of things that you have to deal with?"

Quint looked at her with the same curious look she had seen in his eyes a couple of times before. "I can't imagine that you'd really want to hear about my problems. I think I'd rather hear more about your hopes for your teaching assignment here. Do you really think that your teaching experiences are going to be that much different than those back in the states. After all, these are still typical American kids of American parents attending what are presumably typical American schools. Right?"

Christie took a sip of her drink while she gathered her thoughts. "How long have you been outside of the country?" she asked.

"A couple of years, if you don't count a few brief trips back to the states including the one back in July."

"So you must have some idea about what's been going on back home."

"Sure. I can read the headlines as well as anyone else."

"Then, you must be aware of the spirit of rebellion that's sweeping through the country. It's affecting—or maybe I should say infecting—everything in our culture, including, of course, the educational process. I found that I was spending less and less time teaching and more and more of my time disciplining the students. Not only wasn't that what I got into teaching for but, admittedly, being a woman made it even more difficult than it was for the typical male teacher. That's one of the main reasons that I came out here; I assumed that I wouldn't find the same situation in a military setting."

Quint appeared to be engrossed in making a series of interlocking concentric rings on the tablecloth with the bottom of his glass, but Christie sensed that he had been listening carefully to what she was saying. He leaned back and folded his arms across his chest, while appearing to study the design he had just created.

"You're right. You won't—or shouldn't anyway. But that's an interesting observation. Very interesting, in fact, because it sheds some light on a problem that I've been dealing with. You knew the reason I was back in the states in July was to attend a conference on training issues."

Christie nodded.

"Well, on the flight back to Okinawa I kept thinking that what I had learned at the conference didn't seem to address the problem. But I wasn't sure exactly why. What you just said though was like finding the missing piece to a puzzle." He was quite enthused now, and leaning forward, pressed the fingers of one hand against the corresponding fingers in the other hand, as if he was fitting something together.

"The way I see it . . . ."

"Quint! There you are. Rick said he was supposed to meet you here. I've been looking all over for you!"

Christie looked up as one of the most stunning looking women she had ever seen walked quickly across the room to their table. Quint had barely risen from his seat when she threw her arms possessively around his neck and gave him a long hard kiss on the lips. "You can't imagine how much I've missed you over the past two weeks. It seems like you've been gone for months," she said, as her fingers traced a suggestive path down the row of buttons on the front of his shirt. Quint looked visibly embarrassed as he gently but firmly disengaged himself from Cally's embrace.

"Hi Cally," he said, without much enthusiasm. Turning back to Christie, Quint said, "Meet Christie Atherton. She's a teacher and has just arrived in Okinawa from the states. Christie this is Cally Lameroux."

Cally gave Christie a cursory glance as she nodded in her direction then turned back to Quint and said with a tone of urgency in her voice:

"We have to talk. I want to talk about—you know—that last night. It's important that we clear the air about exactly what happened. Looking down at Christie, she turned back to Quint and motioned for him to follow her over to another part of the room. Quint just as insistently said in a low voice, "Not now. We'll talk later."

Christie wasn't surprised that Quint was involved with someone. With his looks he was bound to be a target for all kinds of women.

Standing up abruptly, Christie turned to them and said, "Look, if you want to have a private conversation why don't you stay here and I'll leave. This is about the last place I want to be on a sunny summer afternoon anyway." Quint reached out to her, obviously flustered by the awkwardness of the situation. "Christie please wait . . . ."

To hell with you, she thought, as she strode decisively across the room to the stairs leading up to the main level. Just before reaching the top of the stairs, Christie glanced back over her shoulder but Quint and Cally were no longer in sight.

Christie had no idea what she was going to do now, but as luck would have it she ran into Sally Rehnquist just entering the O Club.

III

"So tell me what brings you to Okinawa?" Sally was saying, "And please don't give me the line about wanting to serve your country in some small but tangible way and that teaching the children of our men in arms seemed to be the best way for you to contribute to the war effort."

"Okay, I won't. Because it isn't true. And to be perfectly frank, I'm completely opposed to our involvement in Vietnam. In fact, I have a problem with the way the United States asserts its power in a number of places around the world. Including here on Okinawa." Now, having admitted that," she said, light-heartedly, "do you still want me as a housemate?"

"Of course—but on a serious note, Christie—if I were you, I wouldn't go around advertising your views. I'm sure you're not going to be surprised when I tell you that the overwhelming majority of the people here are strong supporters of the war."

"I assumed as much. But what about classroom discussion?"

"What about it?"

"Well, don't your lessons occasionally lead into discussions about current issues? After all, you are a history teacher."

"So far I've managed to waltz around any controversial topics."

"Not to change the subject, but how far do we have to go to get to your house?"

"About seven miles. The area is known as Ojana and we live in Ojana Heights."

"What kind of a neighborhood is it?"

"Mostly Americans with a few Filipino families thrown in."

"No Okinawans?"

"Nope. Not in this particular housing area."

"Where do they live then? Quint said they're scattered all over the island."

"That's true but our house is right squat in the middle of the three biggest population centers on the island. Koza City and Ginowan City to the north of us and of course Naha City to the south."

"Is there any tension between the Okinawan and the American communities?"

"No, not that I know of."

"I just wondered," Christie said, having decided not to tell Sally about her conversation with Quint, "what with the dramatic difference in living standards. Plus the fact that Americans tend to stick to themselves and don't bother to learn the language. And then there's the case that we're squatting on some of their best land. It seems like that would be enough to cause some bad feelings between the Okinawans and the Americans."

"Maybe, but it's not my problem. My eighty odd high school students are more than enough to contend with. I don't have the time or energy to deal with anything more than that. By the way, from a teacher's standpoint, the main advantage of living in this area is that it's conveniently located between the major military bases. If we need to get stuff at either the Commissary or Base Exchange, we have a choice of Kadena, Futenma or Naha."

"And don't forget the 'O' clubs . . . ." Christie added, aiming a gentle dig at Sally's penchant for frequenting the officer's clubs in her free time. Several of the letters Christie received had apparently been penned while Sally was in the Naha Officers Club.

"The 'O' Clubs. Right. And yes, I probably do spend too much time hanging out there," she said, acknowledging, by that admission, that Christie's quip had not slid by unnoticed. Christie had the distinct feeling that Sally had no desire to pursue that particular topic.

Around twenty minutes later they pulled into a small driveway that was barely big enough to accommodate a single car.

"Your new home, Christie."

My new home, Christie thought, rolling the phrase around in her mind. In a way, Okinawa would have to become like a home to her. During the long flight over, she had become more and more convinced that it was an Okinawan who held the key to her father's personality change. That meant that the better acquainted she became with the people and the culture of this small island country, the greater her chances of making some headway in her search for information about her father. If she could get to know some of them and gain their trust the end result might be the opening of doors that would otherwise have remained closed to her.

But where was she to begin this quest? What should her first step be? Who was going to help her? Every time she started thinking about it, more questions popped into her mind. Maybe it wasn't even feasible. Maybe Quint was right and she had greatly underestimated the amount of effort that would be required in order to uncover information on someone who had last been on Okinawa over two decades earlier.

Christie sighed as she reached into the trunk and began tugging away at her oversized suitcase. In any event, it was too soon to begin fretting about it. Her immediate job was to settle down into a routine as quickly as possible and be prepared to start teaching in less than a week's time. It was clear that her quest would have to be carried out in such a manner so as not to interfere with her teaching responsibilities. The first steps in the search for information about her father would just have to wait. At least for the next few weeks. Not to mention her research on the Okinawan woman.

"Go on in," Sally said, pushing the door open with one hand while holding Christie's carry-on bag with the other. Christie was still wrestling with the large suitcase that held virtually her entire wardrobe of warm weather clothing. Once inside, Sally directed her to the spare bedroom. "I'll help you unpack a little later but I'll give you a quick tour of our palatial residence first then I'm going to prepare a stir-fry for your first meal on Okinawa. I got the chicken and veggies ready this morning." Although the tour of the house was really unnecessary, Christie followed Sally dutifully around from room to room.

The back side of the house consisted of two bedrooms with a bathroom in between. The front side included a good size, combination living room and dining area, a medium size kitchen with enough space to hold a small table at which two people could comfortably sit, and a laundry room. Since wood was relatively scarce resource on Okinawa, the floors throughout the house were covered with a flat black tile. The furniture was an eclectic mixture of contemporary American pieces and the ubiquitous rattan style that was common throughout the Far East. Christie soon learned that it was provided gratis to all DOD teachers by the military housing office at Kadena. The picture windows in the living room had drapes and the small windows in the bedrooms, curtains. The drapes were made of fine brocade and had the look of being professionally sewn. The curtains, however, looked as though they had been handmade by someone whose talents lay in another direction. The windows themselves had wooden frames and were the type that opened horizontally by sliding sideways along a grooved path in the sill.

"Do you ever open the windows?" Christie said, as she looked out her bedroom window at their small back yard.

"No. Well . . . once in a while. When it's a little too cool for the air conditioner but not really that cold yet. But I generally keep them closed and locked."

"Why?"

"Well, not to alarm you, but we have had occasional problems with small groups of Okinawan teens that specialize in breaking and entering."

"Are they dangerous?"

"No, not really. And there haven't been any problems with them in this area for several months now anyway. Besides, we pay a local Okinawan man to patrol the grounds each night. Whenever someone new moves into the neighborhood he appears at the door and explains in his broken English that he'll be glad to extend his nightly rounds to include their house."

"That sounds like a form of protection money to me."

"Well, I guess that's what it amounts to, but it's only five dollars a month so what the heck. That's not much to pay for a little peace of mind."

"I suppose." Christie said, following her roommate back out into the living room. As Sally headed for the kitchen to get dinner started, Christie paused for a minute and surveyed the living area with a critical eye. Utilitarian, but comfortable. That was her judgment of the place that would be her home for at least the next ten months. "Sal, I've really got to take shower before I do anything else. I feel absolutely disgusting. I can't imagine how anyone could even stand to be around me."

"I thought you might want to, so I left a clean set of towels and a face cloth in the bathroom. I'm going to do some final prep work in the kitchen for dinner."

"I won't be long at all. And then I'll be glad to help you out." Christie walked into her bedroom, flipped open the suitcase and pulled out clean lingerie, a short sleeve blouse, shorts, and a pair of clogs. She undressed quickly, slipped into a cotton bathrobe, and headed down the hallway to the bathroom. Moments later a short startled cry brought Sally running in from the kitchen.

"What's the matter?"

"That!" Christie said pointing to a small green lizard on the sidewall of the shower.

Without even bothering to take a look at what Christie was pointing to, Sally said, "Those are geckos."

"Geckos?" She had already deduced that it was nothing to be concerned about by Sally's muted response.

"They're small lizards. Harmless little tikes, actually. In fact, I think they're kind of cute."

"What do they do?"

"What do you mean 'what do they do'?"

"Well, are there many of them around the house? Am I likely to find them swimming in my soup or sharing my bed with me at night?

"Nah. They just hang around up near the ceiling and meditate about things like—well, like where their next meal is coming from and whether or not the new lady in the house is going to pose a threat to their peaceful existence. Stuff like that."

"I guess that means I'm not supposed to worry about them, right?"

"You've got it. When you finish your shower I'll give you a complete briefing on what else you can expect to find sharing space with us in the house."

When Christie stepped out of the shower several minutes later it was with a deep sense of relief. Cleanliness may not have been next to Godliness but it was right up there in the top tier. Dressing quickly, she walked back out into the kitchen. As she did, Christie mentally ticked off the number of air conditioning units she had observed so far: one in each bedroom, two in the living room, and one in the kitchen. Only the large unit in the living room and the one in the kitchen appeared to be running right now and it felt and sounded as though they were on low cool. That was a good sign. She hated everything about air-conditioning while reluctantly admitting that it was a necessity in certain places and at certain times of the year.

"I'll start working on the salad," Christie volunteered, as she opened the refrigerator door and began removing the salad greens. "And by the way I'm glad you aren't one of those people who need to have the house air-conditioned cold. I couldn't live like that."

Sally had poured a little peanut oil into a wok and was swirling it around to make sure the surface of the pan was evenly coated. "Well, even if I liked it frigid—which I don't—the expense of running the darn things would prevent me from doing so."

"Why? How much is your monthly electric bill anyway?"

"In mid-summer it runs around two hundred and fifty dollars a month. For people like you described, who keep it really cold, it's more likely to be in the four hundred dollar range. Then once it gets cold we have to heat the place. Most people use electric heaters to warm the rooms but that's probably the most expensive form of heat."

"Are there any other options available to us?"

"Yes. Some people use small kerosene heaters."

"Why don't you?"

"Well, they create a fairly strong residual odor which tends to hang in the air unless you make a point of opening all the windows at least once a day. This of course makes no sense at all."

"By the way, Sal, what are those light bulbs doing down at the bottom of the closet? Is that so you can find your shoes?"

Sally laughed and shook her head. "No. Those are there to help keep the mold down."

"Mold?"

"That's right. Mold. Since this is an island with a sub-tropical climate it's an ongoing problem. In fact, I go through a few gallons of bleach during the winter months. I use it on the walls on a fairly regular basis to keep the mold under control."

Christie was silent for a minute while contemplating the prospect of having some of her best summer clothing ruined by mold. One of the less obvious costs of an overseas assignment on an island. "So what other utility expenses do we have?"

"There's the monthly water bill, but that's not too bad."

"How about telephone service?"

Sally snorted. "Telephone service! Forget about that. The average wait is about a year."

"So Quint was right about that."

"Yep. And even if you manage to get one installed the service is so unreliable that it's a major achievement just to complete a local call."

"What do you do if you're in the military and someone needs to get in touch with you?"

"Usually, someone in the neighborhood has a phone and it's that person's responsibility to contact other military types in his immediate area. On the other hand, if you're really important, whatever unit you're attached to will set you up with a direct line to the command post on base."

"What about teachers? What happens if someone needs to get in contact with us?"

"One of the assistant principals lives in Kishaba Terrace; another in Machinato Point. Neither of those housing areas are more than ten or twelve minutes away by car.

"By the way, we need to go shopping tomorrow for more salad makings, plus some staples. And it will give you an opportunity to pick out some things that you like to eat—and cook," she added. "You do like to cook, don't you?" There was a slight edge to her voice but Christie quickly put Sally's mind at ease about shouldering her share of the household chores.

"Yes. I like to cook and, not to boast, but I've won a few awards in the last few years with some of my specialty dishes."

Sally's eyes lit up at that revelation. "Now, that's what I call exciting news! It will be a real treat to eat something other than my own cooking. Especially something that comes from the hands of an accomplished cook." Sally had returned to the stove, added some garlic, ginger and various other spices and was now beginning to add the pieces of chicken. "The other thing that's a real pain is trying to prepare a meal for only one person. There just aren't that many recipes that are designed with a single person in mind. It's sort of like being left-handed in a right-handed world. No one cares about us. Anyway, dinner will be ready in a few minutes," Sally said, as she added the vegetables to the chicken. "What do you want to drink? There's a little white wine in the fridge if you'd like that."

"Do you have any ice tea?"

"Sure. I drink it by the gallons so I generally have a jug of it brewing out on the back wall. But getting back to the subject of non-human sharers of our space, are you especially squeamish about creepy-crawly things?"

"No . . . I don't think so, although I'm not exactly enamored with spiders—especially the large black disgusting ones."

"How about snakes?"

"Now, that's something that does make me nervous. Well, some of them anyway. Up in Northern Maine there weren't a lot of snakes—just the little garter snakes—but I nearly stepped on a timber rattler one time. They're supposed to be rare but that's an experience I won't soon forget." After a brief pause, she continued, "I remember reading in the guidebook that there are snakes on Okinawa and that a couple of the species are poisonous. Do I need to look where I plant my feet every time I step outside?"

"No. Not hardly," Sally said, smiling reassuringly as she handed Christie a plate and motioned her to a seat at the dining room table. "There are places where they're found but I doubt if it would be anywhere around here. At least, I've never heard of anyone encountering one in Ojana Heights."

"Good. That's a relief. So our little wall-climbing housemates are the only new thing to be experienced then."

"Well . . . not exactly—remember: this is a semi-tropical climate."

"Okay. So what else am I going to have to contend with?"

"For one thing, cockroaches—big ones! Not like the small ones you find stateside."

"Cockroaches! I thought you only found them where there was a lot of dirt!"

"And then there's the centipedes," Sally continued, ignoring her comment about the dirt, "one of my friends went into her kitchen to get a drink one night and when she flipped on the light she found her cat and a centipede in a face-off. And the cat was the more nervous of the two! Like I just said a minute ago: there are a number of critters that flourish in this type of climate. Anyway, enough of this talk about bugs, snakes and other unwanted pets. So what would you like to know about the day-to-day life of a government-sponsored teacher? Any questions that I didn't answer in my letters?"

"I do have a few but before I ask you about that I want to compliment you on this dish. It really is a delicious tasting stir-fry. I especially love the effect that you got from using that particular mix of spices."

"Thanks. It's one of my few cooking successes. I'm sure that your worst meal is probably several levels above this effort."

"Don't be so quick to downplay your own efforts. You haven't even tasted my cooking yet!"

"I don't need to. You already told me that you were an award winning cook."

"Yes, but that was at a regional cook-off in central Maine. Not some national contest."

"That's still magnitudes better than I've ever done—or would ever hope to do. Anyway, now that I have some food to fortify me I'm ready for the interrogation to begin."

Christie set her fork down next to her plate, picked up the napkin from her lap, and wiped the corners of her mouth. "Well, I hope it falls considerably short of being that. One of the things I forgot to ask was how much latitude I have with regard to the way I teach—and what I teach."

"Well, up until the arrival of horrible Harlan you had pretty much complete freedom in those areas."

"Who is 'horrible Harlan'?"

"Harlan Price is the new area superintendent for DOD. Didn't Joe Magnuson mention anything about him when he wrote to you?"

Christie paused with her fork in mid-air. "No. Well . . . he did say there was a new superintendent on board but nothing beyond that as far as I can remember."

"Probably didn't want to scare you off."

"What's so bad about him?"

"Basically, his problem is that he thinks he has all the answers. In fact, there's another expression going around about him."

"What's that?"

"The Price is Right. At one of his first meetings with the teachers he made it known that he rather liked the expression but preferred it even more when the adjective 'always' was placed in front of 'right'. Although he chuckled when he told us, you could sense the arrogance underneath."

33

Christie nodded. "So what you're telling me is that if he disagrees with my methods or my subject content then he can make my life pretty difficult."

"Uh huh. And another problem with this guy is that he's ex-military. He flew bombers during WWII. Apparently he's still a major in the Air Force Reserve so he brings the military mindset to his position: everything has to be done by the book and if you don't do that you'll end up in big trouble."

"So how do people manage to work with him?"

"It's not easy. Some don't. A few of our veteran teachers and two of our best administrators have already requested transfers to other DOD schools in the Far East."

"I gather Joe Magnuson is not one of them?"

"No, thank heavens. I don't know what we'd do without Joe to run interference for us and deflect all of the flack that Harlan regularly aims our way."

"I would think that a strong department chair could also make one's life easier."

"That's true. And by the way, you're lucky because Jim Martin, the English chair, is cut from the same cloth as Joe Magnuson is. Everybody likes and respects him. In fact, I would have assumed that you'd received a letter from him before you left the states."

"I did. He wrote me a very nice letter."

"So what did he say in it?"

"Well, among other things he promised me a couple of sections of junior honors English and one creative writing section that would be open to all three grades."

"No kidding! Hey, you really did well, Christie! Most new teachers get the cast-offs—you know: the classes no one else wants. Jim must have seen something in your resume that really impressed him."

"I suppose it might have helped a little to have published an article in the English Journal," she said.

"You published an article in a national journal!"

"Well, actually, I shouldn't have said published. It's been accepted for publication and is due to appear in the January '67 issue."

"Come on Christie, don't be so modest, 'Accepted for publication' is pretty much equal to 'published' in my book. And in everyone else's for that matter. That is so cool! I am really impressed! And this is only your what—third year teaching?"

Christie nodded as she leaned across the table for the pitcher of iced tea.

"Of course, I'm sure it also helps that you're going to be working on your doctoral thesis."

"But that doesn't have anything to do with my teaching ability."

"Maybe not," Sally acknowledged, "But it does show that you're ambitious and determined to continue your professional education. And one of the reasons you chose Okinawa was because you wanted to do some research on Okinawan women?"

"Yes."

"So how did that come about?"

"While I was at Harvard, I became close friends with a member of the anthropology department who was an expert on societies that are still largely matriarchal. A number of them are, not surprisingly, in pretty remote areas of the world. We had lunch on a number of occasions and she suggested that Okinawa might be a good place to carry out some research on gender roles. I knew that I would need a job to support myself while I was here so I applied to DOD for a teaching position. You know the rest of the story."

"Tell me a little about what you already know about Okinawan women."

"Not a lot. Although Okinawan women are subordinate to the men in certain areas, in others they hold the decision-making power. Since I'm particularly interested in the whole area of woman's rights, Professor Soroka encouraged me and said she would be glad to be a kind of long distance mentor. So there you are."

"How about your search for information about your father?"

"That makes three major tasks I have to carry out and I'm already beginning to have second thoughts on the practicality of handling just two of them."

"So what's the order of priority?"

"It's obvious that my teaching responsibilities come first; after that probably my search for information on my father; and third, doing some research if time allows."

"As far as I can see, how much you can accomplish depends partly on how well organized you are and also on whether or not you're going to limit your stay here to just a single year."

Christie nodded.

"So how do you intend to start your search for information about your father?"

"Beats me," Christie acknowledged, "but I do know that I've got to try and establish some contacts in the Okinawan community as soon as possible."

"That could be easier said than done, Christie."

"Tell me about it. Quint's already pointed that out."

Christie put her glass down and resting her elbows on the table, cupped her chin in her the palms of her hands. "Anyway, it's too soon to begin fretting about things."

"I agree. And back to the more immediate concern. I have one very strong suggestion to make with regard to your teaching assignment. If you follow it, you shouldn't have any problems with Price or anyone else for that matter."

"And what's that?"

"Like I said before: don't raise any controversial issues in the classroom. That's sure to get you into trouble. Especially, anything to do with our involvement in Vietnam." "But that's simply ridiculous, Sal! Opposition to the war has been growing by leaps and bounds in the past six months, especially among the young people. You know what's happening back there. It's been in all the papers and on the nightly television news programs: demonstrations, draft-card burnings are becoming the norm. Of course, it's mainly the college kids, but even in Bar Harbor the high school kids were asking hard questions. And demanding straight answers. And I don't blame them. After all, many of them are only months away from being drafted."

"I hear what you're saying, Christie, but this is not Bar Harbor. It's Okinawa and the kids you're going to be teaching are largely the dependents of career servicemen and women. I'm giving you fair warning: if you encourage the kind of free-wheeling discussion that you apparently did back home, you might find yourself on a boat headed stateside."

Christie nodded thoughtfully as she finished the last of her ice tea. Although she would not completely disregard Sally's warning, there was no way she was going to try and muzzle her students. If they wanted to talk about a controversial topic, she'd let them. She'd just make sure that it was kept within the limits of the classroom. That way it wouldn't cause any problems for her or her students.

As Christie lay in bed a few hours later, mulling over the events of the day, a sudden brief surge of anxiety mixed with joy washed over her. She didn't know where it came from, but took it as a sign. A sign that her stay on Okinawa would be a time of trial as well as a time of growth. And hopefully a time of discovery as well.

IV

Quint tossed the draft of the safety report back in the in-basket and leaned back in his chair, staring absentmindedly at the stack of paperwork piled in the center of his desk. Holding his pencil like a drumstick, he tapped out a random rhythm on the arm of his chair as he mentally sorted out the tasks that lay before him on this September morning. Abruptly tossing his pencil on the desk, he swiveled in the chair and glanced out across the tarmac to the coral reefs beyond the edge of the runway. Vertical heat waves shimmered in the distance, giving visual confirmation to the weather officer's prediction that the day would turn out to be a scorcher.

A taxiing C-130 cut across his vision, the high-pitched whine of the four turbo-prop engines barely penetrating the double-thick windows of the hanger. It was one of only half a dozen aircraft left on the field due to a maximum effort launch of almost the entire Wing the previous day in support of the army's latest effort in Vietnam.

Quint rubbed his chin thoughtfully, as he made a mental note to remind Chief Master Sargent Ferris to prepare for a dramatic increase in maintenance problems. And that, of course, would put a greater strain on his already overworked maintenance force which, in turn, would make the training and safety issues stand out in even greater relief. This also meant that the old man would be pressing him even harder for some kind of solution to these problems. The inevitability of the chain of cause and effect made Quint even more frustrated. *Damn,* he thought, *is there no end to this cycle?*

Normally, after allowing himself a few minutes to silently grumble about his plight, Quint would have turned back to his desk and brought his considerable powers of concentration to bear on the various matters which lay before him. Today was different; in fact, not just today, but for the past several days personal matters kept interfering with his ability to focus on professional issues.

The C-130 which had taxied by moments before slid across his line of vision again as it lifted off the runway and headed south on the sixteen hundred mile trip to Vietnam. He wondered if Cally was on board that flight. Quint knew she had received temporary orders to the Air Force hospital at Cam Ranh Bay and was supposed to be leaving within the next few days. What to do about Cally; that issue was definitely one of the major distractions of the past few weeks.

Callista Lameroux. Tall and blond with exquisitely sculpted features and a flawless figure that flattered even the plainest of clothing. Regal in bearing, oftentimes imperious in manner, she was that rare woman who turned the heads of both men and women no matter where she went. A Grace Kelly with fire. That's how one admiring male had once described her. It was an apt description. The thought had crossed Quint's mind more than once that she should be ruling over an eighteenth century manor house or better yet a medieval court instead of the Intensive Care Unit of a large military hospital. But then the possibility that the positions might require some of the same qualities had not escaped his notice either.

Typically, whatever reservations he felt melted away in the heat of his desire for her. That was exactly what had happened when he returned from the week spent at the training seminar back in the states. In spite of the still vivid memories of the violent argument which they had the night before he left for the seminar, he had succumbed to her charms within an hour of first seeing her again. It was shortly after the scene with Christie at the officer's club. He and Cally had ended another long argumentative discussion with an equally intense period of lovemaking on the small beach off the end of the runway. Quint shook his head as memories of that afternoon filled his mind. Cally, of course, assumed that the sensual ending to their tension-filled discussion meant that everything was all right between them. But Quint was beginning to think that their relationship had been built upon nothing more substantial than a strong chemical affinity which enabled them to fulfill each other's sexual needs.

In the past that may have been sufficient, but he was now beginning to look at Cally and his relationship with her in a different light. Furthermore, at some level of his thinking, he sensed there was more than one reason behind his new-found willingness to acknowledge its deficiencies.

Leaning back in his chair, Quint put his hands behind his head and stared up at the ceiling, his thoughts turning back again to his encounter with Christie Atherton. He couldn't quite put his finger on it, but there had been something special about that whole episode. In spite of the clash of wills back at his sister's apartment in Portland and the more recent incident at the O Club he found himself attracted to her. She was certainly very different from any other woman he had met. In fact, he sensed that Christie might just be the woman who he had begun to doubt even existed —except in his own imagination.

There was one minor problem: the last time he'd seen her she had walked away in a fit of pique. Based on that incident, it seemed unlikely that any interest he might have in her was likely to be reciprocated. Of course, he couldn't be absolutely certain about that. There were a couple of occasions when he had caught her looking at him in more than just a casual way. But then, maybe he had misread those clues entirely. He had to admit that he hadn't shown any great skill in figuring out where Cally was coming from. It had taken him months to get a correct reading on her.

The insistent jangling of the phone finally penetrated his reverie and he spun around and grabbed for it somewhat guiltily.

"Major Brewster."

"Quint, it's Rick."

"Hi Rick, what's up?"

"A couple of things. First the boring stuff. The old man will be looking for that safety report on the maintenance facilities at Bangkok. Where do you stand on that?"

"It's in a final draft right now. I just looked it over about a half an hour ago and it only needs a couple of minor changes before it goes out to Doris for final typing. Colonel Crane should have it in his hands by tomorrow afternoon."

"That's good. That takes care of the first item. The second thing. The old man wanted me to be sure and remind you that this max effort in support of the army will probably put even greater pressure on our maintenance resources."

"No kidding," Quint said sarcastically. "Was this profound observation accompanied by any original suggestions about what to do about it?"

"Sorry, Pal. You're supposed to be the idea man."

"I seem to be running short of ideas lately. Is there anything else? Specifically, have you got anything uplifting to tell me; something which will bring a little relief to my overburdened psyche?"

"Of course. I saved the best for last. The old man asked me to be the Wing representative at the annual new teacher's cocktail party at the Shuri Hills Club. It's tonight at 1900 hours. What do you say we check it out?"

Although intrigued at the thought of seeing Christie again, Quint's interest was tempered somewhat by the prospect of getting involved in another verbal fencing match with her.

"I don't know Rick. My in-basket is filled to overflowing from the trip stateside. I probably should stay here and attempt to tackle some of it."

"Come on. That stuff can wait another 12 hours—except for what I need from you, of course."

"Of course," Quint echoed. "Okay. I'll go. Who's going to do the honors?"

"I'll drive. Are you going to stay here at the base or go home and change first?" Rick asked.

"I won't have time to go home because I've got to finish up a couple of APRs that were due over to the base personnel officer yesterday. Two of my top NCOs are going before a promotion board in October and I want to make sure they have the latest efficiency reports in their folders. But I do have a change of clothes in the car, so that should work out all right."

"O.K. See you about 1845 in the front parking lot."

"Roger."

That evening, as they headed up island on Highway I, Quint began to have second thoughts about the whole idea of attending the party. The more he thought about it, the more uncomfortable he became at the prospect of encountering Christie after the way he had treated her.

Rick looked over at him and said, "You're unusually quiet tonight—even for you!"

"I'm thinking."

"I can see that," Rick said, "What about?"

"Odds and ends. Just mulling over a few things that have been bothering me."

Rick glanced over at him. "What's the scoop on you and Cally, anyway? Are you still going with her?"

Quint shrugged. "I don't know. Every time I try to have a serious conversation with her we get sidetracked and never get back to the original discussion."

Rick looked over at him and grinned mischievously. "Let me guess. The interruption typically takes some form—or forms—of non-verbal communication. Right?"

Quint slumped back in the seat and closed his eyes. "No comment."

Rick started whistling some ribald tune while keeping beat with his fingers on the steering wheel.

Without opening his eyes or changing position, Quint said: "You're off-key and off-color tonight."

"At least I'm consistent."

"That you are, my friend. But you know what Emerson said about consistency, don't you?"

"You mean Ralph Waldo?"

"Who else would I mean?"

"You could have meant Liz Emerson."

"Who the devil is Liz Emerson?"

"Only a stunning looking blonde who happened to be Miss New Hampshire a couple of years ago."

"And why would I have meant her since I've never even heard of her?"

"Well she's a darned sight better looking than Ralph is—or was, rather."

"I would hope so. So tell me: how do you know her?"

"I don't exactly know her. I happened to meet her when she was touring the state—I think it was in North Conway. Then I got a photo of her from my cousin who's a press photographer with The Manchester Union Leader."

"So how does Sandy feel about you keeping a photo of a beautiful blonde around the house?"

"She doesn't care. She feels pretty secure about our marriage. And she should. I'd never stray. I love her too much to do anything like that. Besides, Emerson's picture, along with those of several of my old girlfriends, resides in a folder in the bottom drawer of a dresser.

"And speaking of good-looking women," Rick continued, "word has it that this new crop of teachers is supposed to be one of the best in recent years. Although I doubt if any of them can match Christie Atherton. So anyway, tell me more about her."

"Well, for one thing she's a real activist."

"What do you mean?"

"Christie's always been a real do-gooder. You know the humanitarian type. Lisa told me that she spent two years in Somalia with the Peace Corps teaching English in a small town outside the capital city. According to my sister, Christie raised a real ruckus shortly after she got there."

"Why?"

"I gather that the area Peace Corps administrator was pretty inept. Apparently the morale of all the volunteers was at rock bottom. So Christie decided to take the bull by the horns and do something about it."

"What did she do?"

"She found out Sargent Shriver was going to be in the capital city of Mogadishu and after hitching a ride into the city from the small town where she was based, managed to get an audience with him. Word has it she told him in no uncertain terms what the problem was and what he needed to do to correct it. Whatever she said must have made an impression on him because the administrator who was causing all the problems got booted upstairs into a job where he had no contact with the volunteers and Shriver replaced him with someone whose real strength was in handling inter-personal relations."

"She sounds like a pretty impressive lady to me, Quint. At least one with a lot of moxie—which is something I would think that you'd appreciate."

"Yeah," Quint said, "that's what Lisa keeps telling me."

A few minutes later they pulled up to the stoplight at the turnoff to the Machinato

Service Area. Quint glanced at his watch. It had taken less than ten minutes to get there. During the rush hour it would have taken three times as long. He looked over at Rick.

"At this rate we might actually get to Shuri Hills by seven."

Rick nodded. "Traveling on Highway One isn't so bad at this hour. That's one advantage the enlisted troops have—the ones who work the swing shift anyway.

"So what else can you tell me about this mystery lady?"

"Well, she didn't come to Okinawa just to teach—or even mainly to teach."

"No? So why did she choose this place? Seems like she could have done just as well—maybe better— throwing a dart at a map of the world."

"Tell me about it! Anyway, she   came here to try and track down information about her father."

"Her father was stationed here?"

"Apparently he served as a medic during the battle of Okinawa and as a volunteer at one of the refugee camps shortly after the war ended. End of chapter one. Beginning of chapter two: enter Christie twenty plus years later to try and find out what happened to him when he was here. That's the whole story so far."

Rick said nothing at first while he pondered the feasibility of launching a search for information about a man who had last been on Okinawa twenty years earlier. After a moment or so he looked over at Quint.

"Are you going to try and help her?"

"I'd just as soon not considering how busy I am these days. Besides, as far as I'm concerned it's a wasted effort. But it occurred to me that I could at least put her in touch with Mitch McGuire."

"Mitch McGuire?"

"Yeah. You know—the civilian who works for me in the structural repair shop."

"I know who you mean. I don't think I ever knew his name. So why do you think he can help?"

"For one thing, he's been here ever since the end of the war. In fact, he came over with the first Seabee battalion. They were on the beach only a few hours after the first troops landed. For another thing, he's married to an Okinawan woman."

"I didn't know any of that," Rick said. "It's worth a try I guess."

Moments later they pulled into the parking lot at the Shuri Hills club. Rick looked around and exclaimed, "I think we got the last parking spot in the place. Looks like the word got out about the quality of this group. Either that or the rest of the single officers got word that a particularly desirable teacher has arrived on the scene," Rick said, glancing in the rear view mirror as he ran his comb through a thatch of unruly red hair a couple of times.

V

As Quint followed Rick through the door of the club into the lounge, they exchanged looks of mild astonishment at the size of the crowd. Even taking into account the fact that this was the first major cocktail party of the fall season, the sheer magnitude of the numbers was impressive. Quint estimated that there were over two hundred people at the party. Considering the fact that each year's influx of new teachers typically numbered fifty to sixty—virtually all of them female—that meant that there were roughly three officers to every one teacher. Not bad odds for a young woman who was interested in picking up a husband along with a couple of year's overseas experience. One inevitable by-product of Quint's quick calculations was the somewhat unsettling thought that a woman with Christie's looks and personality might well have a half dozen or so suitors before the evening was over.

Unlike the subterranean lounge in the officer's club at Naha, the main lounge at Shuri Hills overlooked a panoramic view that included a rolling eighteen-hole golf course in the foreground and the harbor in the distance. Floor-to-ceiling windows provided an unobstructed view of the grounds and on three sides a narrow balcony provided additional space when the weather was good.

"You sure called this one right," Quint said, "It looks like every bachelor officer on the island is here."

"Yes and the question is how are you going to locate Christie in this crowd?"

"Maybe she isn't coming tonight."

"Attendance is considered mandatory for teachers new to the island unless they're sick."

"How would they know if someone didn't show up?"

"You mean you didn't notice that guy at the door checking off names on a sheet as the teachers arrived?"

"I remember seeing a guy at the door but I thought he was just waiting for someone."

"That was one of the superintendent's flunkies, Quint."

Quint shrugged as he scanned the room. As tall as he was, he still could see only a short distance across the room. The only hope of locating Christie was to try and work his way around the room and hope that she wasn't moving around at the same time. If she was, he'd probably never catch up with her. "Maybe the crowd will thin out in a little while then I'll try and circulate around the area."

Rick tugged at his elbow. "Come on. Let's tackle the food first, then make our way over to the bar."

Once at the food table, Rick dived enthusiastically into a plate of shrimp as Quint nibbled half-heartedly on some vegetable slices while continuing to survey the room as best he could. Quint felt a sudden revulsion at the whole scene. It was all so damned superficial and trite. People standing around shouting to be heard above the din and no one caring anyway because they were all thinking about what they were going to say once they could edge back into the conversation. It was bad enough that he had to attend all those mandatory cocktail parties but to voluntarily subject himself to this! Quint shook his head in disgust. He wondered how Christie would feel attending a function like this. Cally would Love it.... This would definitely be her cup of tea; he could just see her holding court as she moved from one admiring group to another.

Quint became aware that Rick was nudging him and motioning in the direction of the bar. As they threaded their way through the crowd, Quint admitted to himself that he had no idea what he would say to Christie if he did run into her. It was probably the first time in his adult life he had allowed another person to impinge to such a degree on his consciousness.

—※—

Nearly an hour had passed and Quint had spent most of that time sitting at the bar engrossed in a lengthy technical discussion with the local Lockheed technical representative about the relative merits of a turbo-prop vs. pure jet engine. When the tech rep finally threw in the towel and wandered away from the bar, Quint glanced at his watch and arched his eyebrows in mild astonishment at how completely he had lost track of time. The three empty glasses lined up in front of him on the bar spoke volumes. Quint rarely had more than a couple of drinks and here he was halfway through his fourth drink of the evening. It wasn't that they impaired his thinking; he had long ago learned that he could handle his liquor as well as the next person—in fact, better than most. But they did have a tendency to make him more responsive to his emotional side. And that was something which he found very disconcerting.

Looking down at the ice cubes as he swirled them in his half-empty drink, he abruptly decided that he needed to get away from all the noise and pretense. Glancing over his shoulder, he saw that Rick was heading back to the bar for a refill. Motioning him over, Quint said: "Look, I really think this is waste of time. Let's cut out and head back to the base. Then I can get those APRs done before midnight and be able to hand them in tomorrow."

After placing his order, Rick turned and gave him one of those looks that parents often bestow upon recalcitrant children: "Come on Quint, the evening is young. Give it a little more of a chance."

Quint thought for a long moment then, acquiesced reluctantly, "O.K but I've got to get out of this overheated place and get some air. If you decide to leave or just want to touch base, look for me out on the balcony."

"Roger. See you in a while."

Picking his way gingerly through a dozen or so conversational clusters, Quint finally made it out to the balcony. After glancing around to see if he recognized anyone, he wandered over to the railing and, leaning back against an upright steel column, looked out over the scene in front of him. The fairways had blurred into the background in the gathering dusk but he could see a few lighter splotches scattered haphazardly around the course. He was mystified for a moment then realized that he was look-ing at the flags on the pins which showed the placement of the greens. Memories drifted to the surface of his mind—particularly of the smell of the greens at the local country club where he had first caddied as a young teenager. There was a special fragrance he associated with them on the first round of the morning just after they had been watered and cut. It was one of his favorite scents from childhood.

On the horizon the sun was almost ready to drop into the sea but, in one last effort to hold off the encroaching darkness, threw off a final shower of light rays which back-lit the puffy nimbo-cumulous clouds in the distance, outlining their edges with a multi-colored border ranging from a deep lavender to a brilliant red. Against that spectacular backdrop, a pair of F-102 fighter interceptors lifted into the sky simultaneously, the tiny darts of flame from their afterburners mere pinpricks of light against nature's lavish canvas.

No sooner was the sun gone than the chorus of night sounds began, echoing and re-echoing through the tropical evening. Myriad small insects and other creatures created a din which made the sounds of a late summer evening in New England pale by comparison. That was something that he still hadn't gotten used to. It was hard to believe that things so small— some of which were virtually invisible—could make such a racket.

As he glanced down at his empty glass, a stray line from something— from what: a movie, a book, a song— passed through his mind: 'a night that was made for romance'. Turning away from the railing with a shrug, he had taken a couple of steps toward the door when the sound of a woman's laughter brought him to a sudden halt. He knew instantly, intuitively, that it was Christie's laugh even though he had yet to hear her laugh. Melodic, joyous, infectious—a sound so distinctive that even if he hadn't known its owner he would have felt compelled to seek out the woman to whom the voice belonged.

He turned slowly and looked towards the far end of the balcony. Although she could not see him because he was standing in the shadows, he could see Christie clearly, the light from a nearby window framing her perfectly. She was surrounded by several young officers and it was obvious that she was enjoying herself. Her casual outfit served only to emphasize what he had long ago learned about attractive women: they made the clothing, not the other way around. She had on a short-sleeve, powder blue, scoop neck blouse which in combination with a white, pleated skirt revealed a full, curvaceous figure. Taking in the white sandals which completed the picture, his admiring gaze traveled back up her figure, noting again the graceful line of her calves and the firm, shapely behind which he suddenly had the strongest urge to reach out and touch. Her hair was pulled back on one side and held in place with a live flower, and her full sensuous lips were deliciously outlined with a deep red lipstick which reminded Quint of the color of burgundy wine. The thought which kept returning to the forefront of his mind was that they were lips which cried out to be kissed.

He felt at that moment that Christie's natural beauty was a hundred times more appealing and alluring than Cally's formal, ice-cold beauty.

Quint hesitated, not sure of what he was going to do next. If he stepped into the light, she would probably see him, but what then? Would she ignore him? Smile and wave while continuing to talk to the officers. Come running into his arms. Yeah, sure. None of the above? He was curious to know how she felt about him at this point and the easiest way to do that was to try to read her expression at the instant that she first saw him. Unlike Cally, he sensed that Christie was too honest to hide her true feelings and that he would get an accurate reading the moment she recognized him.

After taking a few more steps toward the door, Quint deliberately paused in the light that spilled out from inside the lounge. Christie was turned slightly away from him at the moment and he was struck by how attractive she was in profile. It was hard for him to decide what her best feature was: her nose was narrow and straight although slightly up-turned at the end and contributed to the pert air about her. The well-modeled facial bones and firm chin, on the other hand, simultaneously underscored both her femininity and her strength of character. He was trying to recall what color her eyes were when she suddenly turned towards him in response to a comment from someone standing beside her. Quint waited for what seemed like minutes, wondering if she would turn back to the others without noticing him. Staring at her with all of the mental energy he could muster, he thought, *look at me, damn it.* I want you to know that I'm here, wanting to see you. And then, almost as if she had received his unspoken request through some form of mental telepathy,

Christie abruptly looked past the shoulder of the person to whom she was speaking, across the room to where Quint was standing. Their gazes met and locked as they probed each other's minds, trying to read the message behind the outward facade.

Quint started walking slowly towards her and Christie, after excusing herself, moved somewhat tentatively in his direction. Was she walking—or was she floating towards him? It was strange, almost as if time had slowed down and everything that was happening, everything that he was experiencing, was occurring in slow motion. And because everything was happening more slowly, it heightened one's awareness of their feelings and surroundings—of everything that was registering through the senses. Quint wondered if this was just the effect from the four drinks he had or if it was something more than that. Whatever its source, it was an extraordinary experience and not a little disconcerting.

They came face to face in a secluded area of the balcony where the shadows lay deep, although there was still enough light to see each other's faces clearly.

"Hi."

"Hi," she said.

"Having a good time?"

"Uh huh. How about you?"

"Oh fine," Quint said, without much enthusiasm. "So how do you like it here so far?"

"Fine."

"How's school?"

"It's a little hard to judge after only a couple of weeks, but I would have to say that so far there have been no surprises. It's about what I expected. How about you? How are things going for you?"

Quint wondered if he detected a trace of irony in that last question. "About the same—very busy—more so than I care to be." He was trying hard not to show his growing discomfort. Finding himself at a loss as to how he could halt this low-key, verbal fencing he suddenly blurted out, "You know, you look absolutely amazing tonight."

"Why thank you," Christie said, a little bemused at the strange form of his compliment—assuming that's what it was meant to be. Her voice reflected a touch of amusement as she responded, "you look fairly presentable yourself."

Quint looked at her with a half-smile and a nod of his head acknowledging, through those spare gestures, her attempt at injecting some humor into the conversation.

"By the way," she continued, glancing around the immediate area, "where's your girlfriend tonight?"

There was no hint of sarcasm in her voice, just a matter-of-fact tone as if she was asking him the time of day.

"Cally flew down to Cam Ranh Bay on a temporary assignment. He paused for a minute, then added, "But she's not my girlfriend any longer; she's my ex-girlfriend."

"Are you sure about that?" A trace of annoyance registered in Christie's voice—a warning signal which he had already come to learn should not be ignored.

"Yes, I am." Although that wasn't entirely true. Even though dating Cally had turned out to be a superficial kind of experience he still had some feelings for her. That's the way it was with Cally.

"Going out with someone who is a true friend is a much deeper experience. Or at least it ought to be," Quint added.

Christie looked down at her hands so he wouldn't see her eyes misting. She wondered just how transparent her feelings were to him. Neither said anything for a long minute. The silence enveloped them in a cocoon which effectively shut out other people's voices and made them feel as if they were a thousand miles removed from any other beings.

She looked up at him with those luminous eyes. Amber, with flecks of gold. Eyes that could mesmerize if you looked too deeply into them. It was not so much as if they reflected light from an outside source, Quint thought, but instead emitted some inner light from deep within her. In fact, he felt almost as if he was being drawn into her very soul. Her pupils widened, then became larger and liquid, as if they were floating in an azure sea.

He was drowning and he didn't care. Oblivious to what was going on around him, not caring if anyone could see them; he knew that he could not stop himself from reaching out and touching her. Lifting his hand, he let his fingers slowly trace a path from behind her earlobe across her face to her lips. Even that slight point of contact with her skin was enough to send currents of electricity flowing out to every part of his body. His finger continued moving, exploring, gently following the outline of her mouth. She had tilted her head back and closed her eyes, offering her lips to him and he could no longer restrain himself. Cupping her face in both his hands, he leaned over until his lips were so close to hers that he could feel her sweet breath on his face.

His pulse was beating rapidly and he could feel his heart thudding beneath his rib cage. He hadn't been this excited since the first time he had kissed a girl. His lips brushed hers lightly as he moved his mouth in a slow, gentle exploration of her mouth. He felt rather than heard a low moan escape from her as she reached up and slid her arms around his neck. Their kissing became more insistent, Christie's lips parting willingly in response to the gentle but demanding probing of his tongue. He sensed the upward spiraling path of her passion and was pleasurably shocked to find her a willing participant in an ever more sensual oral dance. Their tongues intertwined, then darting, flicking, thrusting, carried them towards dizzying heights of arousal. Just when they were on the brink of being swept away on a wave of ecstasy, the mood was abruptly shattered by a loud and slightly flippant voice just a few feet away:

"So, this is what happens when I take you along to a singles party and let you wander off by yourself."

Quint and Christie had reluctantly disengaged from their embrace, looking more than a little sheepish as they struggled to regain both their composure and their breath.

Before Quint could say anything in response, Rick, grinning good-naturedly, stuck out his hand and said: "Let me guess. It's Christie Atherton— right!"

"Right," Christie said, smiling back at him, and deciding, on the basis of that brief exchange, that she was going to like him.

Quint was still feeling somewhat bewildered at how completely he had succumbed to the tyranny of his feelings. Feelings whose depth and intensity eclipsed anything that fell within his previous range of experience.

VI

Rick couldn't resist taking advantage of Quint's continued discomfit: "Quint's done nothing but talk about you for days now. Ever since he picked you up at the terminal. And I must say," Rick continued, as he bowed in Christie's direction, "Your picture doesn't do you justice."

By now Quint had finally caught up with the other two and was getting more than a little annoyed at Rick, both for exaggerating his feelings about Christie as well as for taking over control of the conversation.

"Anyway," Rick continued, "I assume since I'm now ready to leave you probably are not. So, my friend, I'll leave you my car and hitch a ride home with one of the other guys from the Wing." Then momentarily reverting to his tongue-in-cheek teasing, he added, "That way you and Christie can pick up where you left off when I so rudely interrupted you."

Quint pretended not to have heard Rick's final comment as he turned to Christie and asked whether she had a ride home.

She shook her head slowly from side to side.

"Would you like a ride home?"

Looking up at him from under arched eyebrows, she responded in a deliberately casual tone. "Sure."

Glancing over at Rick, Quint said, and "as long as Christie's ready to go why don't we leave together. You can drop Christie and me off at my car if you don't mind going a little out of your way."

"No problem. Be glad to."

Turning back to Christie, Quint said, somewhat hesitantly, "Is there anyone that you have to say goodbye to—or want to say goodbye to?"

"No," she said, smiling at him knowingly.

He cleared his throat and nodded. "Good. Shall we go then?"

As the three of them walked across the floor, it became apparent that the party had about run its course. The crowd had thinned out considerably although there was still a small group gathered around the piano bar. Quint recognized the pianist as a C-130 pilot from the 35th Tactical Squadron. Word had it that he had given up a promising career as a rising young jazz pianist to join the Air Force. Quint wondered why he had chosen to make such a dramatic career change, especially after showing such promise in a field that he obviously loved. But then people had often wondered the same thing about Quint: his reputation as a rising star in the civil engineering field was not unknown to a number of people. *And just look at me*, he thought, as they walked across the parking lot to Rick's car. *Now I've taken another giant step backward: I'm not even flying anything anymore, just fixing the damn things.*

On the way back to the base Christie and Rick chatted away in the front seat with the easy familiarity of two people who immediately felt comfortable with each other, while Quint sat silently in the back seat preoccupied with his own thoughts. Once in a while he would acknowledge a comment or briefly answer a question that was directed at him, but for the most part he seemed distant and remote.

When Rick pulled up beside Quint's car in the parking lot at the hanger, Quint got out first to open the door for Christie. As he held out a hand to her, she turned to Rick and said:

"I really enjoyed talking to you and I hope I'll see you again soon." She couldn't resist adding, "And I must admit, if I spent a hundred years trying to guess what Quint's best friend would be like, I never would have imagined it would be anyone like you."

Before Rick could respond, Quint chimed in with, "what she means Rick, is that she would have expected me to associate with someone whose class and intelligence were pitched a little higher."

Christie's retort came back like a flash: "Actually, I was really thinking how amazing it was that someone as light and upbeat as Rick could stand to be around someone as heavy and serious as you!"

Rick let out a low whistle of awe and, waving a hand disparagingly in Quint's direction, said to Christie: "Touché', my beautiful lady, It's been all my pleasure."

Disregarding both of their cracks, Quint said, "I'll check in with you tomorrow morning about re-scheduling the Wing training workshop. And, as I promised, the maintenance report will be on the old man's desk by mid-afternoon."

"O.K. Quint," Rick said, solemnly, "talk to you then."

After Rick drove away, Quint walked around to the passenger side and held the door for Christie. When he slid into the driver's side a moment later, Christie turned to him and said:

"I hope you aren't angry with me."

"About what?"

"My comment—crack—about you being too serious."

"Oh that. Only if you meant it." Then he caught himself, "Hey, what am I saying, you did mean it!"

Christie colored slightly, but she wasn't about to apologize for uttering the truth.

Quint looked over with a half-smile on his lips. "Don't worry, I know it's true. Besides, I probably deserved that comeback anyway".

"How long have you known Rick?"

"A little less than a year."

"How did you meet him?"

"There were some administrative matters that I was involved with. He proved to be a real help in getting things pushed through the proper channels—and in a timely fashion."

"That sounds like a good person to know."

"You bet. Especially in the military where there are so many levels in the chain of command and where it's so easy for something to get hung up, misplaced, or just plain sandbagged. Rick knows more people than anyone I've ever met, and more importantly, knows how to get them to move on something. He's a very valuable ally to have and to top it off he would give you the shirt off his back, as the old saying goes."

"Speaking of people who would give you the shirt off their back, your sister Lisa definitely falls in that category."

Quint gave her a quick grin. "That's true. The only problem is she'd give you the shirt off my back too on the assumption that you'd be that much better off with an extra one."

Christie laughed out loud, delighted to find evidence of a sense of humor in Quint as well as amused at the deft way in which he had pinpointed one of his sister's more visible attributes. "It does seem to be true that her generosity knows no bounds."

Abruptly changing the subject, Quint said, "Where are we headed, anyway?"

Christie looked over at him for a long moment, then responded: "I assumed you were taking me home."

"I know, but where is home?"

"Oh, sorry. Ojana Heights. 5C Ojana Heights."

Quint wondered if he had heard a trace of disappointment in her voice. "I guess that's the local enclave for teachers, right?"

She nodded. "I like the location—it's pretty central—and you're right. There are quite a few teachers in that housing area. I don't mind admitting that I do feel more comfortable in that kind of setting."

Quint nodded. They drove the last several minutes in silence. When he pulled up in front of her house a few minutes later, he turned off the engine and sat for a minute staring reflectively at the distant hills.

"I guess I owe you another apology," he said while wiping some imaginary dust off the steering wheel, then continued, ". . . this time for coming on to you so strongly. I honestly don't know what came over me. I've never done anything quite so impulsive before." He struggled to find the proper words. "I don't want you to think that I go around doing things like that. To be honest—and this is one of those times when I wish I could be less than honest—I've never felt quite so out of control before and it isn't something that I feel particularly comfortable with—just losing it like that! Anyway, I do apologize and promise that nothing like that will ever happen again."

Christie stared out the window, partly amused by his response, partly irritated by it, but mainly disappointed in it. She reached down for her purse and as she placed one hand on the door handle, looked over at him and said quietly but firmly, "It's as much my fault as it is yours—that's assuming, of course, that either one of us should feel any guilt over what happened." By the time Quint got around to the passenger side, Christie was already out of the door, waiting for him on the sidewalk.

"Look," he said, as he walked with her up to the front door, "I would like to see you again. And soon, if possible. But the problem is there's so much going on in my life that it's difficult to find any time to socialize. And as you've seen, I haven't exactly been the greatest company lately." A trace of a grin appeared but then was quickly erased again.

Christie was silent as she fished in her purse for her house keys. When she found them she looked down at them, idly fingering the door key for a long minute. Then abruptly looking up at Quint, she said, "You know where I teach, Quint. Now you know where I live. And I don't plan on going anywhere for the next ten months but," she added, firmly, "you should be aware that I have no intention of sitting around while you attempt to find a niche for me in your busy schedule. No offense, but that's just not acceptable to me." Leaning forward, she brushed his cheek with her lips, "goodnight."

"Whoa! Wait just a minute."

"What?"

"Rick and I are sponsoring a party at my place in a couple of weeks. Would you like to come to it—if you don't have any other plans, that is"

"Sure."

"Good then I'll see you a week from this coming Saturday. It will start at 1800 hours. That's 6 o'clock in civilian terms."

"Yes, I know."

As Quint got into the car and pulled away from the curb, he shook his head in mild dismay, acknowledging that he had once again been put in his place—and by someone who was nearly a dozen years his junior! But the worst part was that he probably deserved it.

Fascinating was definitely the right word for Christie. Never before had he met anyone who was such a mixture of softness and strength, of intelligence and passion. And there was something more . . . . Even though he had been with her for such a short time, he felt as though she had reached down and touched a chord deep within him, one that no one had ever touched before. His engineer's mind searched for an analogy and finally settled on the concept of sympathetic vibration. Two chords so in tune to one another that the one can start the other to resonating. Shaking his head to clear out such unsettling thoughts, he was willing to admit that he if he did not see her again he might very well be missing out on something more special than anything he had yet experienced.

VII

Machinato Point really wasn't much different from the housing complex at Ojana Heights where she and Sally lived. That was Christie's observation as she followed the coral gravel road down towards Quint's house. Same mix of two- and three-bedroom houses with tiny yards enclosed by a four-foot cinderblock wall and the ubiquitous Shishi dogs mounted on either side of the gate.

Although it was true that most of the houses in Machinato Point enjoyed a view of the water, the homes in Ojana Heights had larger yards. One thing that Machinato Point shared in common with every other off-base housing complex, however, was the pothole-pitted roads. Anything faster than five miles an hour would probably result in some broken springs and a cracked skull.

Before she was even in sight of Quint's house, it became clear that she had better pull over and park, as both sides of the road up ahead were lined with parked cars. After stopping the car, Christie reached for the door handle but paused momentarily to take a quick look in the mirror. Her shoulder-length hair tended to fall over the edge of her eye, creating a Veronica Lake effect. *Autumn fire*, her favorite color lipstick, enhanced her pronounced cupid's bow, making her lips even more alluring. And some bronze eye shadow intensified both the roundness and depth of color of her blue eyes. The total effect, when combined with her off-the-shoulder peasant's blouse, was captivating. Satisfied with her appearance, she slid out of the car, and moments later she was carefully picking her way between the potholes and parked cars.

Quint's house was located on a narrow strip of land between the crushed coral road and the water. Situated on a low cliff, with the front of the house facing the water, it offered a 120-degree view of the East China Sea. The back wall of the house was only a few feet from the edge of the road, so there was no back yard. However, there were two small side yards and a large front lawn. Gates opened into both side yards. Christie walked up to the nearest one and let herself in. She had barely gotten through the gate when she was immediately surrounded by six young officers. She recognized a few of them as part of the group that had been so attentive at happy hour a few weeks earlier.

"Hey, Christie!" one of them said. "Where were you last night? We were expecting to see you at the club."

"Yeah, Christie" another one interjected. "Do you know how many disappointed guys there were at happy hour the last two weeks?"

"Sorry, guys," Christie said, embracing them all in the warmth of her smile. "I was invited by some of the other teachers to catch happy hour at Futenma and Sukiran, so that's where I was for the past two weeks."

That announcement promptly triggered an outburst of grousing.

"Sukiran!" said one of them. "Does this mean we're going to have to share you with every other officer's club on this island?"

And another one asked why she even bothered to visit those other clubs.

"The Air Force is the most important of the services and the classiest!" he said. "Those other characters will never appreciate you like we do!"

"Yeah," chimed in a third one. "Why waste your time with a bunch of ground pounders who have nothing better to do than run around in the jungle with their faces blackened and a couple of branches stuck in their helmets?"

By this point, Christie was beginning to wonder how long it would take to make her way past the front gate. But all of the commotion hadn't gone unnoticed. It wasn't long before she spotted Quint striding towards them. After pushing his way through the throng to her side, he slipped his arm around her waist in a possessive manner.

Turning to the group of young officers, all of whom he outranked, Quint said in a friendly but firm voice, "Okay, gentlemen. I'm afraid you're going to have to bite the bullet and share Miss Atherton with the rest of the guests."

Shrugging philosophically, they stepped back as Quint extracted her from the group and led her around to the front of the house.

"I got the impression that you knew most of those young officers," Quint said.

"Yes, I met them at Happy Hour a couple of weeks ago."

"Well, you obviously made one heck of an impression on them, Christie."

"Don't worry, Quint. I won't let their adulation give me a swelled head."

While Quint was inside getting her a glass of white wine, Christie made a quick survey of the crowd in the front yard. There were around forty people, roughly two-thirds men. And then there was that adorable little blond girl running around the yard, but she didn't seem to belong to any one at the party. A few minutes later, Christie crossed the yard, stopping briefly to look over the wall. Dense underbrush and scattered outcroppings of coral ledge extended about sixty feet from the base of the cliff to the water. A foot path ran along the edge of the cove, and after crossing over a narrow stretch of coral ledge, wound its way up to Quint's house at the far end of the yard where the cliff tapered off into a gentle slope. In the distance, a line of mostly uninhabited islands, part of the Ryukyuan chain, extended across the horizon as far as the eye could see. The scene presented a picture of tropical beauty and serenity. She wondered what it looked like when a typhoon was hammering away at the island.

Turning away, Christie continued around to the side yard where Rick was overseeing the grilling operation. Although he was obviously glad to see her, it became apparent after a few minutes that this was not the best time to be carrying on a conversation with him. Rick apologized for not being able to chat longer but admitted it was taking all his concentration to monitor steaks on two grills.

As Christie began walking back towards the front of the house, her path was partially blocked by three couples standing with drinks in hand. The women were talking and laughing conspiratorially while the men were watching a B-52 on final approach into Kadena. Christie tried to slip by them, but one of the men stepped aside to let someone else pass and accidentally bumped into Christie, spilling his nearly full glass of wine on her arm and skirt.

"Omigosh! I'm so sorry!" he said, turning red with embarrassment. "I am such a klutz! I'll go and get a towel or something for you."

"It's not necessary," she said. "It'll be dry in a few minutes."

"Are you sure?" he said, continuing to look thoroughly dismayed at his own clumsiness.

"Yes. I'm fine," Christie said. "Just think about it," she added with a wink and a quick smile, "It could have been a red. Then you might have reason to worry!"

That elicited a smile from him as he realized she really was not annoyed.

"That's true," he solemnly acknowledged. After taking a closer look at her, he suddenly exclaimed, "Hey aren't you the woman who was the center of attraction at Naha's happy hour a couple of weeks ago?"

Christie said nothing for a few seconds. That was not the way she wanted to be introduced, particularly in the presence of their wives and girlfriends. However, she had no choice but to say, "Yes. That was me. My name is Christie Atherton."

"Sven Andersen," he replied, taking her outstretched hand. "And these characters to my left are Josh Levine and Mike Ramirez, respectively." Each of them shook her hand in turn. As the wives were introduced, two of them, Robyn Levine and Kitty Andersen, scrutinized Christie with the same combination of fascination and caution that one might give a beautiful but potentially dangerous animal. In sharp contrast, Mike's wife, Maria, an attractive Hispanic woman, greeted her with real warmth as she eyed Christie with a mixture of admiration and curiosity.

"I don't remember seeing you around here before. Is your husband one of the new pilots in the 41st squadron?" Kitty asked, speaking with a pronounced southern lilt, which Christie thought sounded decidedly fake. She reminded Christie of an overdone Barbie doll with her bouffant hair style, too cute clothes, and heavy make-up.

"No," Christie said, matter-of-factly, glancing over her shoulder to see if Quint was en route with her drink. Most people, knowing that a fuller answer was expected, would have continued by explaining who they were and why they were there. Christie resented the way she had been automatically placed in the subordinate role to the man, so she deliberately let the unspoken question hang in the air.

Her lack of response clearly threw Kitty off balance. "Well, why are you here then?"

Although Kitty didn't mean it to sound peremptory, that was the way it came out.

"I beg your pardon?" Christie answered, her tone reflecting a combination of disbelief and annoyance.

"What Kitty means is what brought you to Okinawa?" Sven interjected.

Even though Kitty's husband phrased the question with considerably more tact, Christie was still a little annoyed. If she hadn't taken an immediate liking to Maria Ramirez, she would have been tempted to tell them it was none of their business. *What the hell,* she thought, *I'll give them something to talk about after I've left.* "To teach," then after a deliberate pause, she added, "and to do some preliminary research on a topic for my doctoral dissertation."

Her explanation triggered various responses. The blank expression on Kitty's face said it all. Robyn Levine, Josh's wife, looked annoyed, as if Christie's comment was a personal affront.

But then Christie had a distinct impression that her mere presence at the party was a source of annoyance to Robyn.

Maria Ramirez, however, was obviously both impressed by and interested in Christie's response.

"Is there some aspect of the culture that particularly interests you?"

"Yes, the various roles that women play in Okinawan society," Christie said.

Maria's response was immediate and positive. "I took a sociology class at UCLA a few years ago and ended up writing a paper on the impact that WW II had on the role of women in American society. Unfortunately some of the progress made during the war was erased afterwards, due, in large part, to a backlash from the men returning to civilian life. Anyway, it was a fascinating course and I've been interested in the topic of women's rights ever since."

"Let's discuss it over lunch sometime soon!" Christie said, with genuine enthusiasm. The sour look on Robyn's face was matched by an expression of dismay on Kitty's face.

Just as Christie was about to excuse herself and go to look for Quint, he arrived with her glass of wine in one hand and a bottle in the other. "Sorry I'm so slow in delivering this to you," he said, "but things were getting pretty hectic in the kitchen." Glancing at the rest of the group, he asked if anyone needed a refill.

"I'll pass," Sven said, winking at Christie. "I seem to be having a little problem keeping the wine in my glass tonight."

Quint nodded his head, unaware that there was a second level of meaning to Sven's casual comment. "So . . . I guess that all the introductions have been made?"

"Yep," Sven said.

"Can we assume that your decision to come to Okinawa to teach had something to do with Quint's presence here?" Robyn asked.

Christie shook her head. "I've already told you why I chose Okinawa," she said, trying to keep a lid on her growing irritation.

Robyn persisted. "I've been told that the majority of the single women who come to Okinawa to teach have an ulterior motive: namely, to latch on to a husband." There was no mistaking the supercilious tone in her voice now.

Christie's response was immediate and categorical. "Personally, I think that's a lot of rubbish. It's not only an insult to a woman's intelligence, but it strongly suggests that we're incapable of functioning independently of a man." Christie's tone was as emphatic and uncompromising as the sound of a ruler smacking the top of a desk. It was followed by several seconds of awkward silence, broken only by the sound of Quint clearing his throat and Sven Andersen's self-conscious cough. Mark Levine chose that moment to announce that someone with Christie's looks would probably find herself in just the opposite situation: fending off would-be suitors by the carload.

"That's the way it's been ever since Christie landed on the island," Quint agreed, good-naturedly. Christie however, was watching Robyn's reaction to her husband's comment. She could almost see the smoke coming out of her nostrils. The poor guy would probably pay dearly for that compliment later on when they were alone.

As they were walking back to the front yard a few minutes later, Quint glanced over at Christie and asked, "What the hell was that all about?"

Christie shook her head in frustration. "It's the same old thing, Quint. Another insecure woman who's taking out her insecurities on me. I swear," she added tiredly, "you would think I had nothing better to do than go around making passes at every man that I came in contact with.

Anyway, I've got to go back into the house," Quint said, changing the subject, "and check on things in the kitchen. But I'll come and get you when it's time to eat."

"Okay. By the way, who does that little blonde child belong to that I see running around the yard?"

"That's Kimberly Petersen, Tech Sergeant Petersen's daughter. He's my next door neighbor on the other side. Kimberly spends a lot of time here because she loves Sam."

"How do you feel about that?"

"I love having her here. She's my little buddy. And since Petersen is gone TDY much of the time I'm the primary male figure in her life—right now, anyway."

Hmmm. So Quint likes kids; that's a good sign. At least I know he'd make a good father.

After Quint left, Christie leaned against the wall, sipping her wine. She was beginning to second guess her decision to attend the party. Although many of the guests were around her age, she felt like an outsider who had invaded territory staked out by a closed clique. So who did that leave to socialize with? There was always her fan club, the group of young officers who couldn't seem to get enough of her. But that, too, grew old after a while. Besides, they seemed to be avoiding her ever since Quint had treated her so possessively.

Christie turned away from the wall and walked down towards the far end of the yard where the crowd thinned out to just a handful. At one point she stopped and introduced herself to a couple of women but her attempt at initiating a conversation with them fizzled after a few minutes. One of the women yawned in Christie's face, then excused herself before wandering off, followed by her companion, presumably to seek out a more interesting conversationalist.

A couple of minutes later, two men came over and struck up a conversation with Christie. One of the men made her uncomfortable as he spent more time leering at her breasts than thinking about what he was saying. The other man was less obvious, but Christie sensed that he, too, was interested in her. Within a few minutes the two wives came over to retrieve their errant husbands and they gave Christie the evil eye as if she had been an active pursuer in the drama. Shortly afterwards, the guests all walked back towards the house in response to an announcement that the steaks were ready.

Christie took another sip of her wine and glanced idly around the yard. The sparseness of vegetation of any size was one of the less appealing aspects of this part of the island, particularly the total absence of any shade trees. Other than a few stunted Japanese pines, the only other tree in Quint's yard was located a few feet away from where she was standing. Actually, it was more like a good size shrub than a tree.

Christie walked over to examine it more closely. It was probably about twice her height with bright green, lance-shaped leaves and delicate salmon pink blossoms. In addition to the tree's visual appeal, there was a pronounced candy-like fragrance that emanated from the flowers. She walked around to the other side of the tree and was about to pick a blossom that was within easy reach when a voice from right behind her spoke up.

"Miss! Not good touch any part of tree!"

Christie turned around with a startled look on her face to confront an Okinawan man standing behind the wall in the adjoining yard. Apparently, he had been kneeling down behind the wall, working in his garden, because he was wearing a pair of gloves and holding a trowel.

"What did you say?" she asked with a confused look on her face.

"Oleander very poisonous. Touch bark of tree you get skin rash."

"Really?" Christie said, wondering how such an innocuous looking tree could have such a reputation.

"Yes. More dangerous if inhale smoke when oleander cuttings burning. Most dangerous if eat part of it. You die then."

"Why would anyone eat it?"

"People break off branch to roast hot dog. Sap run into hot dog, and in few hours, too late to help them. Problem mostly back in States or place where many tourists visit. Natives know better than fool around with Oleander," he added, solemnly.

He spoke with such a tone of authority in his voice that Christie unconsciously stepped back away from the tree. As she did so, the innocent looking tree suddenly took on a more menacing appearance. Although she knew it was only her imagination, she saw everything in a different light: the lance-shaped leaves were spears that had been dipped in poison; the bright red blossoms were stained with the blood of the victims who had been pierced with the spears. Shaking her head to clear away the malignant image that briefly clouded her mind, she turned to thank her benefactor who had spoken up just in time.

"My name Ota Nakamura," he said bowing to her.

"And I'm Christie Atherton," she replied returning the bow.

"What bring you to island, if you not mind me asking."

"I don't mind at all Mr. Nakamura. I'm a teacher—high school, that is."

"Welcome to Okinawa, Miss Atherton. I hope your time here most pleasant," he said smiling shyly.

The smile on his face disappeared and was replaced by a neutral expression as Quint strode up to Christie's side, nodded at his neighbor, then turned to her and said, "What are you doing down here? The party's at the other end of the yard." He took her by the arm and led her back to where the rest of the guests were gathered.

When Quint rescued Christie from the group of young officers a short while earlier, she had mixed feelings about the way he had gone about it. She had chosen to overlook the incident, not wanting to be accused of overreacting. This time she was not so tolerant of the gesture, seeing it as a definite attempt to impose his will upon her. Christie gently but firmly removed his hand from her arm.

"I'll be with you in a minute, Quint." There was an edge to her voice which served as a clear warning that he was on shaky ground in acting so possessively. "I want to thank your neighbor."

"For what?"

"For saving me from a potentially dangerous encounter with the oleander tree."

Mr. Nakamura had started to work on his garden again when he realized Christie had returned to say something to him.

"Nakamura-san," she said, pressing her fingers together in front of her chest while dipping her head slightly, "I very much enjoyed talking to you."

Mr. Nakamura beamed at her gesture of respect as he bowed in return and expressed hope that they would get a chance to talk again soon.

As she walked back to where Quint was standing, it was obvious from the expression on his face that he was annoyed with her. On the other hand, she was doubly annoyed with him for trying to control her as well as for being curt with Mr. Nakamura.

"What's the matter with you, anyway?" she said, as they began walking towards the table where Rick was sitting.

"What do you mean?"

"You were pretty impolite to Mr. Nakamura."

Quint frowned. "I wasn't impolite. I'm just not very good at making small talk. Besides, it's not my obligation to go around being chummy with my neighbors. We each mind our own business. That's the way I like it."

"Would you have been that unfriendly to an American neighbor? I doubt it."

"It's like I said before, Christie: we don't have anything in common that we could talk about. Unless you think I should say something about how nice it is that we share space on the same small island."

"You don't need to get sarcastic, Quint. I wish your guests were half as friendly as Mr. Nakamura."

"What's the problem?"

"When I tried to strike up a conversation with two of your women guests, I got the cold shoulder. And a couple of your male guests made my skin crawl."

Quint jammed both hands in his pockets and stood staring out at the distant horizon for several seconds. "So what do you want me to do about it?" he finally asked.

"Nothing. But I am beginning to think it was a mistake to come to this party tonight. I really don't fit in."

"Maybe you need to try a little harder."

"Quint, you shouldn't have to work at socializing when you go to a party."

"Look," he said, lowering his voice so the people sitting nearby wouldn't hear, "Can we talk about this later? I don't want to get into an argument with you right here in front of everyone."

"Who's arguing? I was just making an observation. That's all."

"Fine. You've made your observation. Now, can we go over and sit with Rick and Sandy and see if we can manage to get along for the rest of the evening?"

As they sat down at the table, Christie wondered what Rick and Sandy were thinking. The tension between Quint and her was palpable. They *certainly must sense that something is amiss.*

As Christie pushed aside a piece of overdone chicken and began nibbling at her salad, Sally's admonition about Quint came back into Christie's mind. Sally had reminded her during their last conversation that Christie and Quint were very different people, perhaps too different to ever establish a relationship that was free of contention. It was his damn chauvinism that was the main problem. Would he ever change? If not, then their relationship was doomed. On the other hand, Christie felt the evening was by no means a total loss. Meeting Maria Ramirez had been a pleasant diversion. And Mr. Nakamura was her first real contact with an Okinawan, Maybe he could put her in contact with some of his friends. With that thought to comfort her, Christie decided to try to make the best of the remainder of the evening.

VIII

Wednesday morning, October 5ᵗʰ

"Christie, are you busy right now?"

It was nine-thirty in the morning and ten minutes into Christie's free period when Joe Magnuson called her on the intercom.

"Not that busy. Just looking over some papers."

"Can I see you for a few minutes in my office, please?"

"Sure."

A few minutes later, Christie was knocking on the door to his office.

"Come on in, Christie."

Joe had been a history teacher before moving into administration, so his office shelves were lined with history books. But his expanding library had long since outgrown the available space. Stacks of books covered his desk, his coffee table, the top of his credenza, and all the chairs except the one he sat in. Most students who ended up in his office felt it was a deliberate ploy designed to keep them standing in semi-military fashion. When asked about that, Joe dismissed it as nonsense. But the piles remained. And since he continued to add new books, some of the stacks had reached the point where it seemed as though a good sneeze might trigger a catastrophic avalanche.

"Here," he said moving the smallest stack of books from one of the chairs onto the floor. "Now, you have a place to sit."

After sitting down behind his desk, he reached for his coffee mug and took a quick sip only to grimace upon discovering that it was cold. "I don't know how many times a day I do this."

"Do what?" asked Christie.

"Pour a cup of coffee and then let it sit around until its ice cold." As he leaned across his desk and buzzed his secretary to bring him a fresh cup, he looked questioningly at Christie.

"No thanks," she said. "One cup in the morning is all I allow myself."

"Smart girl. I mean, woman," he said, quickly correcting himself. "Tell me, how do you like it here so far?"

"Do you mean at Kubasaki High or on Okinawa?"

"Well, both I guess, although I was thinking mainly of the school."

"I like it fine," she said. "And that applies to both places. I feel very comfortable on the island. In fact, I did from almost the first day. And the school, well, it seems pretty much like any other high school, except that the kids' parents all work for the same employer."

"The word is out on you, Christie. You know that, don't you? Don't mess around in Miss Atherton's class. That's what the students say. I thought maybe you had discovered some secret formula that could be used by some of the other teachers in the school."

Christie shook her head. "I have no idea what it might be. I treat each of them with respect and require the same from them."

Joe looked unconvinced. "There must be something more than that."

Christie gave him a quick grin. "Come on in and observe the class. Maybe you can figure it out and then we can bottle it and make a fortune from it."

After Joe's secretary delivered the fresh cup of coffee, he took a long satisfied sip and leaned back. He studied Christie briefly over the rim of his cup. "Have you seen today's *Morning Star*?

Christie had a sudden feeling of foreboding. "No. Why?"

"There's a picture of a group of demonstrators outside the offices of the paper. Two of the demonstrators were American high school students."

"Were either of them one of my students?"

"Yes. But not to worry, Christie. It wasn't an anti-war demonstration. It was a number of workers from the *Morning Star* striking for higher wages. Although I would be opposed to our students participating in an anti-war demonstration, I had no problem with them supporting local workers in their campaign for better work conditions."

Christie sighed with relief.

Joe continued. "Have you had any discussions about the Vietnam war?"

"Yeah. It started out with the kids being pretty subdued after hearing about the death of Scott Barlow's father. Then there were a few comments about the war and whether or not we were winning it, whether or not it was even winnable. Most of the discussion centered around the question of whether the students were obligated to toe the line, support the official position, because of their connection to the military, even if they happened to disagree with it."

"Is that it?"

"More or less. But I began to get a little uncomfortable with the direction of the discussion when they started talking about whether they had the right to take some kind of public stand on the issue."

"Meaning?"

"Meaning, I assume, taking part in an anti-war demonstration."

Joe leaned back in his chair and clasped his hands behind his head. After staring at the ceiling for several seconds, he looked over at Christie and asked how she answered the question.

"First, I solicited viewpoints from as many of the students as I could. Jen Coburn took the position that it was important for them to avoid doing anything to embarrass their parents or their country. Keith Ferris asked me where I stood. I admitted that I had my reservations about the war, but said that since I was a DOD employee it didn't seem right to take pot shots at the organization that employed me."

"What kind of a reaction did that produce?"

"None, actually. No one seemed particularly shocked by my answer."

Joe frowned. "You sure don't fit the role of a nervous Nellie, so I'm wondering why you had any concerns about this whole thing to begin with."

"I didn't like the way Lorraine Holloway was eyeing me. Furthermore, during most of the discussion, she had been whispering quietly to Angela Montez, the girl sitting next to her, who I know is the daughter of another high ranking marine officer."

"So what did Lorraine say that raised the hackles on everyone's back?"

Christie proceeded to tell him what Lorraine Holloway thought should be done to all activists and draft dodgers.

"First Lorraine made it clear that she was quoting her father. Apparently General Holloway thinks all those student demonstrators and people who are burning their draft cards should be thrown in jail or shipped to the front lines where the fighting is the worst. And as for those people who go to Canada to avoid the draft, well, he thinks they should be charged with treason and lined up in front of a firing squad.

"And Lorraine said she agrees with him. At that point she crossed her hands across her mid-section and glanced around the room, daring anyone to challenge her."

"What happened then?"

"There was stunned silence for several seconds while each of my students decided whether or not to let her outrageous comments stand unanswered.

"Nick was the first to speak up, and his response was predictable. This is more or less what he said, Joe: 'Way to go, Lorraine. Spoken like a true jarhead! And while we're at it we might as well get rid of all the queers, hippies and other misfits cluttering up the country. Right?'

Joe tried unsuccessfully to suppress a smile.

"What did Lorraine say then?"

"She told him to shut up. Claimed he didn't have a patriotic bone in his body."

"What did he say to that?"

"This is what he said and I'm quoting him 'Patriotic? What bullshit! The word for the mess in Nam is idiotic, not patriotic!'"

That brought a quick grin to Joe's face. "I love Nick's irreverence, but I would never let on to him I felt that way. It would be like handing a pauper a blank check."

"I told him that we could do without the use of swearing to punctuate his strongly held opinions."

After a moment of silence, Joe said, "Christie, short of fomenting outright insurrection, you're not going to get into any trouble, if that's what you're worrying about."

"I was a little concerned about what Lorraine and Angela Montez were whispering about during the discussion. I guess I had visions of them going home and telling their parents I was against the war and that I was encouraging the students to take a similar position."

"You were right in handling it the way you did. So, anything else, or anyone else, bothering you?"

"Yes. The area superintendent."

"Harlan Price?" Joe said with a puzzled expression on his face. "What about him?"

"My housemate warned me more than once that I could get in a lot of trouble with Harlan if I strayed from the party line and allowed any free-wheeling discussion about controversial topics, especially Vietnam."

Joe shook his head slowly from side to side while tapping his fingers on the edge of his desk. "You know, Sally Rehnquist does everything possible to avoid rocking the boat while at the same time refusing to get involved in anything that calls for any extra effort or that interferes with her personal activities. There's no doubt she knows her subject well, but she's unwilling to go that extra mile. In fact, as far as I can see, she lives what I'd call a triangular existence."

Christie looked puzzled. "What do you mean by that?"

"Just that she pretty much limits herself to traveling along the sides of a triangle, her house being located at one vertex; Kubasaki High at another; and the Naha Officer's Open Mess at the third."

Christie nodded in understanding. Although she felt Joe's assessment was accurate, she was reluctant to talk about Sally behind her back.

"Sally warned me more than once about Harlan Price," Christie said. "She said that because of his position as well as his military background, he wouldn't tolerate any kind of controversy in the classroom."

Joe scowled in obvious annoyance at Sally's alarmist comments. "Harlan can be difficult at times," he admitted. But he's a good administrator, and he's totally committed to what's best for the students. They come first in his mind, and it's kind of hard to argue with that. I suppose she also told you that several teachers and administrators have resigned or asked for re-assignment somewhere else because of his so-called overbearing manner."

"That's what she said."

"Well, like most other widely-held fallacies, there's a small amount of truth to that statement, but it's mainly a gross exaggeration. Most of the transfers took place because there was a critical shortage of teaching and administrative staff on both Taiwan and the Philippines. People voluntarily accepted last minute reassignment even though it was extremely inconvenient for them and their families. And one teacher left because of an emergency situation back in the states. Only two of the resignations were related to Harlan's presence and one of those was a definite over-reaction on the part of the administrator. That leaves one teacher who had a halfway legitimate complaint about the treatment he received from Harlan. And speaking of Harlan, I've got to meet with the boss in about five minutes," Joe said, glancing down at his watch.

"One other thing you need to know, Joe, is that I might be house-sitting for a friend who lives on Machinato Point sometime during the next several days. I've already left the phone number with the school secretary."

"Okay. Which reminds me, you probably haven't met Jack Lasalla yet, have you Christie? He's the assistant principal for the West Campus."

"No, I haven't. Why?"

"He lives on Machinato Point, too. A good man to know. I'll make a point of introducing the two of you before the week is out. And, Christie," Joe said, as he opened the door and followed her out into the main hall-way, "I want you to relax, enjoy your success and stop listening to people who like to put a negative twist on things. From everything Jim Martin tells me, you're doing a first-rate job. And that's all I need to know."

IX

By 1030 that same morning, the stack of paperwork in Quint's in-basket had shown no appreciable reduction in size although he had been chipping steadily away at it for the past three days. Part of the problem could be attributed to the dilemma faced by managers everywhere and for which there seemed to be no satisfactory resolution: namely, the outward flow of paperwork inevitably ran behind the inflow of new correspondence. And at the same time, the frustration he was feeling over the whole Cally—Christie situation, was proving to be a major distraction. It was clear something needed to be done and he was pretty certain what that something was. But he needed to see Cally once more to make sure that he was doing the right thing. That he was making the right decision. For that reason, as well as some other job-related ones, he had decided to fly down to Cam Ranh Bay that afternoon.

Actually, there were a number of perfectly legitimate official reasons for visiting the C-130 detachment at Cam Ranh Bay. For one thing, there were the proliferating maintenance problems with the C-130 landing gear. With his background as engineer, maintenance officer, and pilot he could bring a diversity of pertinent training and experience to that particular problem. In fact, since it was his branch that performed the heavy, field maintenance repairs on the planes as they returned from Vietnam there was no other choice but for him to assume responsibility for looking into the matter. He had already placed a call to the Operations Officer at his old outfit, the 41st Tactical Squadron. When Captain Richardson came on the line that morning Quint quickly outlined his need and was told that there was a flight leaving for Cam Ranh Bay at noon on which he could get a hop. The next call he made was to Chief Master Sergeant Ferris asking if he could meet with Quint that morning instead of Thursday morning. Ferris said that he could.

After a quick breakfast at the Officer's Club, Quint returned promptly to his office in order to spend a few minutes organizing his thoughts before Ferris arrived. There was the matter of the APRs and the need to broach the subject with Ferris about improving his writing skills. He was conscious of the sensitive nature of this issue and of the need to pick his way gingerly through this particular mine field.

Shortly before 0900 hours there was a knock on Quint's door and Sergeant Ferris opened it in response to his summons, walked in, and saluted. Quint gestured for him to take a seat while he pulled some written notes from his center drawer and studied them briefly. Leaning back in his chair, he looked over at Ferris and said,

"How have things gone so far today, Chief?"

"So far, so good, sir. We had a problem with balls 002 and balls 004 this morning, but in each case the crew chief was able to handle it with his flight line troops, so the planes got off after only a short delay."

Quint nodded. "At least field maintenance's reputation wasn't on the line that time. But I'm sure it's only a short reprieve, unfortunately. I assume that we're still getting a lot of landing gear problems with the birds that are returning from Cam Ranh."

"Yes sir. I'm sorry to say that they're taking a real beating what with all the unimproved strips the army has got us flying into. The thing is, that wouldn't be such a problem if we could just get enough of a breathing spell to put them back on a regular periodic maintenance schedule. But you know how it's been; we've supported three major operations in the last four months plus the max effort needed for Junction City. The maintenance quality is bound to go into a tailspin under those conditions."

"I suppose so," Quint said, "but there's something else going on here and I'm not sure yet exactly what it is."

"Sir?" Ferris said in a neutral voice.

"I'm flying down to Cam Ranh in a couple of hours to check on things at the detachment but before I go there's one other thing I'd like to discuss."

Quint sat momentarily lost in thought as he idly rolled a pencil back and forth on the desk with the fingers of one hand. Suddenly, as if he had come to some inner decision, he picked up the pencil and dropped it in his center drawer. Looking up at Ferris he said:

"It's about those last two APRs that you sent over for my endorsement—you know the ones on Malinowski and Novak."

Sergeant Ferris shifted uncomfortably in his seat.

"Begging the Major's pardon, but I know what you're going to say about them," Ferris said, leaning forward and running the crease in the flight cap back and forth nervously between his fingers. "Sir, I'd rather wrestle a planeload full of Vietcong soldiers than tackle one APR. Or one report, or one memo for that matter. It's like the worst kind of pick and shovel work, sir. It just doesn't come easily no matter how many times I do it."

"Look chief, I know how you feel. I'm an engineer, not a writer; I feel a hell of a lot more comfortable with a slide rule and a set of math tables, but there's no getting around it. If you're in a position of responsibility, you're going to have to write: reports, memos, and yes, evaluations on people who work for you.

"I do hear what you're saying Major Brewster, but it's different for you. You're a college grad with an advanced degree and you're used to writing—even if it doesn't happen to be your specialty."

"Yes, but that's exactly the way I became a proficient writer, Chief. It wasn't something I was born with. It's a skill, not a gift. I learned early on that I'd need to b e a good writer if I was going to be even halfway successful as an air force officer."

"Point taken, sir," Ferris said, the tone of respect evident in his voice.

"Okay. Remember, there are a couple of reasons why you need to get better at preparing these APRs. Not only are you making extra work for me but you're also weakening the NCOs chances when their file goes before the promotion boards. And I'm positive you wouldn't want to be the reason for someone getting passed over for promotion."

"No sir. That's unacceptable. I guess I'll just have to try harder. But what can I do about it? I mean where can I go to get help?"

Even as Quint was anticipating Sergeant Ferris' response, a half-formed thought in his mind suddenly coalesced into something substantive—one of those flashes of inspiration that seemingly spring out of nowhere, yet often end up solving more than one problem simultaneously. He smiled wryly to himself at the thought that he was definitely sticking his neck out on this one. But if Christie was as dedicated a teacher as he thought, maybe she'd be willing to take on the challenge.

Mentally promising to Christie that he'd make it up to her for what he was about to do, he turned back to Sergeant Ferris and said, "There's a teacher I know who's thinking of running a remedial writing class in the evening for people just like yourself—individuals in positions of responsibility who have a real problem putting their thoughts down on paper. How would you feel about signing up for a course like that if she decides to go ahead and offer it?" Quint studied his expression carefully while Sergeant Ferris wrestled visibly with the idea of going back to school and taking a course which he could easily fail. The very real possibility that he would end up displaying his own ineptitude in front of a group of people he didn't even know—or worse yet, did know—was obviously a discomfiting thought.

After a minute or two of strained silence, Ferris looked over at Quint and shrugged as he nodded in acquiescence. "I'll do it, sir. It can't be any more painful than some of the other things I've had to tackle in my life."

"I would have been disappointed if you had said otherwise. When I get back from Cam Ranh Bay, one of the first things I'll do is touch base with this teacher and find out more of the particulars—you know like when and where it's going to meet."

Taking this as a cue that the meeting was over, Sargent Ferris got up, saluted and was walking towards the door, when he abruptly stopped, turned around and said, "If you don't mind me asking, sir, what's the name of this teacher?"

"Miss Atherton. Christie Atherton." He held Sergeant Ferris' gaze and said in a matter-of-fact tone, "why do you ask? Is there a problem?"

"No sir. I was just wondering, that's all."

As soon as he was gone, Quint called the receptionist at the high school and left a message for Christie to call him as soon as she was free. Next he placed a quick call to Rick.

"Hey Rick."

"Hi Quint. Where have you been keeping yourself? I was beginning to think that you'd dropped off the face of the earth or perhaps were spending an inordinate amount of time with a certain young thing of the teaching persuasion."

"Actually, I haven't seen Christie since the night of the cocktail party. Anyway, the reason I called was to tell you that I'm flying down to Cam

Ranh this afternoon and to see if there was anything that I owed you before I left."

"Nothing that I'm aware of. What's the reason for the trip, if you don't mind me asking?"

"Both professional and personal," Quint said, truthfully.

"Do you plan on seeing Cally?" Rick asked, a hint of coolness creeping into his tone.

"Yes. To be frank, that's one of the main reasons for my trip. I plan on breaking off with her now that I'm going to be seeing Christie."

There was a pause on the line and then he heard Rick saying, "Suppose you find that you can't once you're down there." There was a hint of something else in Rick's voice now, censure perhaps. "I wouldn't want to see Christie hurt, Quint. Suppose Cally tries to seduce you?"

"I have every intention of keeping her at arms-length this time."

"I hope it works out that way—for Christie's sake, as well as your own."

"It will. Look, I've got to get going," Quint said, wanting to end the conversation before either one said something they'd regret. "I'll see you in a few days."

"Okay."

Shortly after the call from Rick, Christie called.

"Hi, Quint. What's up?"

"I'm heading down to Cam Ranh in a couple of hours. I plan on looking Cally up and telling her officially that it's all over. I just wanted you to know Christie," he blurted out.

"All right, Quint I'll see you when you get back."

"That should be Saturday night sometime."

"Okay."

It was after 1100 by the time Quint finished up things in his office and prepared to leave for the flight line. By 1330 hours he was already an hour and a half out of Naha winging his way south at a steady if unspectacular 350 miles per hour. Although he normally sat up front in the cockpit, there had been less room than usual due to the presence of an extra flight crew that was deadheading down to Cam Ranh to pick up a damaged C-130. He probably could have squeezed in anyway but decided the six hours aloft could be put to better use if he sat in the back and plugged away at the paperwork in his briefcase.

The cargo consisted mainly of pallets stacked to the ceiling with everything from canvas bags of mail to a couple of spare engines. Near the back of the ramp the loadmaster had managed to squeeze in a small jeep which Quint chose for his temporary office, stretching out in the front seat with his papers spread out in front of him on the hood. It was bound to be more comfortable than the pull-down canvas mesh seats which lined either side of the fuselage and which had no equal when it came to providing maximum discomfort in an innocuous looking package.

About an hour before they were due to land at Cam Ranh Bay, Quint put the paperwork aside that he had been working on, leaned back in the seat and closed his eyes. Although the earplugs had served to lower the decibel level from the threshold of pain to a dull roar, even his powers of concentration were gradually eroded under the relentless barrage of noise and vibration from the four big turboprop engines. Despite the adverse conditions, however, he had begun to drift off when there was a light tug on his pants leg and, opening one eye, he saw the loadmaster gesturing that they were about to land. He climbed out of the seat and over a couple of pallets to the small porthole shaped windows but quickly changed his mind, electing instead to go up to the cockpit and watch the landing from a better vantage point.

As he watched the coast of Vietnam gradually take form on the horizon, a length of green and white ribbon materializing out of the ocean, he was struck again by how accurate the description was about it being a land of dramatic contrasts. Cam Ranh Bay itself was a fairly good example of that truism. A barren landscape devoid of everything except a smattering of scrub growth inhabited by an indigenous population of lizards. Its most ubiquitous feature was sand: hundreds and hundreds of acres of the whitest, purest sand found anywhere in the world.

Ironically, the crystalline structure of the local sand did not provide the necessary adhesive quality needed for concrete, so sand had to be imported from elsewhere when they began to construct the roads and runways. But that deficiency notwithstanding, Cam Ranh Bay had some of the most beautiful beaches to be found anywhere and also had one of the best natural harbors in the world. Quint decided that it was the latter attribute more than anything else, which led the Department of Defense to choose this out of-the-way place as the main logistical support base for the Vietnam theatre.

The plane banked over the ocean and lined up with one of the twin, twelve thousand foot runways that stretched like parallel ribbons from one side of the peninsula to the other, dividing it into what had informally been termed Cam Ranh East and Cam Ranh West. The west side was only recently developed and to date the C-130 detachment from Naha was the only unit located in the new facilities. The east side housed the various support units such as the hospital, Officer's Club and personnel quarters as well as the rest of the operating units including the 12ᵗʰ Tactical Fighter Wing whose home base was back at Kadena Air Base on Okinawa.

After the C-130 taxied to a stop in front of the small flight operations building, Quint grabbed his travel bag and briefcase and headed over to check in with the maintenance dispatcher to arrange for the use of a small pick-up truck for the next few days. Following that, he arranged for a room that could be used the following day for a series of meetings as well as a review of the maintenance and training records and then decided to call it a day.

The detachment maintenance officer had offered him the use of an empty bunk in his hooch for the next two nights. A crude, ridiculous sounding word, Quint thought idly to himself as he was driving around to the east side of the base early that evening, but hooch was probably as appropriate a term as any to describe the primitive huts that served as living quarters throughout Vietnam. Wooden slated sides set on a concrete base with an opening at the top to allow for some movement of the air—that's all they amounted to. Quint was reminded of the typical pavilions that were found in parks back home. The main complaint about them was that they allowed sand to filter in every time the wind blew, which at certain times of the year was almost continuously. Aside from that and the fact that they afforded very little if any privacy, he supposed they were adequate for a subtropical climate like Vietnam.

Dinner at the Officer's Club was typically the high point of the day, one of the main reasons being that it was one of the half dozen or so buildings on base that was actually air-conditioned. Throughout the meal, Quint found himself scanning the crowd somewhat apprehensively, expecting to see Cally walk in at any minute. When it seemed likely that she was not going to show up, he felt a mixture of both relief and irritation. On the one hand, he really wasn't in the mood to tackle any personal issues after the long tiring day, but on the other hand there was a part of him that would like to have dealt with it that night so that it wouldn't be hanging over his head any longer. The problem became a moot one a few minutes later, however, when he happened to overhear a couple of nurses talking, one of whom mentioned that Cally was up at Danang for the day and probably wouldn't be back until the following afternoon.

He decided at that point that he might as well get to bed early in order to be completely rested for the following day's demanding schedule—one which he had to ruefully admit, was of his own doing.

An hour later he was still lying awake, shifting from one position to another in an attempt to get comfortable. Part of the problem had to do with the condition of the old metal bunks which he was certain were of World War II vintage. The other problem was that the general noise level on the base was about as bad at night as it was during the day. The biggest culprits were the engine test pits which were located about a quarter of a mile away; they typically operated 24 hours a day, testing the big turbo-fan engines that powered the phantom jets. Quint had always thought the sounds emanating from them had an other-worldly quality, transformed at night through a combination of the atmosphere and one's imagination into what he pictured a wounded dinosaur would sound like, roaring in its death throes.

Sitting up on the edge of the bunk in disgust, he decided that there was no point in lying there any longer. He probably should have stayed at the Officer's Club and had a couple of drinks before attempting to get any sleep. Since it was still relatively early he decided to hop in the pick-up and go back over to the club for a while—the chances were always better than even that he would run into someone from Naha with whom he could pass the time.

Even before he turned the corner and saw how full the parking lot was he could tell by the noise level that the place was in full swing although it was only a week-day night. Once inside the building, the reason for all the activity immediately became clear: a large group of fighter pilots were lined up three deep along the bar, gesturing and talking boisterously as they swilled down bottle after bottle of the local Vietnamese beer. Apparently, the 12th Tactical Fighter Wing had flown a sortie over the North that day and had lost a couple of their planes to the Russian ground to air missiles which the North Vietnamese were employing with such deadly effect. Fighter pilots by nature were an unruly bunch anyway; it didn't take much to set them off—in either an explosion of anger or a frenzy of joy—and the end result in both cases was often about the same. On several occasions in the recent past they had tried to dismantle the club after an evening of wild celebration or rampaging frustration. Whatever their reasons, Quint never could identify with that type of mentality and really wasn't in the mood for their antics tonight. But since there was nowhere else to go, he decided to stay for a short while anyway.

After managing to get close enough to the bar to place an order for a beer, he worked his way over to the far corner of the room where, miraculously, he discovered a small empty table. Leaning back against the wall, he put his feet up on an empty chair and settled back to watch the proceedings. With a little luck, he thought, maybe someone he knew would wander in and he could try and get their attention. Usually, he didn't mind being alone, but tonight was different; tonight he felt the need to talk to someone—almost anyone, in fact, would do.

X

But that 'almost anyone' didn't include the person who had suddenly materialized out of the crowd at the bar and was moving somewhat unsteadily in his general direction. It was Cally, looking more than a little disheveled, and leaning for support on the shoulder of some officer. Quint was more surprised to see her slightly inebriated than with another man; control was as big an issue for Cally as it was for Quint, perhaps even bigger, and like him she was also leery of placing herself in a position where there was even a temporary loss of control.

As far as her being caught arm in arm with another man, that was hardly a surprise. Although they had dated each other almost exclusively for the previous year, there had never been any discussion—much less stipulation—that they couldn't date anyone else. And although Quint had never opted to do so, he always suspected in his own mind that Cally hadn't been quite so loyal.

He was torn for a moment as to what he should do. He could simply go back to Okinawa and tell Christie that before he had even had a chance to talk to Cally she had shown up at the Officer's Club in the arms of another officer. But that was the easy way out and, never having given into that temptation before, he wasn't about to do so now.

But should he try and get her attention right then and there or wait until tomorrow and deal with her when she was completely sober and rational. He had about decided on the latter course when she happened to glance over in his direction. Quint raised his beer bottle in a mocking salute to her, waiting with a look of amusement on his face to see what she was going to do. It was hard to read her expression in the dim lighting, but he would have sworn that he saw a mixture of annoyance and—most surprisingly—fear, something which he had never observed on Cally's face before.

Disengaging herself abruptly from the officer, she whispered something in his ear which caused him to glance quickly over at Quint then back at her again. She said something else which appeared to make him momentarily agitated, but after a minute he turned away and walked over to the door.

Cally managed to walk over to the table unassisted and sat down in the empty chair that Quint had pulled out for her. By the time she got to Quint's table her look of annoyance had been replaced by a deliberate seductive look which Quint for the first time found not only irritating but also offensive. Wrapping both hands around his upper arm, she blurted out, in a moment of accidental honesty,

"I didn't expect to see you here."

"So I gather," Quint replied, not bothering to hide the sarcasm in his tone.

"Come on Quint, don't be angry with me."

"I'm not but it doesn't really matter anyway. It should have been clear to both of us that things weren't going to be the same after we had that big blow-up."

Glancing around the room she started to rise, saying, "Let's go outside and talk. It's too loud in here to carry on any kind of normal conversation."

"There's nothing really to talk about at this point. We never learned how to talk to each other in the first place and it's a little late to start now."

"Come on, let's go take a walk and then we can talk about us."

Quint shook his head solemnly, "You know what—I don't think there ever was an 'us.' Just you and I. Two separate individuals who shared a few laughs, a few good times . . . ."

". . . . And plenty of sensual times as well," she interjected indignantly. "Don't tell me you've conveniently forgotten those now," an edge creeping into her voice.

"No, I haven't forgotten those times, Cally," he said, his voice clear and unemotional, "but can't you see—by themselves those memories don't add up to very much!"

"How dare you sit there and say they didn't mean anything. That's not the way you felt when you were in the midst of making passionate love to me," she replied, her eyes flashing at him imperiously, reflecting the anger in her voice.

He looked at her with a coolly appraising expression on his face, as if seeing her clearly for the first time. "I can't argue that point Cally," he said, "but unfortunately once the heat of passion was gone there didn't seem to be anything left. In fact, all that was left were the long empty spaces when neither of us could seem to think of anything to say to each other."

"Come on Quint," she said imploringly, "Can we please get out of here and go someplace where we can talk in privacy without having to put up with all this," waving her hand in the general direction of the bar.

Quint shrugged. He was fascinated by the way she could switch back and forth between a conciliatory tone and an angry one. He sensed that it was more of a conscious tactic than any spontaneous emotional response.

"All right. Let's go." Once outside he said, "Where do you want to go?"

"How about back to my quarters? I happen to know there's no one there right now—and won't be for the rest of the evening."

Uh-uh, Quint thought to himself, that's definitely not a good idea. He remembered his promise to himself as well as to Rick to keep Cally at arm's length. That might not be so easy if he was alone with her in a secluded area for any length of time.

"I don't think so. We can sit in my pick-up truck for a few minutes and then I can give you a ride back home."

"That's not a very comfortable place," she said, a tone of disappointment in her voice.

"There's no need to be comfortable," Quint said impatiently, "All we're going to do is have a brief talk."

As soon as they got into the pick-up truck, Cally slid over on the seat next to him and nudged him playfully as she said," actually, this isn't so bad. We've made love in some pretty uncomfortable places—including the front seat of a pick-up truck just like this. Don't tell me you've forgotten that!"

Quint shook his head tiredly. "You're beginning to sound like a broken record. Yes, I do remember that but do you know what's really strange about our relationship?"

"What?"

"How little we managed to find out about each other over the course of almost a year's time. I take part of that back: I know a lot about what you do but you know next to nothing about what I do. In fact, I don't remember you ever expressing any real interest in what exactly it is that I do. I suppose I could have lived with that, but what was really telling is that we didn't know the first thing about each other's personal lives, except for the most superficial stuff."

"So what would you like to know about me? Come on," she said, still trying to make light of everything by being playful, "I'll tell you whatever it is you want to know."

"For Pete sakes, Cally," you don't find out the things like that through some kind of interrogation process. It comes about naturally through everyday conversation—or at least it's supposed to in a normal relationship. Besides, it's too late anyway."

Quint felt the sudden chill in the air as Cally slid across the seat to the other side of the cab. "You never seemed to mind the fact that we didn't have these kind of conversations before. Why is it so important to you all of a sudden?"

"It doesn't matter anymore." He said, disregarding her question for the moment. "But I still want to know," she said, a puzzled look on her face, "why does it matter all of a sudden?"

Quint sat silent for a minute, running his finger idly around the inside of the steering wheel.

"Because I've found someone who I want to know everything about. Someone more special than anyone I've ever known." As the words came forth from his mouth, hanging heavy in the enclosed space of the cab, he wondered if he was being cruel. And even as that thought formed in his mind, he realized that it didn't matter at this point. As Quint watched her, she flipped back, chameleon-like fashion, into yet another mood. The look of seductive playfulness was wiped clean in an instant and replaced by—not anger, but something worse—a coldness, an indifference, which in a flash of insight made him feel stronger than ever that Cally could only ever love Cally. And there was probably nothing that would ever happen to change that fact.

"So there is someone else," she said, her voice colder than he had ever heard before. "I should have guessed based on the way you acted that day at the club."

"No," he said firmly, "You're wrong. There was no one else at that point," thinking to himself that he really wasn't lying to her; that he had not at that moment been aware of being attracted to Christie—in any romantic sense anyway. "I simply came to realize that there were fatal flaws in our relationship."

"You and your analytical ways," she said, her voice thick with sarcasm. "Can't you ever accept things as they are, instead of taking something apart piece by piece until there's nothing left of it."

"Come on, Cally, that's a stupid thing to say. No one ever got any- where sticking their head in the sand and pulling that ostrich routine. Anyway, that's the way I see it and that's all there is to it. So you can go find someone who's still on a fast track to success."

"If that's the way you feel about it then maybe I'll do just that," Cally said, as she reached for the door handle. Closing the door behind her, she added, more as an after- thought than a cutting remark, "You know, I think maybe I will go back into the club, there are probably any number of men in there who can appreciate my so-called superficial qualities."

Quint, struck by the unconscious irony in her response, was momen- tarily overcome by a feeling of sadness—of loss for something that had never really existed to begin with. Twisting the side view mirror until she could see her face reflected in it, Cally studied herself for a moment before applying a fresh coat of lipstick. As she moved the mirror back to its original position, she said out of the corner of her mouth, "I hope you're happy now Quint, we finally had one of those in-depth conversa- tions that were so important to you."

There was a moment before she turned away and disappeared into the shadows that her face was illuminated briefly by the headlights from a jeep that was pulling out of the parking lot. Quint could never be sure, but although it seemed unlikely, in fact, highly improbable, he would have sworn that her eyes were glistening with tears.

XI

When he got back to his quarters a half an hour or so later, Quint lay down on the bunk feeling completely drained and more than a little surprised at the way the evening had ended. It would certainly have made it a lot easier if Cally had flown into one of her infamous tirades and completely lost it all, although a heated argument clearly had its down side as well. The fact that she didn't respond in typical fashion made Quint wonder if, in fact, there wasn't more depth to Cally than he had been willing to give her credit for. He lay on his bunk for what seemed like hours trying to make sense of what had been said and, equally importantly, not said. Shortly before he finally drifted off into a restless sleep, the thought passed through his mind that he might have been wrong about Cally; that maybe he hadn't given her—them—a fair chance. It was not the kind of thought he would have chosen to have in his mind at the moment that he finally lost consciousness.

—m—

When Quint awoke the next morning, it was to the accompaniment of a pounding headache and the realization that he wanted out of Cam Ranh by Friday at the latest. There was no way he was going to stay there and chance another encounter with Cally, no matter how innocuous it might turn out to be.

Between meetings he was able to determine that the first C-130 flight back to Naha was departing around 1400 on Friday, which he quickly calculated would get him back into Naha about 2000 hours. Although far from ideal, it was highly likely that he would be able to sleep all the way back what with only getting about four hours the previous night. There was no question that he intended to be on that plane, providing he could get the meetings out of the way by late morning and start digging into the maintenance records immediately afterwards.

By Thursday afternoon, Quint felt that he had a realistic shot at catching the Friday flight. In fact, the meetings were proceeding so smoothly that he felt comfortable skipping the last one and jumping right into the records review. If he could only get rid of the damned headache. But unfortunately it seemed impervious to even the strongest medication that the flight surgeon's office could prescribe.

His first important clue surfaced mid-afternoon when he was about half way through his examination of records from planes that had suffered heavy structural damage during their flights into unimproved army strips such as those found in the northern highlands and the delta. Two things struck him: they had all recently returned from major maintenance back in the states; most significantly, they all had been to the same repair facility in Ohio. He thumbed rapidly through a stack of records looking for those planes that had been back at that particular repair facility in the past several months. In virtually all cases, the same planes had been in for major field maintenance repairs at Naha within a relatively short time span following their trip back from the depot. It looked increasingly like the problem's roots could be traced back to quality control problems with the depot-level maintenance performed by civilian contractors back in the states. Col. Crane, he was certain, would find this to be a most interesting bit of news. It clearly indicated that the training deficiencies were taking more of the blame than they should have. Not that they were without fault, because clearly there was a need for improvement in that area. But this information at least allowed for a more balanced picture of the whole situation.

Quint spent Friday morning in a concentrated burst of activity in which he managed to put together a package that included several pages of analysis along with photocopies of sample records which would corroborate his findings. Stuffing them into his briefcase, he grabbed his flight bag right after a hurried lunch and hitched a ride out to the C-130, which already had three of its four engines running at full rpms and was just turning over number four.

Less than ten minutes later they were off the ground and climbing out over the ships anchored in the harbor. As Quint settled on top of a stack of mail he realized that no burden—professional or personal—was going to keep him awake on the long flight back. Just before he slipped away into a deep and untroubled sleep, Quint acknowledged to himself that he had never before felt so connected to anyone as he did to Christie—not even to Lisa. Of course, she was only his sister. This was different. Much different. Christie. You . . . beautiful . . . creature. I would love to make mad . . . pash . . . . His thoughts fragmented and slipped away into nothingness as consciousness faded into unconsciousness.

XII

Christie put the red marking pencil down on the pile of essay papers, got up from her desk and walked over to the window. Standing with her arms folded, she looked out over the playing field in the middle distance to the low hills which blocked her view of Tomarii port and Naha Air Base—the base at which Quint was stationed. She wondered what he was doing at that very moment. Presumably he was on his way back from Vietnam by now. Was he thinking about her as his plane drew closer to Okinawa, looking forward to seeing her? Hopefully he'd had it out with Cally.

It was 3:30 on a Friday afternoon and the main reason Christie was still in her classroom at that hour was due to a request from one of her students. Keith Ferris had stopped at her desk after 5th period English Honors class and asked if he could talk to her for a few minutes after school. Although she never refused such a request, today was one of those rare days when her energy and motivation levels were both unusually low. Part of the reason, of course, was that she was pre-menstrual. That always sapped her energy and dramatically reduced her tolerance for other people's problems.

That in itself was frustrating enough, but she knew that her moodiness today was not due solely to the monthly rampage of her hormones. Christie was missing Quint more than she imagined she ever would. It was more than a week now—ten days, to be exact—since he had dropped her off after the cocktail party at the Shuri Hills Club. Of course, he had warned her that he was busy with a number of pressing issues that were demanding virtually all of his time. And so far, she reluctantly acknowledged, he had been true to his word. It would be easy enough to convince herself that she was wasting her time—that he would always end up being too busy. But there were two reasons why she held on to the hope that things would change.

For one thing, he made it clear in their phone conversation that he intended to break off with Cally permanently. But the most telling piece of evidence was the way that he had kissed her that night on the balcony. The way he had looked at her before he kissed her. She closed her eyes and pictured the scene again for the hundredth time. The sheer sensuality of their kissing was so strong an image in her memory that she could almost feel the warmth spreading throughout her body, could almost re-create the passion which swept both of them away in a fierce melding of their lips and tongues. She was drifting on a current of ecstatic memories when she realized that a voice was calling in the distance.

"Miss Atherton. Miss Atherton?"

Shaking her head to clear away the web of memories, she turned away from the window to face a solemn-looking, smooth-faced teenager of about sixteen.

"Hi Keith." Pulling a chair up to the desk, she motioned for him to sit down. Deciding to momentarily skirt the reason for his being there, she pulled an essay paper from the pile on her desk and after looking it over for a minute, said to Keith:

"This first paper that you did—it's really an excellent piece of writing. To be frank, I don't usually see work of this quality from a junior—especially this early in the school year. It's not just that the punctuation and spelling are flaw-less, but the writing is smooth; it flows and is easy to read. Obviously, you have a real gift for writing; you should feel very proud of your accomplishment."

Keith smiled and thanked her but it was clear that something was bothering him. Something that prevented him from fully enjoying his suc-cess. He ran his finger nervously along the edge of his book, then after five or ten seconds of strained silence, looked up at her and said:

"I realize that school is only a few weeks old but I knew from the first day that you were going to be someone special; someone I could trust."

Christie sighed inwardly, wondering now if his apparent discomfit was nothing more than one of the first symptoms of a teenage crush. If so, that was certainly something with which she could identify.

"Thank you, Keith," she said, trying simultaneously to sound sincere but neutral. "If this is any indication of the type of work I can expect from you, then it's going to be a pleasure to have you in my class."

"Thanks, Miss Atherton, I guess you already can imagine how much a compliment from you means to me. I just wish my father felt the same way as you do about my writing."

Christie suddenly felt a little like one of those characters in the comic strip whose moment of revelation is depicted by a light bulb flashing on over their head. "You mean to say that your father isn't proud of you when you produce excellent work such as this," she said, pointing to the paper in her lap.

Keith shrugged. "Not really. The only thing that really makes him happy is when I get As in math and science. He always calls those the hard subjects."

Christie frowned slightly. "I can't imagine why anyone would think that an English Honors class is easy."

Keith shook his head. "No. That's not what he means by hard. It's not hard vs. easy. It's more like hard vs. soft. Math and science are hard—they're good. English and history are soft; you know, like sissy stuff."

Christie nodded, the light of comprehension dawning on her face. "I see," she said, thoughtfully, as she unconsciously rearranged the pile of essay papers in front of her.

"What does your father do?"

"He's a senior NCO . . . ," Keith started to say, then looking at her questioningly, and asked, "You do know what I mean by NCO, right?"

Christie smiled and said, "Yes, a non-commissioned officer, right?"

He nodded and continued, ". . . with one of the squadrons at Naha."

Christie wondered momentarily if Quint might know him, then dismissed the possibility as remote and irrelevant as well.

"He wants me to go to the Air Force Academy."

"Does your father know that the Academy is like any other college or university? They teach you a lot of things in addition to math and science and you're not going to get very far unless you do well in the so-called soft subject areas as well."

Keith nodded, somewhat impatiently. "He knows all that, Miss Atherton, but it doesn't make any difference to him. He just keeps stressing the importance of doing well in math and science, and no matter how well I do in English and History he just shrugs it off."

Christie nodded sympathetically. "Believe it or not, Keith, I think I know what you're going through."

"You do?" he responded, in a somewhat doubtful tone.

"Yes. You see my stepfather is a very well-known aeronautical engineer—in fact, actually famous within his field. He had always planned for his son to follow in his footsteps. When it became clear that wasn't going to happen, he tried to make me to fit into that mold. But all I wanted to do was write and that was a source of major frustration for him—and conflict between us, I might add."

Keith shook his head, unconvinced. "But it's different for you. It's okay for you to like things like drama and poetry. You're a girl—I mean a woman. But I'm not supposed to be interested in stuff like that."

"Come on Keith. You're too intelligent to start pigeonholing people because of their gender. Besides, I'm sure you're well aware of the fact that the majority of the great writers and poets to date have been male, not female."

"Sorry Miss Atherton," Keith said sheepishly, "I didn't mean it that way. I mean it's not like I feel that way. You know—it's my father."

Christie glanced down at her watch and wondered idly what Quint's advice would be in a situation such as this. At this point, she didn't have any idea what she could do to help Keith out of his predicament. Of course, it was always possible that he just wanted a sympathetic ear—that he didn't really expect her to do anything. But then that wasn't her way. She wanted to help but at the moment didn't have a clue as to what her next step would be. She needed some time to mull it over.

"Why are you telling me all this, Keith?" she said, hoping to gain more insight into the reason for his visit. "Is there something specific you wanted me to do? Something that you were hoping I could do?"

Keith sighed and looked at her somewhat dejectedly, "I really don't know, Miss Atherton. I mean it's not like I came here expecting you to pull off some kind of miracle; you know like change my father's attitude with a single phone call. And honestly, I had no intention of putting you on the spot either. I guess I just wanted to talk to someone and you seemed like the person who was most likely to listen to me and—and take me seriously, if you know what I mean."

Christie got up and walked towards the door. Keith, taking the cue, followed suit. When she got to the door, Christie turned around and faced him. "I know you didn't mean to put me on the spot," she said, smiling supportively. "But the fact is, as much as I'd like to help you, I'm not sure that I can do anything. However, give me a little time to think it over."

Keith thanked her and turned to go then stopped abruptly and said: "I almost forgot, I found a novel to write my paper on. Here's the title and author and a list of the few critical studies that I could find on the author's work. It includes your essay, of course. Miss Rehnquist thought you would be a good person to critique what I've done so far since you had the article to your credit."

"I'll take a look at it over the weekend, Keith. When is it due?"

"First draft is due next Wednesday."

"Okay. I'll read it with the idea of checking on how well you support your thesis."

"Thanks a bunch, Miss Atherton. See you later."

"Goodbye, Keith. Enjoy your weekend, and thanks for sharing your concern with me. I'm honored that you felt comfortable enough to trust me with your feelings and frustrations."

Christie walked back to the desk and stood in front of it, idly sliding the sheet Keith had given her back and forth between her fingers as she stared unseeing out the window. Keith's frustration with his father troubled Christie more than she might have imagined; she assumed it was because of the memories it brought back of the turbulent relationship she had experienced with her own stepfather. One of the biggest problems any child had to contend with was the guilt brought on by the feeling that they had somehow failed their parent. Even now, years afterward, it was difficult for Christie to confront her own feelings in that area because they were still there, unresolved after all that time. She wondered if there was anything that could be done to prevent Keith from having to go through the same emotional turmoil.

"Christie?"

She looked up from her reflections to see Sally Rehnquist poke her head through the half-opened door.

"Hi Sal. Come on in."

"Have you got a minute?"

"Sure. I've got plenty of them," she said, a tone of frustration show-ing in her voice. Sally looked at her with a questioning look on her face. "What's the matter? Problems with your students or maybe with your love life?"

Christie grinned at her. "A little of both, actually."

Sally Rehnquist had been Christie's sponsor from the moment that Christie had first signed a contract to teach on Okinawa. It was her some-times rambling, sometimes tongue-in-cheek, but always wonderfully-descriptive letters that had done more than anything to pique Christie's interest in the teaching assignment. And it was Sally who had first offered Christie her spare bedroom when she discovered that her own housemate was returning to the states.

Short blonde hair and a winning smile in combination with an upbeat personality and self-deprecating sense of humor were Sally's most attrac-tive features. Although somewhat on the plump side, Christie thought Sally quite pretty, particularly on those rare occasions when she went to the trouble to dress up. It didn't take her very long to realize, however, that Sally's battle with her weight was far from a recent one and was probably destined to go on forever: hard-won, minor victories inevitably wiped out by successive failures of will power.

Nevertheless, in the few weeks she had roomed with Sally, Christie had grown very fond of her and quickly came to appreciate both her wis-dom and wit, neither of which was dispensed in a heavy-handed fashion.

"Was that Keith Ferris you were just meeting with?"

"Yes. How did you know?"

"I just saw him walking out of the building a few minutes ago and it's highly unlikely that any of the other teachers would still be available at this time on a Friday afternoon." She perched nonchalantly on the corner of a desk and glanced around the room before continuing. "I had him last year and . . . ," shaking her head in amazement at the memory, she added, ". . . he produced such outstanding work that I wondered at first if he was plagiarizing it. But as far as I could tell, it was all his own work."

Christie nodded in agreement. "I just got through correcting a short paper I asked the class to do. There's no doubt about it: both his analytical and writing skills are absolutely superior for someone of his age." She had picked up his paper and was looking it over again, wondering whether she should mention the reason for Keith's visit.

"Did you ever get any indication from Keith that he was having problems at home?"

Sally thought for a moment before answering. "Well, not exactly. But I did get the idea that he was under a lot of pressure to excel—to get the top grades in his class. But I was never sure whether the pressure was self-induced or came from somewhere or someone else—like his parents." Sally paused and looked at Christie curiously.

Christie nodded thoughtfully. "Apparently the pressure is coming from his father. And I gather that he's one of those people who don't put much stock in a subject that emphasizes words instead of numbers."

"I get the picture. Another student caught between a parent's wishes and their own desires."

"Exactly."

"What did he expect you to be able to do about it?"

"I don't know. He didn't say."

"What are you going to do about it?"

"I honestly don't know. I told him that I needed time to think about it. That maybe I could come up with some strategy—some way of dealing with it."

Sally got up and wandered over to the window. Running her finger along the sill, she looked down and frowned at the dust on her fingertips.

"You know, Christie there probably isn't anything you can do in the first place. And in the second place, I don't think it's your responsibility anyway. That's what the school counseling service is for."

"I realize that. And, of course, my first thought was to direct him to Mr. Fontana or one of his colleagues. But the fact of the matter is, Keith came to me. He knows there's a counseling service; if he wanted to talk to a counselor, he would have gone there.

"Anyway," she continued, "there's nothing more I can do about it today. And to be frank, I'm not up for dealing with anyone else's problems right now anyway." As she talked to Sally, Christie had been placing the papers she wanted to take home in various manila folders and stuffing those, in turn, in a worn canvas tote bag. Glancing around the room as she walked to the door, she said to Sally, "I'm sorry; I completely forgot you must have had a specific reason for coming to my classroom."

"Oh," Sally said, "I just wondered if you could bring some things home for me. You remember that I'm headed up to the R and R center at Okuma for a weekend workshop."

"Of course. Just bring them out and put them in the trunk of your car."

"Thank God it's Friday. There's always so much administrative crap— pardon my French— to take care of during the first few weeks of school."

Christie nodded in agreement as she pulled the door shut behind her. Halfway down the hallway she suddenly remembered that she had left the paper Keith had given her on the table next to her desk. She debated for a minute whether it was worth going back for. But then she had told him she would read it over the weekend. Returning to her classroom, she quickly retrieved the paper from the table, and caught up with Sally at the entrance to the school.

As they made their way down the hill to the faculty parking lot, Sally looked over at Christie and said, with a touch of amusement in her voice, "So far you've only answered one of my questions."

Christie glanced over with a puzzled look on her face. "I don't know what you mean."

"You haven't told me about your most interesting problem; the one with your love life."

"You mean Quint Brewster?"

"Well, he's the one who drove you home from the cocktail party last week, isn't he?"

"Yes, but how did you know?"

"I peeked from behind the curtain in my bedroom window. I was just getting ready for bed. You're not angry with me, are you?"

"Of course not. I would have done the same thing if it was you."

"Fat chance of that happening," Sally said. Then suddenly struck by the unconscious irony in her word choice, she hurried on, "he must be a good ten years older than you, isn't he?"

"Yep."

"Where did you meet him?"

"That's a long story, Sal, but the short version is that he's the brother of a good friend of mine: Lisa Brewster. And she's a high school classmate who I've kept in touch with during the years since graduation."

When Christie let herself into their house a few hours later, she was relieved to find that Sally had left the living room air conditioner on low cool. Usually, in the interest of keeping the electrical bill from climbing to astronomical levels, they turned it off during the day. But there was no getting around it; it simply wasn't feasible to go without air conditioning on Okinawa at this time of the year. She hadn't been this uncomfortable since she spent a few weeks visiting with a friend in Houston a couple of years back.

Dropping her bag on the couch, she went down the hallway to her bedroom, slipped off her shoes, and sat down for a moment on the edge of the bed. Glancing at the clock on the bureau, she was mildly startled to see that it was nearly 8 o'clock. Sally was right on target when she said that Christie was likely to find Friday night Happy Hour at the Naha Officer's Club an intoxicating experience. From the moment Christie had walked into the lounge she had been surrounded by a cluster of young officers who spent the next two and a half hours plying her with food, drinks, and compliments. Although she had enjoyed their camaraderie—and their attentiveness was admittedly very flattering— time and again her gaze had been drawn to the entrance to the room where she hoped to see Quint's large frame suddenly fill the doorway. As time slipped away and he failed to appear, she decided that he must not be back from Cam Ranh Bay yet. After turning down a handful of invitations to dinner, Christie managed to break away from her throng of admirers, but only after promising that she would return again the following week.

Standing up, she walked over and opened the closet door, her mind busy turning over various strategies for getting Quint to be more attentive to her. Reaching behind her back with one hand, she nimbly undid a row of buttons and let the dress slide off her shoulders, catching it before it fell to the floor. Although it wasn't exactly her style, maybe the best tactic was simply to put on a show for him. Partly appalled, partly intrigued by the notion, she walked across the room and stood for a minute in front of the full-length mirror.

Slowly and seductively, she traced a path with both hands from her inner thighs, over her stomach, curving around her breasts, up past her neck and with her fingers apart, through her hair until her hands ended up clasped over the top of her head. At the same time, she tilted her head slightly to the side, opened her mouth, and ran her tongue suggestively around the edge of her lips. Fascinated by the unfamiliar image reflected back at her, she turned sideways, stuck out her behind in a suggestive pose, and looking over her shoulder, blew a kiss at the mirror while lifting her hair with the other hand and letting it fall in a sensual tangle around her face.

Suddenly embarrassed, she dropped her hands by her side and self-consciously looked around to see if anyone could have been watching her. Struck by how out-of-character her actions had been, she stuck out her tongue, child-like, at the mirror, signaling her return from a brief excursion into a corner of her being with which she was not entirely comfortable.

As she padded down the hallway into the kitchen, barefoot, and still wearing only her bra and panties, she acknowledged that it was nice to have the house to herself for an evening. A streak of shyness still held sway in her mind, even now in her late-twenties, so it would not have been possible for her to wander around half-dressed in front of Sally. Once in the kitchen, Christie contemplated, with distaste, the prospect of preparing a meal just for herself. Opening the refrigerator door and poking around among the leftovers extinguished any remaining interest she had in eating. Besides, she had already eaten too much that day anyway. The Happy Hour hors d'oeuvres had proved more alluring than she had anticipated. Deciding that she could allow herself one more beer, Christie removed a bottle from the shelf inside the door, and walked back into the living room to tackle the homework papers in air-conditioned comfort.

Curling up on the couch, she opened the carry-all and pulled the stack of folders out onto the pillow next to her. The paper that Keith had given her slid out and fell on to the rug. She started to put it aside after retrieving it from the floor, then changed her mind and decided to see what he had written thus far.

The title was *America in the Post War Years: Champion of Freedom or International Busybody?* The first few paragraphs traced the rise of America from its pre-war, isolationist stance to its de facto role as the leader of the free world. Much of the information was familiar to her, but not all of it—particularly that which related to the military. She had no idea that the United States Army was in such a deplorable state prior to the start of World War II.

Christie was impressed by the way Keith marshaled his facts and went on to discuss America's increasingly activist role in the world during the late nineteen-forties and fifties. Although it was a quality effort, his writing wasn't without its flaws.

Keith tended to use a more complex word where a simpler one would have served just as well. It was a common enough weakness in high school writing, particularly among her brighter students. She frequently had to remind them that the primary purpose of any piece of writing was to communicate, not to show off the size of one's vocabulary.

Her second criticism was a more serious one and dealt with the tone of the piece. As she read further into the paper, his rhetoric became increasingly more strident. And his contempt for America's interventionist philosophy became increasingly more obvious. In the final page his criticism of U.S. policy reached the militant stage as he went off on a tirade about U. S. involvement in Vietnam.

Christie knew that much of what she was reading could be explained as the normal passion of youth for an idea that had caught the writer's fancy. And she knew it was not uncommon for the more articulate students to become enamored with the idea of seeing their own thoughts about an issue appear on paper. But she also remembered Sally's admonition. It would be important to strike a balance between encouraging Keith's intellectual growth while reining in any tendency to go overboard in expressing his dissent. And it might take an extra effort on her part, since she agreed with much of what he had written. Particularly about Vietnam.

Christie was still thinking about the paper when she reached across the corner table and pulled the phone over onto her lap, picked up the receiver, put it down, picked it up again quickly, held it for a minute, then put it slowly back down on the base. The question was would Quint be back yet and if he was, would it be logical to find him in his office? Probably, considering his dedication to the job. But she hesitated about calling him. After all, he said he'd call her when he returned from Cam Ranh Bay. Shaking her head in mild agitation at her own indecisiveness, she picked up the phone purposefully and dialed his office number. It seemed as though there had barely been time for the phone to ring before she was listening to that rich voice which always sent a tremor of excitement through her, now sounding somewhat harried and brusque:

"Major Brewster."

"Hi Quint. It's Christie."

There was a sudden change in tone, one almost of embarrassment.

"Christie! I was just thinking about calling you as soon as I got back to Naha." There was an awkward pause on the line as if he was suddenly struck by how trite that must have sounded. "I know, I know, don't even bother to say what you're thinking.

"'What does he think—I was born yesterday?' But I'm serious," he rushed on, "I was going to call before I left here tonight."

"And what time might that have been?" she said, the teasing quality in her voice partially removing the edge from the question.

"I don't know," he admitted, "But, honestly, that's been my intention ever since I first got up this morning."

"What makes you think I'd be here when you called? It's not as though I don't have any social life, you know." Christie was having a good time at his expense, and she wasn't about to let him off the hook yet. "Do you remember the warning I gave you the night you drove me home?"

"Yes, I haven't forgotten. Lord, does this mean I owe you yet another apology?"

Christie chuckled. "No. Not this time anyway. So tell me, now that you did get around to calling me what were you going to say?"

"I was going to see if you wanted to go out to dinner tomorrow night. Now don't get mad at me, I know it's not much notice, but it's the best I can do right now. So, how about it?"

Her pulse started beating faster following the rush of feelings which accompanied his invitation but she couldn't resist teasing him about his choice of words. "Mad doesn't apply to people, Quint; there are mad dogs but people get angry."

"Great. Just what I need: somewhat who's going to be on my case about my grammar. I suppose you're going to bug me about my spelling and punctuation too. Right?"

More than anything, she had hoped for an opportunity to spend an evening with Quint alone. But correcting his word usage sure as the devil wasn't going to win her any points with him. As she made a mental note to avoid annoying him any further an even more exciting possibility was forming in her mind: why not invite him to her house for dinner? With Sally gone for the weekend, there was no need to worry about anyone intruding on their evening together. They would have total privacy. Aside from the attractiveness of that prospect, Christie was excited about the opportunity of showing off her cooking skills.

Quint had already gotten some sense of her intellectual abilities, perhaps too much so. It was time to correct the imbalance. Furthermore, she could take that opportunity to ask him if he would help her try and locate someone who remembered her father.

"I have an even better idea."

"What's that?"

"Why don't you come here for dinner? My roommate is gone for the weekend so we can have the house to ourselves." As these words tumbled out of her mouth, she wondered in passing what he would think of her offer; would it sound as though she were being too forward. Oh well, it was too late to worry about that now. "Besides," she continued, "I think it's time to show you that I can do something other than indulge in verbal sparring matches."

"Oh, I've already learned that you have gifts other than those required to be a good English teacher," he said.

Quint's tongue in cheek response caught her off guard, although she realized that it shouldn't have. She had left herself wide open on that one.

Before Christie could think of a suitable response, Quint continued on: "anyway, I accept your offer, but under one condition."

"What's the condition," Christie said, cautiously.

"That I can help you prepare the meal."

There was a moment of silence while Christie digested the implications of his offer. That's even better, she thought; I get some unexpected help in the kitchen and at the same time have the chance to spend more time with him. "I must say, I'm impressed. It isn't often that one gets that kind of an offer."

"You can thank my mother for that. She raised me with the idea in mind that I was to be something other than the typical dependent male. Being a woman of farsightedness and having a generous heart, I think she was also planning that I would be a boon to the woman I would eventually marry."

Christie, for the first time, allowed herself to hope that she might be that woman, but then immediately reigned in such thoughts as being a little premature. "Your mother sounds like a wonderful person. I would love to meet her someday."

"Yes," Quint responded, noncommittally, "she's a delightful person."

Christie brushed away her sense of mild disappointment at his response. She was not about to let anything put a damper on her enjoyment of their first official date. In fact, she was going to enjoy every moment of the next twenty-four hours anticipating the details, imagining what they would say and do in a long evening together. The romantic possibilities were, she had to admit, uppermost in her mind.

"Is there anything that I can bring?"

"How about a couple of bottles of white wine. Maybe a chardonnay or Sauvignon Blanc. You make the choice."

"Ah ha! A lady of the world. A sophisticate!"

"Before you get carried away with some imaginary conception of my level of sophistication, you should know that even as we speak I'm balancing a bottle of San Marcos beer on my lap while wading through the weekly homework papers."

"So much the better. A sophisticate with her feet planted solidly on the ground."

"I'm glad that you approve."

"From what I've been able to see so far, I don't think you're likely to give a hoot whether I approve or not."

Christie smiled at the receiver. "Touché, Major Brewster. You get ten points for that one."

"What time do you want me to come over?"

How about first thing in the morning, she thought to herself. *Why don't you arrive in time to greet me with a long sensual kiss while I'm still only half awake. But, on second thought, I need time to at least get my teeth brushed and make myself semi-presentable.*

Stepping back into reality she said, out loud. "How about six?"

"Fine. See you then."

"Goodnight.

"Goodnight Christie."

After the line went dead, Christie held the receiver for a long minute before placing it back on its base. She drew her legs up, wrapping her arms around them and rested her chin on the top of her knees. She looked around and tried to picture what it would be like to have him there. His commanding presence and masculine strength would completely alter her perception of the room. It was hard to contain her excitement as she pictured being in such close quarters with his body, his scent, his lips . . . .

She suddenly felt unaccountably lonely. A quick shower was in order she decided and then perhaps a little reading in bed. Certainly not the homework papers. Maybe one of those romances that Sally had stacked around the house. Something that required no thought. Something light and uplifting and—yes—romantic.

A few minutes later the phone rang again. This time it was Sandy Jamieson, Rick's wife.

"Hi, Sandy. What can I do for you?"

"I'm calling to see if you have time to chat since we didn't get much of a chance to do so at the party. Is this a good time or are you busy?"

"No. I'm not busy."

"Good. First of all, tell me how you like it here so far."

"I like it a lot. Just wish I had more time to go wandering around and do the tourist thing."

"I'm sure you'll find the time. After all, you're going to be here for close to a year—or maybe longer."

"That's true."

"So Rick tells me you knew Quint Brewster back in the states."

Christie was sure that Rick must have told Sandy about the passionate kiss he interrupted so she was bound to be curious about the nature of Christie's relationship with Quint. But then there was that friction at the party. Sandy had to have noticed that, so she must be somewhat confused at this point.

"Yes. I first met him when I was a sophomore in high school."

"It's obvious that you're younger than him."

"Quite a bit. Ten years, actually."

"So how did that come about—your meeting him, I mean?"

"He had a younger sister, Lisa, who was still in high school at the time. She was a senior and captain of the debate team. Although I had no experience in public speaking, I had a reputation for being outspoken and difficult to defeat in an argument, so I got picked for the team—the only other girl on the team I might add.

"Anyway, Lisa more or less became my mentor so we ended up spending a lot of time together preparing for our debates. In the process, we became close friends. That winter she went skating with Quint and one of his friends and took me along. And that's how I got to meet him."

"I can picture the scenario: you ended up having a wicked crush on him and he didn't even know you existed."

Christie laughed out loud. "You're right about the wicked crush but not about the other part I'm afraid."

" No?"

"He knew that I existed all right. You might say that I made a lasting impression on him. Not just that weekend but the following summer as well. I'm not sure he's forgiven me yet. Especially after our confrontation at his sister's apartment a couple of months before I came to Okinawa."

"What was your confrontation about?"

"Let's put it this way, we ended up disagreeing about everything from my drinking habits to the United States' role in the Far East and Okinawa in particular.

"I felt kind of badly about it afterwards. A lot of the verbal skirmishing can be traced to a real stubborn streak in me. And unfortunately we got off on the wrong foot here as well."

"So I noticed."

"Yeah. I'm sure everyone else at the party did too. Anyway, I'm pretty tired, Sandy, so can we continue this conversation on another day?"

"Of course. I'll look forward to that. Give me a call when you're available; maybe we can meet somewhere for lunch."

"Okay. Goodnight, Sandy."

"Good night, Christie."

A few minutes later Christie was back in the bathroom turning on the shower. She unhooked her bra, then wiggled out of her panties. Turning to face the full length mirror on the bathroom door, she ran a critical eye up and down her figure, coolly appraising her body, feature by feature, as she was often prone to do. Her face was definitely her best feature, or so she thought, although most people generally ranked her hair as her most stunning attribute. Most women anyway. The men, of course, had been enraptured with her full breasts for as long as she could remember— which was over a dozen years now because she had the unfortunate luck of developing a woman's figure by her early teens. The thought of having had to wear a size 34C bra from the time she was fourteen brought a quick frown to her face. At least they were firm, and didn't sag—not yet at any rate.

Her tummy was flat, her thighs and calves shapely, and she had been told by more than one boyfriend that her behind jutted out in such a way as to literally drive them crazy. She twisted sideways and looked back at the mirror, but, as always, could only get a hint of what apparently was one of the more provocative parts of her anatomy. The thick, triangular patch of curly brown hair was a source of both frustration and pride. She never could understand why oriental women were clean shaven in that crucial spot, much less what oriental men saw in such antiseptic beauty. On the other hand, the dark hair was prone to creep down the upper part of her thighs, so keeping her bikini line under control was a never-ending process.

As she stepped into the shower, Christie momentarily regretted not having taken a bath instead. But that would be something to treat herself to tomorrow afternoon after she had gotten everything ready for the evening. And that would also insure that she would be as relaxed as possible by the time Quint arrived.

She took her time washing, then after a few minutes leaned back against the side of the shower, cupped her hands just beneath her chin and let the stream of water flow over her breasts and down her abdomen tracing a path between her inner thighs before free-falling in a cascade to the tops of her feet. The sensation was at once both tranquilizing and arousing. Her thoughts began drifting and inevitably focused on Quint. She imagined what it would be like to take a shower with him. At first, she pictured him taking a bar of soap and starting with her back, gently, and lovingly washing her, gradually moving to ever more intimate areas of her body.

Without consciously willing it, she let the fantasy unfold in her mind step by step; soon it took on a life of its own, blurring the line between fantasy and reality. She could almost feel his glistening masculine body pressed to hers, his mouth seeking hers, his hands caressing her body, seeking out her secret places, taking liberties that inflamed her passions and sent her spiraling farther and farther along a path of sensual ecstasy. Christie moaned audibly at the image which was rapidly lifting her to new heights of arousal. One hand slid gradually down to her nipple and began stimulating it in a circular motion while the other dropped down to the seat of her sensuality, gently reaching between the folds, finding the spot which now became the focal point of her being. As rising passion swept all focused thought from her mind she succumbed to the tidal waves of ecstasy which rolled through her one after another, lifting her to ever higher plateaus until she felt as though the rhythmic shuddering of her body would never cease. Just before it reached the point beyond which it would have been unbearable, she heard herself call out his name, then accompanied by moans of delight there came the sudden release as the floodgates opened to the outpouring of all sensation. As her pounding heart slowly returned to normal, Christie turned off the shower before sinking down, weak-kneed and exhausted, to a sitting position on the shower floor. Unable to move for a moment, she sat there and, as focused thought once again became possible, suddenly grasped something of the depth of her hunger for Quint.

After managing to get herself out of the shower and toweled dry, she stumbled into the bedroom, slipped into her teddy, and collapsed on the bed. Forget about reading anything tonight, she thought. As she reached over to turn off the lamp on the bedside table, a final thought imprinted itself on her fading consciousness: she wanted Quint to need her as much as she needed him; he needed to know that she could fulfill his every desire. As she slipped off into a deep and tranquil sleep, she called out in her imagination: Oh Quint . . . . . please come to me and envelop me in your love.

XIII

By nine Saturday morning, Christie had been up for almost two hours and was on a cleaning spree such as hadn't been witnessed in the house in several months. At least that's what her educated guess would be. After having spent over an hour cleaning, vacuuming, and dusting, she had barely made a serious dent in the overall condition of the place. Well, that was probably an exaggeration, Christie thought, as she sipped the last of her second cup of coffee. For one thing, it wasn't so much the dirt—although there was enough of that—as it was the clutter. It was just now beginning to sink in that Sally was a true collector—one of those people who can't bear to throw out anything. Actually, that was probably the reason the dirt and dust had gone unnoticed. Virtually every available tabletop, counter-top, chair seat—she even had to clear off a spot on the couch when she wanted to sit down—was buried under stacks of magazines, newspapers, homework papers, and books—especially books: hard cover and soft cover; textbooks and novels, but mainly romance novels. Christie would guess that there were forty or fifty of them scattered around the kitchen and living room. And heaven knows how many more there were in Sally's bedroom.

Still, Christie recognized that it wasn't all Sally's fault. At least part of the blame could be traced to the living habits and abrupt departure of Sally's previous roommate. And Christie herself had to take a certain amount of responsibility for the house being like it was; after all, she had been there almost three weeks now. And it wasn't as though she wasn't aware of what was needed; it was simply a matter of not having any time so far, she told herself, except for the most cursory cleaning. In fact, if it wasn't for Quint she probably wouldn't have initiated anything of this magnitude even now. Except for the refrigerator. Clearly, that needed some immediate attention and, in fact, she had made a preliminary pass at it a few days after moving in. But today, she decided, there would be an all-out assault upon it.

As she began moving the chairs back into the kitchen after a thorough cleansing of the tile floor, Christie went over the menu possibilities in her mind for the hundredth time. The choices had been narrowed down to two: a favorite pasta dish or a shish-kabob using chicken instead of beef. Since Quint didn't know she was a vegetarian and she had no intention of telling him—at least not yet—Christie decided she would break her own rules and serve the chicken. The decision was, in effect, made by default when she discovered that there already were some boneless chicken breasts in the freezer. A recipe from Sally's cookbook which included limes, sesame oil, soy sauce, rice vinegar, honey and garlic sounded like the perfect marinade. She pulled up a chair to the kitchen table and rested her chin on the heel of her hand while scribbling out a grocery list which included small onions, cherry tomatoes, mushrooms, and green bell peppers. Wild rice would complement it nicely but what to do for dessert, that was the question. She was familiar, of course, with the old adage about the way to a man's heart being through his stomach; her tolerance, however, for anything that tended to enhance the man's position while even implicitly denigrating the woman's wasn't very high. It really was unfair; after all, she enjoyed a good dessert as much as any man. What nonsense!

But what about the dessert, she thought, idly tapping the pencil between her teeth. Her pie crust definitely left something to be desired, so that was out of the picture. And anyone could make a cake what with all the mixes that were available nowadays. She got up, pulled another cookbook from the shelf over the refrigerator, and started rifling through the pages.

There was nothing more boring than a cookbook that was all recipes and no pictures. Half the pleasure of leafing through them was drinking in the color photographs of mouth-watering entrees and desserts. Of course, all of this was typically accompanied by a certain amount of cynicism as she wryly noted the many times in the past that the actual result had failed to match the image on the page.

Nothing captured her fancy or if it did it was something that she considered to be outside her zone of competence. In desperation, she flipped to the index in the back of the book and started reading through the desserts in alphabetical order: brownies, cheesecake, cobbler, crème Brule—that was a possibility— gingerbread, Indian pudding: hmm, how about pudding; no, too common, mousse, mousse—that was it; chocolate mousse, she said out loud. Who could resist chocolate mousse!

By late morning the house was—if not immaculate—only a few degrees shy of her mother's standard of perfection, which was to say about the same thing. A light lunch of tuna fish on a few lettuce leaves while standing at the sink reviewing her revised grocery list was followed by a quick shower—her first of the day. From her closet, she quickly selected a sleeveless, white cotton blouse and a pair of khaki shorts; she then slipped into a pair of tan sandals. A brief look in the mirror confirmed that that she looked presentable enough for a quick trip to the commissary. Christie pulled her hair up off the nape of her neck with a barrette; yet another small tactic in combating the relentless mid-day Okinawan heat.

By 2:30 she was back at the house, having made a couple of extra stops: one at the local glass factory to obtain two new wine goblets—the only two that Sally had were mismatched—and the second at another outlet to pick up a matching set of napkins and table mats. She had definitely decided on the screen porch instead of the dining room for their dinner; not only was it pleasantly cool in the evening but it also provided complete privacy, being bordered on two sides by a cinder block wall and on the back side by a steep coral ridge.

Shortly before five she glanced at the clock, noting that there was still a full hour before Quint was due to arrive. As far as she could see, everything that needed to be done had been done. Except, of course, for the preparation of the food, which Quint had made her promise to postpone until his arrival. Standing in the doorway between the kitchen and screened in porch, she studied the end results of her decorative efforts with some pride. The table settings reflected an oriental motif which in her mind definitely added to the romantic atmosphere she had been trying to create.

The centerpiece was a floral arrangement of her own design and was balanced by two candles which should provide sufficient light in combination with the indirect lighting from the kitchen. The most frustrating part had been trying to roll the napkins up into the elaborate configuration depicted in one of the cookbooks. But that was finally accomplished on the third try. In fact, they looked quite attractive standing upright in the wine goblets; she was glad she had persisted until she had them looking the way they were shown in the diagram.

A sour cream, dill dip was chilling in the refrigerator along with some vegetable slices. They could munch on those and sip their wine while slicing the ingredients for the shish-kabob. She hoped he would be organized enough to have at least one of the bottles already chilled. Oh well, she thought, although a connoisseur might turn up their nose at such a practice, she wasn't above utilizing a couple of ice cubes to chill them should it be necessary.

When she found herself moving from the living room through the kitchen to the porch and back again, adjusting things which needed no adjustment, and checking things which had already been checked a half dozen times, she knew that it was time for a bath. That would serve the dual purpose of enabling her to freshen up and also help her to unwind.

—∞—

A half hour or so later she stepped out of the tub, dried herself off and slipped into a particularly sexy, peach colored lace bra and panty set which she had purchased for just such an occasion. Sitting down in front of the vanity a minute or two later her thoughts returned to those things which had been the focus of her reflections while relaxing in the bathtub. Or perhaps the word was trying to relax. The mild state of anxiety which had persisted throughout the day was still present, although in somewhat more muted form. It wasn't anything like those occasions in the past where the feeling of butterflies in her stomach had been accompanied by an extra trip or two to the bathroom. Just a slight edginess which under other circumstances would probably be written off as simply one facet of her pre-menstrual state. But it wasn't just that; and knowing herself as well as she did, she had a pretty good notion about the origin of her concern.

It was simply that she had loaded so much into this hoped-for relationship that she couldn't tolerate the possibility of failure. All of her life she had been involved with men in relationships which in the end had fallen short—far short—of her hopes and expectations. First her step-father followed by her half-brother, high school boyfriend, and the half dozen or so college men that she had dated. In a sense, of course, she was the one to blame for setting such high standards; how could you realistically fault someone for not being the perfect father, or the perfect brother, or perfect boyfriend. Supposedly, such an animal didn't exist anyway.

But she was convinced that Quint was the one that could fill the void—if he could conquer his chauvinism. That was the question. After the confrontational luncheon at Lisa's apartment and Quint's belligerence on the drive back from Kadena, Christie had her doubts. But she couldn't deny the strength of the feelings she had experienced the night of the cocktail party.

Her thoughts slid back to the face staring back at her from the mirror. A hint of taupe eye shadow, a little mascara and a slight redefining of her eyebrow with the pencil was all than was needed in the line of make-up. Her hair needed only a little touching up; that was a third reason for taking the bath instead of yet another shower; there was no need to redo her hair. Remembering that it had been pulled back on one side for the cocktail party, she decided to set the back of it off with a ribbon this time. After a careful scrutiny of her dress collection, she chose a sleeveless white dress with a pastel blue and peach floral print and a bow that tied in the back. In the bottom of the closet she discovered a pair of white, open-toed flats that would nicely complement the dress. For jewelry, she selected a favorite topaz pendant which was suspended from a necklace made of tiny golden rectangles. A matching bracelet completed the ensemble.

The final crucial step was the selection of the appropriate lipstick. The shape of her mouth was also considered one of her most attractive features, particularly enhanced by a rather pronounced cupid's bow. Remembering the look in Quint's eyes that night as he ran his finger lightly around the outline of her lips, she was determined to wear something that would recreate that same seductive effect. With that image burned into her mind, she reached tentatively for the autumn fire then just before applying it decided on passionate plum instead. Not that there was much difference between the two shades; however, the second sounded more appropriate for the type of evening she was hoping for!

—◆—

A few minutes later she was completing her final inspection of the house. A quick look around the living room revealed a stack of romance novels piled on the floor behind a rattan footstool. Just as Christie was returning from Sally's room, having deposited them in the middle of her bed for lack of any other space, the phone rang. She held her breath as she picked up the receiver, hoping that it wasn't Quint calling to tell her about some last minute change in plans.

"Hello."

"Miss Atherton?"

"Yes."

"This is Chief Master Sergeant Ferris. Keith's father."

"Oh yes. How are you."

"Frankly, Miss Atherton, I've been better."

"Oh. What seems to be the problem?"

"It's about Keith—or actually, it's more about you and your treatment of Keith."

"My treatment of Keith? What do you mean? I don't follow you."

"You've been filling his head with a lot of nonsense about the importance of poetry and symbolism and stuff like that. I'll tell you right now, Miss Atherton, I don't buy it. Knowing that stuff is not going to get him anywhere. It's the science and math that counts. Why all you have to do is look around and see who the people are that are getting ahead in today's world. It's the people with technical training; people with engineering and math degrees. I intend to see that Keith is one of those people."

Christie reminded herself to remain calm, watch her tongue, and curb her natural instinct to go on the offensive. It wasn't the easiest of tasks.

"As I was saying to uh . . . someone recently, Sergeant Ferris, colleges expect applicants to be able to think clearly and write effectively. Furthermore, that's even truer once you get out of college into the real world and begin looking for a job." Christie realized that she had nearly slipped and referred to the conversation with Keith. Not only would that be a breach of confidence, but it also would be a serious mistake in light of Sergeant Ferris' feelings about this issue. She had to proceed very carefully from this point on.

"I'm not arguing against the importance of good writing, Miss Atherton. I understand that. But I sure as the devil don't see the need for studying poetry and trying to dig out all the symbols that are supposedly buried in those stupid novels he has to read."

"There is a lot of accumulated wisdom in those so-called stupid novels. Great men and women have discovered universal truths which they then presented in narrative form so we can apply their insights to our own lives. These are wonderful things for young people to be exposed to. Superior students like Keith can learn a lot from studying such literature." Christie sensed that her efforts were going to prove fruitless, but for Keith's sake she had to try.

"He can find out about life through the school of hard knocks—just like I did. That's the best way to learn about those things; by living them not reading about them. But math and science and subjects like that have to be studied in school. And the more time spent on them, the better. That's what I say. That's what he needs to get a good job and be a success in life. I'm not going to have him end up like me."

Trying to sound like an advocate and not an adversary, she countered with, "I can't imagine that anyone knowledgeable about the service would consider you to be anything less than a success."

Ferris refused to be mollified. "Well, it's not success by my measure. And even if it was it's not good enough for my son."

Christie sighed audibly. "So what is it you want from me, Sergeant Ferris?"

"Stop piling on all those papers, poetry exercises and whatever! It's taking away from the time he should be giving to his math and science homework."

Christie decided that enough was enough. "I'm sorry to disappoint you Sergeant Ferris," she said firmly, the coldness in her tone plainly evident, "but Keith is in an honor's program and as such is expected to produce a significant amount of writing—expository as well as creative—writing that shows good analytical as well as good communication skills. And I have no intention of watering down the content of the class for anyone—or for any reason. Do I make myself clear?"

"I hear what you're saying Miss Atherton, but don't forget, I could have him yanked out of your class and put in a regular English class."

"And that would be shortsighted and plain stupid," Christie said, still trying to contain the anger bubbling up within her. "His successful completion of an honor's English program will count heavily when colleges are reviewing his application."

"I can see where I'm not making any headway talking to you about this. But I'm warning you: I won't put up with anything or anyone pushing science and math into second place. And that's that!"

"That has never been my intention, Sergeant Ferris."

"Maybe not. But you stand warned, Miss Atherton."

"Yes, you've made yourself very clear," the anger now plainly evident in Christie's voice.

"Good day, Sergeant." She slammed the phone down on the receiver and stood there for a minute, staring unseeing across the room, as she waited for her racing pulse to slow down and her frayed nerves to stop jangling. Quint would be knocking at the front door at any moment and she didn't want her surging emotions to contaminate any part of their first evening together. Damn! Not only hadn't she been able to help Keith's position, she may have even have aggravated it after that confrontation.

A few minutes later she heard a car door slam followed by a man's footsteps marking his passage up the slate sidewalk to the front door. It was Quint, of course; even his footsteps reflected his decisive nature. Her heart was thumping against her rib cage as she nervously opened the door to greet him. *Lord*, she thought, *he was gorgeous!* No wonder she'd had a crush on him from the time he first came into her life. He was wearing a dark green, short sleeve, polo shirt which, if anything, emphasized rather than masked his beautifully proportioned upper body. His perfectly-fitted tan slacks reminded her of how much value she placed on a trim waistline and the argyle socks and worn penny loafers suggested a collegiate bent to his make-up which she found rather appealing.

"Hi!"

"Hi! I'm not late am I?"

"No. You're right on time—to the minute, in fact."

"Well that's good. Just as I was getting ready to leave I suddenly couldn't recall whether you had said 6:00 or 6:30. On the way over here I got to thinking about it: what was worse from a woman's standpoint—to be late or to be early. What do you think?"

"It depends," she said, then added as an afterthought, "You do tend to analyze everything, don't you?"

"I guess so," he reluctantly admitted. "If you listen to what Rick says about me, I over-analyze just about everything."

"Here," she said, taking the package of wine bottles from his hands, "let me relieve you of these first of all, then give me a minute to think about your question," smiling at the boyish quality which surfaced in him from time to time and which she found irresistible. As she walked into the kitchen Quint followed along behind, glancing around the room as he did so.

"Boy, you sure keep this place immaculate. I'd be embarrassed to have you see what my place looks like after seeing this," he said shaking his head in disbelief as ran his finger along the top of the TV. Glancing down at his finger, he looked up at her quickly and smiled. "Clean as a whistle. If there's one place you're guaranteed to find some dirt, it would be on the top of my television set since I rarely ever go near it."

"Our set doesn't get much use either except . . . ," she added ruefully, "as another convenient storage site for my roommate's magazines."

"Anyway, in answer to your question, it all depends: if you arrive too early then your date might not be ready and. . . ."

"And that wouldn't be a very auspicious start to their evening, would it!" he added, completing her sentence.

"That's true," she agreed, nodding her head. "On the other hand, if she had a meal ready and was timing it to your arrival, then that also could be a problem."

"Actually," he said teasingly, "that was the real reason I suggested that I help prepare the meal. If I just happened to be a little late I wouldn't be the reason for a burnt dish—or a cold one." He crossed his arms and looked at her with one of those self-satisfied looks that she had seen on more than one occasion when a male friend thought he had very cleverly wiggled out of a tight position.

Glancing over the top of the refrigerator door with an amused but skeptical look on her face, her expression clearly suggested that she wasn't about to be taken in by that line of reasoning. Handing him back one of the chilled wine bottles, she said, somewhat surprised at her own daring: "Here, make yourself useful. The corkscrew is in the top left drawer and there are a couple of wine glasses chilling in the freezer. By the way," she continued, "I was taking bets with myself as to whether or not you would remember to chill one of the bottles before you got here. I'm impressed. You remembered!"

"Why is it that I can never tell a lie when I'm with you?"

"What do you mean?"

"I did forget. But luckily I was able to scrounge a couple of chilled bottles from Rick. "

Christie clucked her tongue in mild reproof. "Have you, by chance, ever been referred to as . . . how shall I say this tactfully . . . the absent-minded professor type?"

Quint looked up as the cork popped free of the stem of the bottle and grinned at her. "Can I take the fifth amendment on that one—for the moment anyway?" He then

proceeded to pour out a scant half glass for each of them and handed one to Christie.

She eyed it doubtfully for a second then looked at him with a raised eyebrow. "Is this is all I get?"

"Well, I suppose you can have more if you want. But I better not have anymore. At least not if I'm planning to get all this food ready in a reasonable period of time," he said, a little uncomfortable with the thought that he was, in fact, lying to her. The problem, as usual, was not about his capacity to function effectively but about his emotional response to an excess of liquor. As he topped off the glass in response to her complaint, he did so to his own, thinking 'to hell with the consequences.' He had already spent too much of his life driven by the need to act rationally under all possible circumstances. Maybe it was time for a change.

Christie had brought out the vegetables and chicken from the refrigerator and set them down on the island next to a cutting board.

"Your work, sir, is cut out for you—no pun intended. The cutting tools are next to the board."

"How about the skewers."

"They're right in front of you—under your nose so to speak."

"Well, so they are. Of course, you realize I did that on purpose. I felt it was only decent of me to give you a chance to see my absentmindedness in action," he quipped.

Christie chose to ignore that comment, for the moment anyway. In fact, she liked people who were organized and had little tolerance for those who were not. Of course, being a little absentminded didn't necessarily equate with or imply disorganization—or did it? Now she was getting too analytical. It was time to focus on the most important issue anyway, which was impressing—no, make that convincing—Quint that Christie was the best thing that had ever happened to him.

"I think it might be a good idea if you put on an apron to protect your clothes from any stains. Unless, of course, you have some objection to wearing one."

"I guess not. At least not as long as it isn't one with any frills or flowers on it."

Christie had been rummaging around in the small kitchen closet and turning to him said, "How about this one?"

At first, Quint looked a little askance at the ribald picture on the front then grinned broadly when he read the caption beneath the drawing. Holding out his arms, he said in an amused tone, "I wonder what it's like to barbecue in the buff?"

Satisfied that the apron was clean, Christie looked over at him and nonchalantly said: "I often barbecue in just bra and panties—sometimes just my panties, actually. That's if I'm home alone, of course."

Quint scrutinized her face for a minute to see if she was teasing him. "You're not kidding, are you?"

"No. Why should I make up something like that. According to my parents, when I was very small I hated wearing clothes and would shed them whenever and wherever I could. Of course, I'm a little more circumspect about where I do it nowadays. But with a very private back yard and a roommate who is often out gallivanting . . . ," she shrugged, letting his imagination complete the picture.

"Frankly, I would have thought that you were a little too conservative for such . . . ," he gestured with his open palms while searching for the right word, ". . . uninhibited behavior."

Wrinkling her nose at him playfully, she responded in a tone which was both bantering and a little suggestive as she approached him to slip the apron over his shoulders. "Even conservative types have been known to let their hair down under the right conditions."

"And their clothes as well?" he added, without so much as a trace of a smirk.

"That too," she agreed, "but only in the right company, of course."

"Exactly," he said, mimicking her tone, "it has to be the right company."

It took a supreme effort on her part to keep from wrapping her arms around his neck and pulling his lips down onto hers as she reached up and tied the string behind his neck. Especially during that brief moment when her mouth was only inches from his. Walking around behind him to tie the apron strings at his waist made her realize once again that being close to him was almost akin to moving within the orbit of an energy field, or some kind of magnetic field. Was it only her, or did other people feel that pull when they were in his presence? She wondered.

"There. You're all set. Go to it."

"What are you going to be doing?" he said, in a slightly accusatory but jesting tone, "sitting down with your wine and taking it easy?"

"You know, that's not a bad idea. The only problem is I happen to like more than simply a one-dish meal. I guess you might call that one of my idiosyncrasies."

"Hmm," he said with his lips pursed together. "Do I detect a touch— just a hint—of sarcasm in your voice?"

Ignoring his retort, she continued, "So I thought it might be nice to have something to accompany the shish kabob as well as something to complete the meal."

"Are you by chance referring to a dessert?"

Continuing in the light bantering vein which they had fallen into, she said, "I believe that's the customary term to use when referring to the final course of a meal. In America anyway," she added. "By the way, I'm impressed with the way in which you're making such short work of that chicken. I can see that you're no novice in the kitchen."

"I told you about the training I got from my mother. She insisted that both Lisa and I take turns helping to prepare the meal from the time we were in our early teens. And that didn't mean simply setting the table or filling the water glasses either."

Christie nodded approvingly as she stirred the wild rice and then opened the refrigerator door, glancing in to see if the mousse was chilling properly. Satisfied that everything was under control, for the time being anyway, she decided to pitch in and help Quint with the vegetables. He was drying his hands after having finished cutting the chicken into small chunks. As she reached for the apron hanging from the peg next to the kitchen door, a pair of strong arms encircled her waist and a low but deliberately seductive voice said, "Now it's my turn to return the favor."

After slipping the neck loop over her head, she momentarily leaned back against his chest and let her hands rest on his arms. A ripple of excitement spread out through her body, starting in her stomach and rapidly traveling to more erotic areas, lighting a small fire as it passed by each of them, one by one. She felt her nipples harden with desire, then a few seconds later became conscious of the increasing warmth between her thighs. It seemed to her that her breathing grew shallower and at the same time more erratic. Her mind reeled at the ease and rapidity with which his closeness had brought her to a state of arousal.

He had barely touched her so far! She felt a little self-conscious about how easily it would be for him to seduce her right there in the kitchen but even as that thought formed, another part of her mind was trying to estimate whether the dinner could be postponed for a half an hour without any serious consequences to its success. She needn't have worried! After brushing the nape of her neck with his lips, he tied the apron strings with a flourish, gave her a friendly pat on the behind, and went over to start dicing the vegetables.

She closed her eyes for a moment and fought to bring her surging emotions under control. Walking around to the other side of the island, she picked up a knife and started quartering the onions, afraid for the moment to meet his gaze.

"There," he said, "that takes care of the peppers. By the way," he continued, smoothly shifting to another topic without missing a beat, "do you remember me saying how great you looked that night on the balcony?"

She nodded without looking up. "I believe the precise phrase was 'absolutely amazing.'"

"I have to confess, that really wasn't what I wanted to say."

She looked up at him with a questioning look on her face. "It wasn't?"

"Nope, and I guess now is as good a time as any for you to hear the truth." As he said that, he walked around the island and placing his hands on her shoulders, gently turned her so that she was facing him.

Christie looked up at him with a mystified look on her face. "The truth?" she said, feeling a little bit like an idiot as she mimicked him for the second time in a row."

Cupping her chin in his hand, he studied her face for a few seconds before saying, "What I wanted to say is that you've got the most kissable looking lips I've ever seen.

Christie looked up at him thoughtfully for a long minute then said, "So kiss me."

"I fully intend to," he said, grinning at her.

"Well, for heaven's sake," she said, shaking her head in mild exasperation. "Just do it. We don't have all night! Then impatiently taking the initiative, she pulled his lips down onto hers in a long hard sensuous kiss which left them both gasping for breath after a few minutes.

After barely catching his breath, his mouth reached down hungrily for hers again only to be met by her probing tongue which sought out the deepest recesses of his mouth, exploring with an erotic urgency which he had never experienced in a woman before. Just as his hands slid down her back and curved around her behind, molding her body to his, she suddenly pushed back against the flat of his chest with both hands and said in a startled voice, "Damn it! I don't believe this is happening"

"What do you mean?" Quint said abruptly, a hint of nervousness suddenly evident in his voice.

"We completely forgot about starting the grill."

"Oh, is that all," Quint said with a sigh of relief, "I thought for a minute that you were upset at something I'd done," wondering if he should be feeling a little guilty about having taken liberties with that gorgeous body in front of him.

"Don't be silly," she said, reaching up and giving him a quick kiss, "After all, I was the one who initiated it." She paused and gave him a knowing grin, "this time anyway. But come with me," she said playfully, pulling him along by the hand. "If we don't find that electric starter we're not going to eat tonight."

"Where do you normally keep it?" he said as he tagged along behind her.

"It's supposed to be hanging on a hook just inside the screen door," Christie said, sounding more than a little annoyed at the fact that it was not in its accustomed place.

Quint stopped and glanced at a small stack of photographs that were lying on the kitchen counter, then began leafing through them idly. "What are you doing with these things?"

"What are you talking about," she said over her shoulder, while poking through a storage box in the back of the kitchen closet.

"These glossy photos. It looks some kind of an official ceremony at the Pentagon."

"You're right, it is—or was rather—an official ceremony. They were honoring my stepfather after his retirement from NACA—or rather NASA. I was sorting through the pictures, trying to find a couple that would be suitable for framing."

"You never told me your father worked for NASA."

"You never asked."

"Well, I remember you telling me he was an aeronautical engineer. I just assumed he worked for a private company."

"Actually, he worked as an engineer at Langley Aeronautical Lab in Virginia from 1944 to 1960."

"Oh. Which one is he?"

Christie sounded a little exasperated as she answered, "He's the only civilian in the picture; the one wearing a medal around his neck.

"Here it is," she said triumphantly, referring to the electric starter which she had found buried in the back of the closet. "I don't know how it ended up in here. Anyway, the charcoal is in a bag by the door to the back yard. The grill is around the corner; you'll see it when you open the screen door to the porch. Why don't you get the charcoal started and I'll finish putting the kabobs on the skewers."

"Yes ma'am," he said, throwing her a playful salute." A few minutes later he returned and announced that the coals would probably be ready in about ten minutes.

"Here," Christie said, removing the dip and sliced carrot sticks from the refrigerator, "try some of this while you're waiting."

"Wow, this dip is delicious," he said after the first mouthful, "what's in it?"

"Oh, just a little of this and a little of that," she said mysteriously.

"Can't you be more specific than that?"

"Sure, but I don't want to give away all of my secrets—at least not all in the same evening."

"I wasn't aware that you had given any away yet."

She put her hands on her hips and tilting her head to one side said, "I beg your pardon, sir, but do you think I go around telling every Tom, Dick and Harry whom I meet what I wear—or don't wear—when I barbecue!"

He chuckled, "I'd forgotten about that for a moment."

Great, she thought to herself. Out loud she said: "Forgetting to chill the wine is one thing; forgetting a tasty little morsel about my private life—about my personal habits," she added emphatically, "isn't so easily forgiven—or understood!"

She had turned back to the stove and was giving the rice a final stir when he slipped up behind her and started nuzzling the nape of her neck. She started to push him away playfully but he was insistent. "Do you want me to burn the rice?" she asked, as shivers of excitement rippled through her body. Damn, she thought, he could do anything he wanted, whenever he wanted, and she wouldn't be able to put up even a pretense of any resistance. Not that she had any plans along those lines anyway.

Placing the spoon down carefully on the stove, she turned around and slid naturally into his arms. Their kissing this time was a little more restrained as they both recognized that their mutual desire had brought them to the edge of the abyss before and that the next time they ventured to its edge there would be no turning back. After coming apart, they stood facing each other for a moment, his hand gently enclosing hers and their eyes locked in a visual embrace.

Clearing her throat, she said softly, "do you think the coals are ready?"

Quint nodded, either unable or unwilling to say anything at that moment. Picking up the plate of shish-kabob he walked to the screen door and stepped out to the grill. Within a few minutes Christie was commenting on the delicious aroma that filled the air as she stuck her head out the door and handed him a brush with which to apply the remainder of the marinade. After about fifteen minutes she looked out and announced that the rest of the meal was ready.

"So is this," he said, I'll be right in."

Christie had lit the two candles in order to fend off the deepening dusk which by then had enveloped the yard and was filling in the corners of the porch, effectively sealing them off from the rest of the world. While she was bringing out the plates which she had prepared buffet-style at the island, Quint opened the second bottle of wine and began filling their goblets. After checking to insure that everything was in place she said, "I guess we're all set."

Quint walked around and held the chair for her while she sat down.

She smiled appreciatively: "Thank you kind sir."

Quint smiled back: "Anything for you, milady."

As he sat down and looked across the table at her expectantly, a troubled look briefly crossed her face. "Do you mind—would you mind," she said awkwardly, "if I said a blessing before we started eating?"

"No," he said matter-of-factly. "I don't mind."

Bowing her head, Christie briefly gave thanks for their health, their food, and asked for God's protection and guidance in all matters relating to their future.

As he slid the chicken and vegetables off the skewer with his fork, Quint volunteered: "I didn't know that you were especially religious."

"I'm not," she responded, "It's simply that I feel overwhelmed at times and need to turn to something beyond—this," taking in everything around them with a sweep of her hand.

Quint nodded thoughtfully as he began eating his meal. "This **is** delicious," he said enthusiastically, "in fact; I don't think I've ever tasted anything quite so good before. I especially like the wild rice. What's in it, if you don't mind me asking, or is that another one of your well-kept secrets?"

She smiled back at him and said: "It's a mixture of wild rice and an Indian—as in India—rice, plus a few herbs and vegetables.

Thoughts about her father suddenly surfaced in her mind and on a hunch she decided to broach the subject once more, taking the chance that Quint might be more sympathetic than he had been that day at Lisa's apartment.

"Can we talk about my father?"

"All right. What ever became of him anyway?"

"My father had an aunt who lived outside of Phoenix. They had kept in touch over the years and occasionally exchanged visits. So it was arranged for him to go to a sanitarium in the area. My great aunt made all the arrangements and pretty much looked after dad for the remaining time that he lived."

"How long was that?"

"Less than two years. He died in the spring of '48."

"So his stay there didn't really help that much."

"According to Aunt Jane he should have improved because his case wasn't that advanced. Other people who were in worse shape than him regained their health. The doctors apparently couldn't find any physical reason for his continued decline. So, it seems as though there had to be some deeper reason. Some non-physical factor . . . ." Christie's voice trailed off as her thoughts brought her to the same dead end that they had a thousand times before.

"What kind of a relationship did your parents have?" Quint asked.

"Not very good," Christie admitted. He was thirty-four when he went into the service. Between his age and the fact that the war was winding down, the chances of him being drafted at that point were just about nil."

"So that would have aggravated their relationship."

"Yes and as the years went by I finally decided that they were actually a very poorly-matched couple."

"What made you come to that conclusion?"

151

"Oh, certain comments made in unguarded moments when my mother accidentally let her true feelings slip out into the open."

"Such as?"

"Such as the time she was going through some stuff she'd found in an old shoe box in the back of her closet. One of the things she found was a poem my father had written to her when they were going together. She mocked it as an example of the worst kind of pie-in-the-sky-romanticism. Those were her exact words as I recall."

"What did she do with it?"

"Started to crumple it up and throw it away but I objected so strenuously that she handed it to me with the comment that I would probably appreciate it because I was cut from the same cloth as my father."

"Like I said before, Christie, what with the trail being twenty years old it seems like an impossible task to try and locate someone who knew him and can tell you anything about him. My advice is still the same: forget the whole thing!"

"Maybe I am wasting my time, Quint. But I know that I'm not going to be able to let go of this until I make an attempt to find some kind of answer. Will you help me, please?"

"I don't know how I could help but I do know someone who might be able to."

"Who is that?"

"A guy named Mitch McGuire. He's a civilian who works in one of the maintenance shops. And he's married to an Okinawan woman. His wife might be willing to meet with you although it seems unlikely she'd have any information about your father. But what the heck. It's still an Okinawan contact, which is what you were hoping for. So it might be worth taking a ride up to Nago. That's where they live. I'll check with him next week and see if it can be arranged."

"Do you want another helping?" Christie asked.

"No, I'm fine. And I have to say, Christie, I don't think I've ever tasted such a delicious chicken meal before."

"It was the marinade that made the difference, Quint," she said while starting to clear the dinner plates from the table.

"Here. Let me help you with those. In fact, why don't you sit and relax while I clean up everything."

"No, that's O.K. Really. I don't mind doing it after all the help you gave me in preparing the meal."

"I insist," he said, as he took the dirty dishes from her hands and led her over to the kitchen table where, after gently pushing her down into a chair and planting a soft kiss on her lips, he added: "End of discussion." As he began scraping dishes into the garbage can and placing them in the sink he asked where her detergent was.

"Under the sink."

She started to get up from the chair. "Let me help now. You've got everything ready for washing."

"No," he said stubbornly, then grinning at her, continued, "if you want to make yourself useful why don't you find some containers to store the leftovers in."

She stuck her tongue out at him and grumbled under her breath as she rummaged through the cabinets above the stove. "I really despise leftovers," she said. "As far as I'm concerned, if you don't finish a dish the same night, then you should dump the remains right then and there."

"No way," he said indignantly. "Especially any part of this meal. If you're not going to eat it, then I'll take it home and eat it myself."

"Be my guest," she said playfully, but her heart warmed at his thoughtfulness and the many considerate gestures which she had witnessed so far. Watching him working away at the sink, meticulously washing and stacking the dishes made her love him even more. Her thoughts began drifting as she pictured them exchanging wedding vows, then in the next frame saw them with their own children—a boy and a girl. No. Make that two boys and a girl—or maybe two girls. The boys would be tall, handsome and smart like their father. And the girl—what about the girl? Would she be like me, Christie wondered. Would Quint want a daughter? Of course he would. He would make a wonderful father. Her eyes watered and a warm glow spread throughout her body as she allowed herself to momentarily taste—at least in her imagination—the sheer joy of having a dream come true.

"Christie?"

Her thoughts returned to the present as she became aware that Quint was staring at her with a wondering look on his face. "Where were you just now? I'll tell you this: wherever it was, it wasn't in this world," he said laughingly, answering his own question.

She still had the dreamy expression on her face when she got up and walked over to the refrigerator to remove two glasses of mousse for their dessert. "It's not your fanciest dessert," she said dismissively, as she brought them over to the table, "but to tell the truth, the other choices were either too complicated for me or simply too mundane to serve at a special dinner like this. Besides, I figured you can't go wrong by serving chocolate in some form—unless you're one of those rare people that hates it or is allergic to it."

"Neither case applies to me," Quint said enthusiastically. "Let's get to it." It seemed like only minutes later that he was pushing the empty dish aside and staring pointedly in the direction of the refrigerator.

Christie noticed the direction of his gaze and said teasingly, "I had no idea that you were going to like my dessert so much, otherwise I probably would have made some more."

"You mean that's it?"

"No silly," she said, leaning down and kissing him wantonly before making her way over to the refrigerator to take out the last two dishes. "Oh shoot," she said, after opening it, only then remembering that there had been a minor accident when she was putting them away to set.

"There's only one left, so I guess we're going to have to share it."

They sat across from each other with their knees touching and although initially used their own spoons, somewhere along the way Quint began feeding alternate spoonful's to her. As the moments went by Christie could feel the erotic tension gradually building up again and marveled for the nth time at the effect his presence had on her. She wondered if he had any sense of what he did to her. Could there possibly be anything deliberate about it? She doubted it; that wouldn't be Quint's way. Or would it? Maybe she was the one who was being naïve.

After they finished the mousse, Christie took the empty dish over to the sink, followed by Quint.

"Thanks again for all your help," she said, spontaneously throwing her arms around his neck.

"My pleasure, my beautiful lady, "he said, his sensual voice caressing her ears.

As their eyes locked briefly, they read the same message in each other's expressions.

Fanned by the flames of their mutual desire, first their hands, then their mouths cooperated in an intoxicating tactile exploration of each other's bodies. She moaned softly as her nipples responded to the heart-stopping touch of his fingers as he reached beneath the edge of her bra strap and began gently massaging them. Smothering each other with a flurry of open mouth kisses, their hearts pounded wildly and senses reeled as they careened madly towards the edge of the abyss. Quint's inept fumbling with the buttons of her dress brought a moment's reprieve as she found herself laughing giddily at his increasing frustration. As they tottered in a frenzied embrace halfway down the hallway to her bedroom, she reached down and started pulling his shirttail out from beneath his pants. By unspoken mutual consent they pulled apart long enough to stumble into her bedroom where she dragged him down on top of her, pressing his hardness against her until her body literally ached for the ultimate intimacy.

Christie lay on the bed in a completely disheveled state, with her arms spread out on either side of her and one leg drawn up as if she had just stretched after awakening from a nap. Her eyes had an erotic glaze which in combination with her rapid breathing and partially open mouth triggered yet another step up in the strength of Quint's desire. Everything about her position exuded such sensuality that the rising curve of his passion was almost instantly matched by the accompanying bodily response. His gaze feasted upon the flawlessly smooth flesh of her golden thighs and his breathing grew heavier at the tantalizing sight of the thick mat of hair beneath the transparent material of her lace panties. Bending over her, he began tracing a liquid path up the inside of her legs with his tongue, stopping now and then to retrace the path or explore another one. As he moved ever closer to the vertex of the golden triangle, the fire which was burning in his loins became almost unbearable. Her soft moans turned deeper and more guttural as his mouth began gently probing into the core of her womanhood; her breathing became heavier and more rapid, joining his in an erotic rhythmic duet. Reaching up, he grasped the edge of her panties and began sliding them down over her abdomen, pausing for a minute until she arched her back, automatically cooperating in the irreversible journey towards fulfillment. His heart was pounding so loudly in his ears that he began to imagine he heard it echoing throughout the room. But it wasn't his imagination; it was someone at the door!

Sitting up abruptly on the bed they exchanged looks of consternation and frustration as the erotic excitement of the previous moment dissolved before their eyes. "Damn it," Christie said, springing up off the bed and slipping on a bathrobe with a few quick movements of her hand. "I can't believe it. Who the devil would be pounding on the door at this hour?" As she ran her hairbrush through her hair she yelled out, "I'll be right there!"

Quint thought he heard her mutter a few choice expletives under her breath. Turning to Quint as she applied a quick dab of lipstick, Christie said, "I'll just tell whoever it is that you were using the bathroom."

Quint looked at her with an irritated look on his face and said somewhat grumpily, "Why bother to lie about it. Who gives a damn what they think anyway. As far as I'm concerned you can tell them I was about to screw the pants off you when they so rudely interrupted us." Then he looked at her and grinned sheepishly.

She winked at him as she started towards the bedroom door, looking back over her shoulder to acknowledge that maybe that's exactly what she would say.

That wasn't what she ended up saying of course. But it wasn't really necessary anyway because it was Sally. Good old Sally who had the decency not to let herself in quietly with her own key but who announced her arrival in unequivocal terms so they would have a minute or two to gather their wits about them—and their clothes. Her explanation was brief and pointed: a violent reaction to a bad meal that morning had pretty much destroyed any prospect of enjoying the weekend workshop, so it was an easy decision to make when she received an offer of a ride home from one of the other people who was leaving the conference early. After being introduced to Quint, she sat with them in the living room for about five minutes then excused herself and retreated to her bedroom.

After she left the room, Christie and Quint turned to each and exchanged tired smiles in unspoken acknowledgement of the frustrating ending to their evening. He reached out his arms and she slid compliantly into the warmth of his embrace. Looking up at him, she said in a emotion-filled voice: "Thanks for a wonderful evening."

"Hey, I'm the one that's supposed to be doing the thanking, after all it was you who had me for dinner."

She smiled up at him, her eyes sparkling with appreciation, "Every woman should be as fortunate as I am to have such a thoughtful and helpful date. If more men were like you, there would be a lot more dinner invitations being offered and fewer complaining women."

He lowered his mouth onto hers for a long gentle goodnight kiss and when he lifted his head a few minutes later he stepped back and studied her pensively for a long minute before speaking.

"What?" Christie said, tilting her head to the side questioningly.

"Look Christie I've been trying to get away to Okuma for a long weekend now for a couple of months. With everything that's been going on, I've had to postpone it two or three different times, but I'm determined to get there next weekend come hell or high water. Taking her face in both hands, he looked down at her and asked, "Will you come with me. You'll love it there. It's so peaceful and romantic; it's a magical place! And I promise you there'll be no one to interrupt us there."

Christie had never been so torn in all her life as she was at that moment while Quint waited anxiously for her answer. This had been her dream for the past twelve years. To spend an enchanted weekend with the man of her dreams in a tropical paradise. She moaned inwardly at the cruelty of fate. That she should come this close to having that dream fulfilled. As she looked up into his loving gaze, the tears forming in her eyes, she heard herself saying that she couldn't.

"That will be my time of the month, Quint."

Minutes later, as his car was pulling away from the curb, she closed and locked the front door, turned off the lights in the living room, and walked slowly down the hallway to her bedroom. Only the fact that she was suddenly overcome by a profound wave of exhaustion enabled her to enter the room which still reverberated with the echo of their passionate lovemaking. Just before falling off to sleep, Christie vowed that they would plan a getaway to Okuma for the near future just as soon as it was feasible for both of them.

XIV

Christie's stepfather had always warned her that fear was the most insidious of all man's enemies and it must be held at bay at all costs. But it was getting more and more difficult to fend it off as she struggled to make some headway against the violence of the storm. An unbroken mass of dark clouds scudded across the sky just above her head. If only she get a glimpse of where she was in order to get her bearings, but the horizontal rain was driving directly into her face, making it almost impossible to see. It seemed like she was on a high plateau-like area, but there were no landmarks of any kind, nothing that was familiar. Where was she? How had she gotten there? Why wasn't there anyone else around?

As the wind got increasingly stronger, it became a challenge to make any headway against it. At first, she seemed to be making some progress, but before long it felt as though she was being blown back a step for every two she took forward. Then after a while it became one step forward, one step backward. She crouched down lower to get out of its path, but there was no avoiding it, no protection from it. To make matters worse, it was becoming more difficult to breathe. The wind was so fierce that it hurt to inhale and was almost impossible to exhale. Furthermore, it was unseasonably cold. She was beginning to shake uncontrollably. Panic enveloped her as she realized she could go no farther. She was going to die alone in this unknown place, and no one would even know. She fell forward on her hands and knees, buffeted by the relentless force of the storm. It was no use. She couldn't go on. The sobs that racked her body were swept away in the fury of the storm. Quint! Where are you! Oh God, please help me! Quint! Quint!

"Christie! What's the matter?"

Christie sat upright in bed as the door to the hallway flew open and Sally burst into her room. As soon as Sally flipped on the wall switch, the room was bathed in light, and Christie was momentarily startled to see that she was safe in her own bedroom. Sitting down next to her on the bed, Sally took both of Christie's hands in hers and asked, "Are you all right? You screamed so loud that I thought maybe someone was murdering you."

Christie's heart was pounding in her chest, and her pulse was racing. As the seconds slipped by, her breathing slowly returned to normal, and she felt calm enough to speak.

"Sorry to scare you out of your wits, Sal. It was just another one of those nightmares." She shuddered as the aftershocks of the fear reverberated briefly through her mind and body.

"What do you mean another one of those nightmares? Are you one of those people who have the same nightmare over and over again?"

"Yes. Well, no. Not exactly. But I have had the same nightmare three times in the past two months."

"What is it like?"

"Basically, I'm caught outside in a violent storm in a place that I don't recognize."

"Sounds pretty much like the garden variety type of nightmare to me."

Christie nodded. "Still, I can't help thinking that I'm being given a glimpse of something I'll experience in the future."

"You mean like a typhoon?"

"I suppose."

"We normally get hit by a couple of typhoons each year, however there's no danger if you stay inside. But there's a certain amount of anxiety, especially if you're new to the island. That's a good reason for riding it out with a friend. And since we have each other, there's nothing to sweat."

"Thanks for the words of comfort," said Christie.

"You know, Christie, it's kind of interesting that you called Quint's name, in light of the fact that you've only recently established good relations with him."

"It's not surprising at all to me."

"Oh? Do I detect a story here?"

Christie looked up at her and shook her head. "More like an incident."

"Is it something you're comfortable talking about?"

Christie shrugged. "I don't know. The topic hasn't come up in years. Besides, Quint and Lisa are the only people I'm still in contact with who were there that day."

"If you'd rather not talk about it, forget I asked."

"It's all right, Sal. I think the time is long overdue that I talk to someone else about it," Christie said as she slid over to the edge of the bed and stepped into her flip-flops. "But first I'd like something to calm my nerves. Maybe a cup of warm milk."

"Okay. Let's go out into the kitchen and I'll warm some up for you."

Christie took her bathrobe out of her closet and put it on while following Sally out to the kitchen.

"So anyway, I've already lived through one real life nightmare, and believe me one is enough," she said. "The difference between my nightmares and reality is that when I called out for help I was fortunate there was someone to come to the rescue."

"Rescue? Rescue from what?"

"From drowning or freezing to death — or both."

"Sounds to me like this is more than just an incident," Sally said as she measured out a cupful of milk and poured it into a shallow pan. After turning the burner on low, she stood over the stove monitoring the milk. "It doesn't take much to end up with scalded milk."

Christie sat down on the kitchen chair and pulled her feet up on the chair and wrapped her arms around her legs.

"Here you go," said Sally, as she placed the warm milk on the table next to Christie. "Why don't we go and sit in the living room where it's more comfortable."

Sally settled into a rattan chair while Christie curled up on the end of the couch across from her. Christie lifted the cup to her mouth and blew gently on the milk before taking a sip. Sally had poured herself a glass of cold water and set it down on the coffee table. She looked inquiringly at Christie.

"By chance am I going to get to hear any of the details of this so-called incident?"

Christie ran her finger around the rim of her cup while considering whether she wanted to go into all the details. But it was too late, since she had already agreed to do so.

"The story really goes back to the time shortly after I became close friends with Quint's sister, Lisa," explained Christie. "At that time, Quint was a grad student at U Arizona. He was home on winter break, and although he was spending most of his time studying for his comprehensive exams, he decided to take Lisa and a few friends ice skating on a large lake several miles outside of town. I was one of those friends. Anyway, not only was the lake in the middle of nowhere, but there had been a slight thaw the previous week, and the ice wasn't that safe. At least along the edges, it wasn't. But we weren't aware of that. If we'd been using our heads, we would have considered that possibility."

"I'm listening. Go on," said Sally.

"The sun had just set when I skated a little further up the lake than anyone else had. Quint had brought along his friend, Ben, the only other guy in our group, and they had built a bonfire which gave them enough light to see me. But a few minutes later I disappeared into the deepening dusk. Shortly after that was when it happened. There was a brief warning crack, and the ice splintered under me and I went right into the water."

"How deep was it?"

"Not very. Between four and five feet. I probably would have been able to make it to shore if I hadn't gotten my skate caught in a submerged tree branch. I started yelling for help and kept trying to work my foot loose but I couldn't. My head was above the water, but whenever I moved I'd get a dunking."

"What was running through your mind at that moment?"

"Nothing was running. Everything was moving at a crawl. Believe or not, I didn't panic. The main thing I remember thinking was how numb-ingly cold it was. In fact, after a few minutes it was even hard to think. It was almost as if every part of me, even my mental faculties, were being brought to a standstill by the exposure to that frigid water. I really believe I would have frozen to death before I got to the point of drowning."

"Your story gives me the chills, Christie, even though I'm sitting in a comfortable house in a semi-tropical climate!"

Christie continued. "Luckily for me, Quint took his skates off and ran along the edge of the lake to the point where he had last seen me. He was calling my name, and I kept yelling, 'I'm over here.'" Christie shook her head slowly. "To make matters even worse, a strong wind suddenly come up, and it started snowing heavily. I guess it was what they call a snow squall. But for a short while it created nearly white-out conditions. Between the heavy snow and the coming of darkness Quint couldn't see me. And with the wind gusting he couldn't hear me either. I didn't think I was capable of calling out again, but somehow I managed to squeeze out one more call for help. By then the snow had stopped falling and Quint had backtracked a short distance, realizing he had probably gone past me during the white-out conditions. All I can say is that I was certainly being watched over that day."

Sally let out a sigh of relief. "So how did he manage to rescue you?"

"He had to wade out to me, breaking the ice each step of the way. He had a rope tied around his waist, and Ben was holding on to the other end in case Quint needed any help. Once Quint reached me, it took three attempts before he managed to free my skate. By then I was so cold I couldn't move my legs so he carried me back to shore and to the bonfire. Within a couple of minutes, Lisa started the station wagon and turned on the heater full blast and Quint and I squeezed into the front seat. As soon as we got in the station wagon we took off our coats. Lisa took off her coat and put it around me. Then someone handed Quint an old woolen blanket that was in the back seat and he wrapped that around me. Ben took off his coat and gave it to Quint."

"And that was it?"

"More or less," Christie said, finishing the last of her milk. "Except for the fact that Lisa got stopped by a cop while driving at breakneck speed back home."

"Don't tell me he gave you a ticket."

"No. When he heard what had happened, he took pity on us and simply gave us a verbal warning."

"So Lisa reined in her natural inclination to exceed the speed limit again. And we got home safely."

"And what happened to you after all that?"

"Amazingly, I didn't get sick! Oh, I was chilled to the bone all right, and I mean that quite literally. It was several weeks before I felt as though most of the chill had finally left my body."

"And what about Quint?"

"He got the worst of it. He came down with a raging fever which turned into a case of pneumonia and as a result he had to postpone his comprehensives. It was a long time before he forgave me for that," Christie said, stifling a yawn. "If he ever did."

"Why? It wasn't like you did anything wrong."

"He said that I shouldn't have been doing any exploring. Especially with darkness rapidly approaching. I suppose he was right."

"Are you ready to go back to bed yet?"

"Yes, the warm milk did the trick," Christie said as she followed Sally back into the kitchen, rinsed out her cup and walked down the hallway to her bedroom. But in the back of her mind there was a small pocket of anxiety which no amount of verbal reassurance could sweep away. And that anxiety sometimes crystallized into the image of a typhoon bearing down upon the island and Christie caught outside in the middle of it.

As she returned Sally's goodnight before closing her bedroom door, Christie reminded herself that she was once again in danger of falling into the habit of creating situations to fret about. That had been one of her mother's failings and one for which Christie never did have much tolerance. When she slipped into bed moments later, Christie vowed that she would not end up echoing that particular behavior pattern.

XV

Two weeks later, Saturday morning dawned hot and sticky, with both temperature and humidity promising to be well up in the discomfort zone before noon. Shortly before ten, Christie emerged from her bedroom into the kitchen and greeted Sally cheerfully as she headed over to the counter to pour her morning cup of coffee for that all-important caffeine jolt. Sally was sitting at the table nursing her third cup of coffee as she looked Christie over carefully like a mother scrutinizing a child.

Christie was wearing a taupe colored, full length, cotton skirt and an off- white sleeveless blouse with a row of small buttons that ran up the front and ended with a cord that tied at the base of her throat. Her hair was pulled up from the nape of her neck and held in place with a black oriental barrette. Sally couldn't help thinking that the same clothes on anyone else wouldn't be noteworthy, but Christie's beauty gave them a special lustre.

"You look especially captivating this morning, Christie. I just hope Quint's powers of concentration are sufficiently strong to keep his eyes focused on the road rather than you."

Christie smiled and said, "I wouldn't be surprised if he could manage to do both. He seems to be one of those rare men who has the ability to focus on more than one thing at a time."

"Okay. If you say so. Now, tell me again who this person is you're going to see and how you found out about her?"

Christie repeated what Quint had told her. "Apparently Mrs. McGuire was agreeable to meeting with us, so we're going to Nago."

"Realistically, what do you expect to find out?" Sally asked, as she walked over to the sink to rinse out her coffee cup.

"Probably not very much, but Quint figured it was worth a try since she originally came from Kadena village."

"So you and Quint are actually getting along for a change."

"So far," Christie said, rotating the cup back and forth between her thumb and forefinger, a thoughtful look on her face.

"You know Christie I've chatted with Quint a couple of times at the O Club, and he seems pretty closed off to me—like there's a wall that he's built to keep people from really getting to know him." The note of caution in Sally's voice was unmistakable. "He's definitely got some baggage."

"Don't we all, Sal?"

"I know, but all I'm saying is that I'd be on my guard. It's my sense that you two are very different people."

Christie nodded. "I'll keep your words in mind."

"I think he's here. Someone just pulled up in front of the house," Christie said, as she got up from the table and glanced out the kitchen window.

As she walked towards the car she saw that Rick Jamieson was sitting in the back seat.

"Hi Rick."

"Hi Christie. Nice to see you again."

"Rick's car has been getting repaired at the local Datsun dealership. It's ready to be picked up and he asked me if I could drop him off there," Quint said, by way of explanation.

"Yeah, Christie; don't worry I'm not coming along as a chaperone."

She gave him a quick grin.

"How long will it take to get to Nago?"

"About an hour and a half," Quint said.

"I haven't been north of Kadena yet, other than to have dinner at the Foreign Broadcast Information Service (FBIS) Club."

"Well, you're in for a surprise then."

"Why?"

"There's a dramatic change in the scenery."

Several minutes later they pulled into the Datsun dealership and left off Rick to pick up his car.

"Are you sure it's ready?" Quint asked.

"Yep. When I called them they said I could pick it up any time before noon."

"Okay. I wouldn't want you to be stranded here if it wasn't going to be ready until Monday."

"Thanks for the ride, my friend. Christie, hope to see you again when we have more time to chat."

"I'd like that, Rick."

As they drove away from the dealership, Christie turned back to Quint, and asked, "Why the change in scenery?"

"Well, in a nutshell, this is what happened. The heaviest fighting of the battle for Okinawa was from Futenma down to the southern tip of the island. So that's where the greatest damage occurred as well as, of course, the greatest loss of life. Japanese resistance north of Kadena was relatively light. So from Kadena north to the Motobu Peninsula the vegetation escaped relatively unscathed. Just watch. You'll be surprised at the size of the trees and the amazing variety of flowers and plants."

It wasn't long before she discovered what Quint meant. It was almost like going through a magic door into a prehistoric paradise, from a sparsely-vegetated landscape to one with tall trees, tumbling waterfalls, lush vegetation, and countless varieties of flowers and flowering shrubs. As they wound their way through small villages and along the edge of steep coral cliffs, Christie found herself responding with the wonder of a child as each bend in the road revealed new vistas to her eyes.

Turning to Quint, who was driving along with one hand resting on the window sill, she said, "Does this move you, too or have you gotten blasé about it, having seen it so many times?"

Glancing over at her, he grinned and said, "Well, to be perfectly frank, I've been paying more attention to the scenery in the car than to that out-side of it."

After digesting that information for a minute, she said in playful tone, which was part suggestion, part command, "well, it seems to me that one of the advantages you have with the scenery in the car is that you can reach out and touch it." With that, Christie slid over against him, until their bodies were touching from their shoulders down to their calves and leaned her head on his shoulder. As she did so, he slipped his right hand under her skirt and rested it on the inside of her thigh, as high up as he could comfortably reach. Leaning back, she reached up and nibbled gently on his earlobe, murmuring something to the effect that if he found her skirt a barrier to further exploration, she would be willing to remove it.

"Christie, I used to worry about this old Chevy overheating if I pushed it too hard, now the thing that's most likely to overheat is this thirty-six year old engine of mine. Which reminds me," he said, suddenly veering off in a new conversational direction. "I know I should be able to calculate this but how old are you anyway?"

"Well I was fourteen when you first met me, so . . . ?"

"So that makes you, let's see—twenty-five?"

"Yes. I'll be twenty-six in December."

"Hmmm. And that's how old I was when I first met you—twenty-five, that is."

"Much to your regret?"

"At the time—yes. But obviously I don't feel that way anymore."

"You did when we encountered each other at Lisa's place."

"Yeah. I just needed some time to adjust to your adult mode."

"And me to yours," she added.

They rode in silence for the next few miles. There were places where the lush vegetation crowded up on both sides to the very edge of the road. In fact, it seemed to Christie as if every square inch of space was taken up with climbing and creeping vines interspersed with ferns and palm fronds. She thought there was simply nothing comparable to it in the northern hemisphere, and she wondered how so many varieties of plants could survive crammed together in such a confined space.

At one point the road curved toward the water and they abruptly broke out of the thick vegetation into an open expanse overlooking the East China Sea. A flat grassy field extended a hundred feet or so before ending abruptly on the edge of a steep coral cliff, the top and sides of which were covered with eye-pleasing patches of Portulaca, a flowering weed with clusters of purplish red blossoms. From the base of the cliff out to the ring of coral reefs, the water was a stunning aqua. Beyond the reefs, where the deep water began, the color changed to a dark blue.

The beauty of the spot left Christie's mind groping for adjectives that could do it justice. Quint pulled off to the side of the road and shut off the engine. They sat in stunned silence for a few minutes, drinking in the splendor of the scene before them while inhaling deep breaths of fresh salt air.

Christie's head was still resting lightly against Quint's shoulder, her left hand clasping his right, and her right fingers gently stroking his forearm. After a few minutes, she tilted her head back and closed her eyes. Quint, interpreting her posture as an invitation, bent down and pressed his lips to hers and Christie responded with ardor to his impassioned kisses. Their kissing became more intense as her lips parted willingly in response to the probing of his tongue.

A few minutes later, a small, beat-up pick-up truck pulled onto the grass and stopped about a hundred feet away from where they were parked. A young Okinawan couple and two small children piled out of the front seat and quickly began laying out a picnic blanket near the edge of the cliff. Quint sighed, and looking over at Christie said, "I guess it's time to get moving again."

For the next hour or so, they drove past field after field laden with the late summer harvest of sugar cane and pineapple crops. But what fascinated Christie most was the variety of burial tombs they began to see. Some were caves in the hillside sealed with a wall of cement blocks; others were more elaborate, free-standing, turtle-shaped shrines; and still others looked like small houses. And there were paper flower arrangements stacked in front of all of the tombs.

"Why do they use artificial flowers when there's such an abundance of real ones to choose from?" asked Christie.

"Beats me. I do know a little about the reason for the flowers though." He explained that the Okinawans had celebrated Obon just a few weeks earlier, a three-day, sacred festival centering around their belief that the spirits of dead relatives returned to visit their ancestral homes at this time. One of the most solemn of the rituals was the opening of the tomb by the families who then took out the bones of the departed and cleaned them.

"How do you happen to know so much about an Okinawan holiday?" asked Christie.

"Every American on the island looks forward to the arrival of Obon because for three days the traffic jams all over the island disappear while the Okinawans retreat to their family tombs. That's reason enough for the Americans to have their own Obon celebration each year!"

"I see," she replied. "How much longer is it until we get to Nago anyway?"

"We should come to the turn-off in about a half an hour."

XVI

"Does Mr. McGuire actually drive this route twice a day every day of the week?"

"No. He has a permanent room assigned him in the NCOQ (Non-commissioned Officers Quarters). Sometimes he'll go home in mid-week to check on things, but usually he stays on base during the week. I don't know how much time he actually spends in his room though. He's in the shop around the clock. Some nights I wonder if he ever goes to bed. And, by the way, if you start out calling him Mr. McGuire he's going to get annoyed and assume that you don't like him, so you'd better call him Mitch like everyone else does."

"What's he like?"

"Physically, pretty darned imposing. He's about three inches taller than I am and outweighs me by a good fifty ponds. He's also strong as an ox. Heck, I've seen him lift things in the shop that would take three ordinary men to lift. Personality-wise, he's an odd mixture. On the surface, he's gruff, hard-driving, and intolerant of anything less than perfection. On the inside, he's a real teddy bear."

"How do you know that?"

"Because I see the way he treats the young airmen who come to the shop straight out of basic training. Most of the airmen we're getting nowadays are pretty darned inept but Mitch is unbelievably patient with them as long as they try to do their best."

Nago turned out to be a picturesque fishing village located on a semi-circular bay, hemmed in between the East China Sea and the rugged mountains of the Motobu Peninsula. Mitch McGuire's home was a sprawling, multi-level ranch that was built into the side of a steep hill a mile or so outside of Nago. As they wound their way up the steep driveway that led to his house, Christie twisted around to take in the view of Nago Bay that was gradually unfolding beneath them.

"What a magnificent location for a house! Imagine waking up every morning to that scene. I'd end up sitting on the deck with a cup of coffee and never get a thing done."

As they got closer to the house, Christie could see that there was a large deck that ran the length of the front of the house. Actually, it was two sections of deck connected by a flight of stairs which led to the upper level of the house. The front lawn was an undulating series of beautifully manicured terraces, with large areas of lawn set off by a variety of local plants and shrubs. Whoever did the landscaping had a real eye for what was visually pleasing. When she asked Quint about it, he informed her that it was all the work of Mitch. He had designed the house, the lawn, the gardens, everything, and what work he couldn't do himself he had hired local Okinawan laborers to do.

"There he is now," Quint said, nodding in the direction of the house, "waiting for us at the end of the driveway.

As they pulled up and stopped on the side of the circular driveway closest to the house, Mitch walked over to the passenger side, opened the door for Christie and offered her his hand. She accepted his help, not because she needed it, but because it was an old-fashion gesture of politeness that had a strong appeal to her. Admittedly, her hand felt as though it was being enveloped in a bear's paw, but a very gentle one at that.

Quint's description, though basically accurate, didn't do justice to the sheer size of the man. Reflecting on it later, Christie decided that it wasn't just his physical strength that one noticed. He exuded an inner strength which made one feel as though they were in the presence of an elemental force. At least, that's the way he made Christie feel.

Before she could even thank him, Mitch let out a soundless whistle. "I've heard a little bit about you Miss Atherton. Not just from the Major, either. It seems that most of the single officers in the Wing haven't had much else on their minds for the past few weeks. And I sure can understand why. I hope you won't take offense at me saying this but you are one heck of a beautiful woman."

Despite herself, Christie blushed. "Thank you for the compliment, Mr. McGui—I mean Mitch," she said, looking quickly at Quint. "And please call me Christie."

"I'll do that Christie and welcome to my own little piece of paradise," he said, reaching past Christie to shake Quint's hand. "Major B, I've wanted to show you my place for some time now."

"Pretty damned impressive, Mitch," Quint said, as his gaze took in the house, yard and view in one broad sweep.

"Come on. I'll give you a quick tour of the place."

Christie and Quint followed him dutifully around the grounds as he pointed out all the different plants, identifying them without any hesitation by their correct botanical names.

Christie was enthralled. "It's just beautiful, Mitch. You really do have an eye for what's aesthetically pleasing. I told Quint on the way up the hill that I'd be hard pressed to get anything done if I lived here. I'd just want to sit on the deck all day long and stare at the view you have."

Mitch grinned appreciatively. "Yep. It's mighty easy on the eyes and on the mind, too, for that matter. Just sort of calms my spirit right down if I get to fretting too much about something. Anyway, I hope you enjoyed the ride up here, Christie."

"I thoroughly enjoyed it, Mitch. It was a beautiful ride."

"Good. Then your trip wasn't a total waste. I'm real sorry to have to tell you this, but Mitsuko wasn't feeling very well when she woke up this morning. She's really not up for seeing anyone today."

Christie tried, without much success, to keep from showing her disappointment. Mitch, seeing it register on her face, hesitated for a minute, not sure what to say next. "Look," he blurted out, "why don't you and the Major come and sit down on the deck and have a drink. You can spare a half an hour or so to enjoy my view, can't you?" he asked apologetically.

Christie glanced at Quint, then back to Mitch and nodded slowly.

"What would you like to drink? How about a glass of ice tea?"

"That would taste good right about now. I am pretty thirsty," she admitted.

"Major B—would you like a beer? I know it isn't noon yet, but you are off duty."

"Sure—as long as you'll have one with me."

"I'll be back in two shakes," he said. "Why don't you two go around to the front of the house? There's a partly shaded area where you can sit and avoid the direct sunlight. I'll bring the drinks out there."

As they walked around to the front of the house, Christie unconsciously reached for Quint's hand while staring unseeing at the panoramic view which lay at their feet. "Do you suppose she's really sick?" she said slowly, looking up at Quint.

Quint shook his head slowly from side to side. "I don't know. I have to admit that the same thought passed through my mind."

"You did tell Mitch what our purpose was in stopping here, didn't you?" she asked, as they crossed the deck and sat down in two white rattan deck chairs.

"Yep. I told him what you were looking for and he said that he thought Mitsuko would be glad to help you if she could."

"But we don't know whether he actually asked her or whether he was merely assuming that she would—do we?" said Christie.

"That's true—we don't know for certain. But on the other hand, it wouldn't be like Mitch to do that. If he says he'll do something you can pretty much count on the fact that he'll do it."

They sat for a few minutes in silence, enjoying the peacefulness of the spot and the beauty of the view. Quint turned to Christie to say something, but just then Mitch came out with a tray of drinks.

As he handed her the ice tea, Christie said, "I think I hear a faint echo of a southwestern accent in your voice, Mitch. Am I right?"

"You've got a good ear, Christie. I'm originally from Oklahoma. Joined the Seabees in `43 and shipped overseas a few months later. Saw service as a bulldozer repairman and operator at Kwajalein, Tarawa, Pelélieu, and then Okinawa."

Quint let a soft whistle. "Wow! You were in the some of the hottest places in the whole Pacific campaign."

"That's for dang sure. I'm lucky I made it through with my ass in one piece. Sorry, Christie" he abruptly added, "didn't mean to be so crude. I can be a little rough around the edges at times. That includes my language."

"Don't give it another thought, Mitch," Christie said, as she rested her glass on the arm of the chair. "I've heard much worse than that—and with much less reason," she added, pointedly. After a brief pause, she asked, "What made you want to stay here on Okinawa?"

He shrugged as he popped the caps off the beer bottles with the edge of his thumb and handed one to Quint. "Meeting Mitsuko. I always had this feeling of being at loose ends. What do the experts call it—rootless-ness. That's me. It seemed like there was no place where I really belonged. Or at least if there was, I sure as hell had no idea how to go about finding it.

"After the war was over I toyed with the idea of signing on with the big construction companies. The construction business was really boom-ing by then. They were getting all kinds of contracts to build bridges, refineries, and dams around the globe. Not to boast, but I knew that those construction outfits would pay top dollar for a man with my talents and my background in heavy equipment. Plus I'd get to see some parts of the world that I'd probably never see otherwise."

"So what happened?" Christie said, fascinated by how everything about the man was oversized: his body, his talents, his heart, even his voice.

"I was ready to head back to the states to get mustered out when this army colonel from the Corps of Engineers calls me into his office. Seems like they couldn't manage without my services. He asked me to stay long enough to keep the heavy equipment in good repair: the stuff that they were going to need to begin building the new infra-structure. Especially at Kadena. Anyway, that's how I ended up meeting Mitsuko. Once I got up the nerve to ask her to marry me, she agreed to it. The only requirement was that I stay on Okinawa so she could be near her family."

"So how did you feel about that?"

"Well, on the one hand, I had to give up my dream of roaming the world on my own terms. That was the hard part—giving that up. But on the other hand, I knew deep down that it was important for a man to settle down and establish some roots. And I figured that would never hap-pen back in the states."

"Why was that?" Christie asked.

"For one thing, both of my parents were dead by then. And on top of that I'd long since lost touch with my only brother. In fact, that was the case even before the war started. Other than a few distant cousins who I barely knew, that was about it. So what was there to go back to?"

Quint and Christie were both silent for several seconds. Although the circumstances were different, Christie could identify to some extent with his feelings of disconnectedness.

Quint finally spoke up. "Ever regretted your decision?"

"Nope. I've been back to the states a number of times. Mostly on business. You know trips to the big overhaul centers. First time I went back, I took a side trip to Oklahoma to try and find those distant cousins. Never did locate any of them. Of course, I didn't have a lot of time. But I haven't been back to Oklahoma since and never had another urge to do so.

"Anyway, I didn't mean to go on like this about myself. In fact, I can't remember ever doing so much talking at one sitting before. I guess I must feel pretty comfortable in your company. Either that or it's because I've about reached the point where there's more years behind me than there are ahead of me," he said taking in both of them with his smile.

Turning to Christie he said, "Major Brewster told me you didn't know much of anything about your father's disappearance. Did he mention anything specific in his letters like people's names or names of villages, places he might have visited?"

Christie had been an interested listener to Mitch's story at first but after a while she found her thoughts drifting back to that time twenty years ago when a father, whom she hadn't really begun to know and appreciate until her teenage years, left her forever. She had been doing that with increasing frequency lately. Trying to bring him to life in her imagination. She liked to picture him doing all kinds of mundane things but stopping every so often to take out a well-worn picture of a little eight year-old girl at which he would stare wistfully.

But it had taken on new meaning since she arrived on Okinawa. Now, wherever she went, whatever place she was in, she could imagine that she was present in the very place where he might have been. Even here in Nago. Christie looked up suddenly, aware that both Quint and Mitch were studying her closely. "I'm sorry," she said, "my thoughts were elsewhere. What did you ask me?"

Mitch repeated his question.

Christie shook her head. "The only name he mentioned was the refugee camp near Kadena village. At least that's the only one in the few letters that have survived. My mother destroyed most of the letters that he sent from Okinawa. There could have been something helpful in one of them but, of course, we'll never know."

"Well, I'm not sure how much Mitsuko could actually help you, anyway," he said, waving his empty beer bottle inquiringly at Quint who shook his head in answer to the unspoken question. "I told her what Major B. said about your father. She said that there were a number of military people that tried to help her people but there was no one in particular that stood out in her mind. When I pushed her to tell me more she clammed up and reminded me that it was a period in her life that she'd rather forget about. I knew that, of course, but I kind of hoped that she might be willing to meet with you anyway. Once she feels better, I'll try again. Another thing I can do is to ask her if there was anyone else from that refugee camp who she knows is still alive and might have some information for you."

Christie smiled warmly at him. "Thanks, Mitch, I appreciate it."

Quint looked down at his watch. "I think maybe Christie and I better be hitting the road. We'd like to get to Okuma before mid-afternoon."

Mitch walked them around to the car. "Let me apologize again for bringing you here on a wasted trip," he said, as he offered Christie his hand.

"Your apology isn' t necessary, Mitch. I don't consider it wasted time at all. Not when I get to meet someone who's gotten as much out of life as you have. I hope I can say half as much about my own life twenty or so years from now."

Mitch shook his head in amazement as he opened the door for Christie. He glanced over the top of the roof and said to Quint. "You're one lucky man, Major B! On top of everything else she's got going for her, this woman's a born diplomat. By the way, did you show Christie our famous Gajumaru tree before you came up to my place?"

"No, but I'll be sure and drive by it before we leave Nago."

"How about Todoroki Falls? Did you stop there?"

Quint shook his head. "Nope. Didn't show her that, either."

Christie looked inquiringly from one to the other. "Did I miss something special?"

"Not yet. But I'm glad I thought to ask the major. Those two scenic wonders are Nago's claim to fame. Along with my house, of course," he said, winking at Christie.

As they wound their way back down the hill towards Nago, Christie asked, "Are we going to stop at those spots that Mitch mentioned?"

"You won't be missing much if we don't stop. A weird looking tree and a small waterfall. That's all you'd see. Incidentally, you sure made a heck of an impression on him. And he's one guy who's not easily impressed—either by high ranking officers or good-looking women."

All Christie could manage was a weak smile. She was really discouraged that her first opportunity to find out something about her father had turned out to be a dead end. And the worst part was hearing how Mitch's wife felt when it came to talking about the war years. Was that the attitude Christie was going to encounter wherever she went? If so, her search was doomed even before it began.

Quint, sensing her thoughts, gave her hand a squeeze.

"Remember what I told you, Christie. This was a long shot. But it's a step in the right direction. Anyway, change of subject. I have a problem.

The people who take care of my house while I'm away are heading back to the states next week. And I have to head back down to Cam Ranh again for a couple of days so there's no one to feed Sam."

"Who is Sam?"

"My cat."

"Your cat! You have a cat?"

"Yeah, I do."

"You," she said, emphasizing the 'you', "have a cat!"

"That's what I said. What's so strange about that anyway? Aren't single men supposed to have cats?" he asked, indignantly.

"No, of course not—I mean of course you can!" she said, quickly correcting herself. "It's just that—well, I don't know. . . . I guess I never thought of you as a cat person."

"And what the hell is a cat person supposed to be like?" Quint said, sounding more than a little miffed at her response to his revelation. "Is there something different about them? I mean can you spot them in a crowd?"

"For heaven sakes. Quint," she said, laughing out loud, "There's no need to get defensive about it. It's just that you took me by surprise with your announcement—that's all. And I wasn't making fun of you. I identify with people who like cats. Anyway, if you were going to ask me to house sit and take care of Sam, I'd be glad to except for one little problem."

"What's that?"

"I still don't have a car yet. I usually rely on Sally to get me to and from school." "That's no problem. You can use mine while I'm gone. I'll arrange to have my car left in the school parking lot for you that Monday morning. There will be an extra set of keys under the driver's seat, including a house key.

"You do remember the way to my place, don't you?"

"Of course. So tell me, how did you end up with Sam?" Christie asked.

"He showed up at my door one morning back in early spring. It isn't unusual for service people to acquire pets then pass them on to some other family when they ship out. A few like Sam manage to fall through the cracks. Maybe they couldn't find a home for him because of his appearance. A lot of people would probably be turned off by that."

"Why? What does he look like?"

"Cinnamon colored. Kind of scruffy looking with one ear that flops down. An old battle wound probably. He definitely looks somewhat disreputable, but he's not that old. Just looks old because of the tough life he's led. On the positive side, he's real affectionate. You know—what they call a lap cat." He rubbed his chin and reconsidered. "Actually, come to think of it, he's more like a shoulder cat."

"A shoulder cat?"

"Yeah," Quint said. "He likes to get up on the back of the chair or couch right behind your neck. Then before you realize it, he's got his two paws draped over your shoulder with his head right next to yours."

Christie smiled at the image of a cat perched contentedly on Quint's shoulder.

As they headed north from Nago Christie asked Quint to fill her in on his background.

"How did you end up in the Air Force? I gather you were originally headed for a career as a hydrologist," she said, prompting him a little.

"All of my life I've been fascinated with airplanes. I was one of those kids that bought every available book on aviation and flying, built countless models, and spent as much time at the local airport as I could manage.

Somewhere along the way I decided that I wanted to know what it was like first hand to pilot a plane. So I applied for the air force pilot training program. Of course, a lot of people thought it was a waste of time; some of my favorite professors—top researchers and teachers who considered themselves my mentors—thought it would at best postpone my career as a hydrologist and at worse permanently derail it. In other words, by the time I got out, the field would have developed to the point where I might be too far behind the latest thinking and research to catch up." He shrugged. "In light of what's happened, it makes their advice look even more appropriate."

"You mean getting grounded."

"Yep."

"By the way, what was your family's reaction to this news?"

"Lisa felt badly, of course; I don't know how my parents felt when they heard—my father, anyway."

"What do you mean?"

"Just what I said. I don't know how he felt and furthermore, I don't care. "

"Why don't you care?"

"Okay, this is why: up until I broke the tradition, all the male Brewster's had gone to Colton College and majored in either English, history or in a few instances, theology."

"And you were pressured to follow in your father's footsteps."

"That's for sure. In my case, I had to resist the pressure not just from my father, but from this seemingly endless stream of generations that had gone before. It was like pushing against the weight of history—sacred history too, at least from my family's standpoint. From the day when I first entered grade school it was made clear to me, in a variety of different ways, that the legacy of the past was a living legacy which each Brewster male was responsible for carrying forward. Anyway, I first threw the glove down when I went to Tulane instead of Colton. Of course, that sent a clear message to my family: I was going to major in engineering and not enter one of the fields that was considered acceptable for a Brewster heir. Well, I never heard the last of that—and still haven't for that matter."

Christie nodded sympathetically. "It never fails to amaze me how many parents there are out there who think that they know what's best for their children and, worse yet, think that by being parents they have some kind of right to direct their children's lives and make major decisions for them. It's so unfair."

"Yeah. Well, that's my family for you—or rather my father and his side of the family."

"So you and he were in more or less continuous conflict from what—high school on?"

"That's the picture. But little did I realize that the worst still lay ahead."

"What do you mean?"

"Well, ever since I can remember he's been in the forefront of all the peace movements, rallies, demonstrations, and marches! He was appalled when I joined the air force—that was the final insult—and naturally his views on Vietnam are about 180 degrees apart from mine. More in alignment with yours actually," he said, in a quick aside. "Anyway, we haven't spoken in a couple of years. Of course, this upsets Lisa and my mother, but I figure—what the hell—it's his problem, not mine. I mean I didn't stop talking to him."

"Do you see your father as weak, as someone you don't have a lot of respect for?"

" No. Even though he was a conscientious objector during WW II he performed a tough job up near the front lines.

"What was that?"

"He was a member of a graves registration team."

"That must have been a rough assignment for someone who was strongly opposed to violence."

"That's for sure. Anyway, my more immediate problem, from a career standpoint, is that I'm stuck on a plateau and I'm not sure there's anything I can do about it."

Christie looked at him sympathetically. "I wish I could help."

Quint gave her hand a quick squeeze. "Thanks Christie but I'm afraid this problem is all mine to deal with. So where does this leave me? It's probably too late to start a civilian career but on the other hand, how much of a career can I have if I'm not on flying status?"

XVII

"So this is Okuma! What a beautiful place!"

Quint looked over at Christie and smiled at her enthusiastic response to the vista which opened up before them, as the narrow road they had been following abruptly widened into a large grassy field, revealing a panoramic view of the harbor in the near foreground and the rugged mountains of the Motobu peninsula in the distance. Adjacent to the field was a long crescent shaped beach whose gradual curve seemed to stretch on for miles before it merged with the distant horizon. Directly ahead were a number of low buildings that were set amidst a stand of Japanese fir trees. As they got out of the car and walked along a crushed coral path to the registration office, Christie was entranced by the open, park-like area whose lighted pathways, small goldfish pools and widely-scattered wooden benches seemed like the perfect place to linger after a romantic dinner.

Within a few minutes of arriving, Quint had checked them in, picked up the keys to their room and was giving Christie a quick tour of the grounds. "Basically, it's a narrow peninsula about a mile long and half a mile wide with a beach on each side, a nine-hole golf course in the middle, and the dining area, recreation room and guest quarters at the tip."

"What do most people come here to do?" she asked, then flushed a little when she realized how her question would most likely be taken.

Quint laughed good-naturedly, as he said, "Well, in addition to that, they come here to relax. In fact, there's not a heck of a lot you can do around here except hang out and relax." Then hedging a little, he added, "well, that's not completely true; there are a few activities: there's golf as you've seen, glass bottom boats, snorkeling, I think there's a tennis court or two, and . . . and you can rent bikes for a dollar a day and explore the area. That's it in a nutshell."

"At least we won't have to worry about anyone pounding on the door when were in the middle of lovemaking. On the other hand, I hope the walls are soundproof," she said, smiling suggestively at him.

In the few minutes that it took to put their clothes away in separate dressers, Quint wondered again at the sometimes contradictory impulses that seemed to drive Christie's thought processes—and moods. One minute she was showing her embarrassment at making a comment which might be taken as slightly suggestive and in the next making one which was openly and deliberately suggestive—if not seductive. It almost seemed as if there were two Christie's housed within a single body: the one shy and conservative, the other bold and sensual. He had noted her mix of qualities before, but by this point had begun to think that he had her reasonably well pegged. Obviously she was far deeper and even more complex than he had realized.

"What would you like to do?"

Christie thought for a moment then said, "Actually, it would be nice to spend an hour or so at the beach. I've been so busy lately that I haven't had any time to work on my tan."

"Sure. Now's a good time to go because we're past that point when you chance getting a burn. Besides, by the time we spend an hour or two there then get back here to the room and shower, it will be about time for dinner."

There was a moment of awkward silence then Quint, realizing its source, said, "Why don't you go ahead and use the bathroom. I'll change right here."

When Christie reappeared a few minutes later Quint took one look and let out a soundless whistle. She was wearing a white, two-piece swimsuit with navy and gold trim which would have turned the heads of men and women both on any beach in the world. Unlike many of his male peers, Quint had always preferred a figure that was somewhat on the slender side; Cally had been a perfect size 6. But Christie's lush figure was so striking that it literally took his breath away. Seeing the look on his face she flashed her most seductive smile and said:

"I gather you like what you see."

Pulling her into his arms, Quint answered her question with a long passionate kiss, in the midst of which, he somehow lost his balance and fell back onto the bed with Christie still in his arms, then rolled off onto the floor with her on top of him. They stared at each other in total shock for a minute, both trying to figure out how that had happened, then simultaneously broke into laughter.

A few minutes later, as they walked hand in hand to the beach, still chuckling about what had happened back in the room, Christie abruptly looked up at him and said in a tone of mild amazement, "Do you know something?"

"What?"

"I just realized that's the first time I've ever heard you actually laugh. A smile, an occasional grin, yes, but I've never ever heard you laugh up until a few minutes ago."

Quint shrugged in acknowledgement. "I know. Everybody says I'm too serious. And you know what?"

"What?"

"I really don't care. I enjoy my life. But at the same time I don't really see a heck of a lot to laugh about—either in the world at large or in my own immediate world."

"But that's a terrible way to be, Quint," she said, the sincerity of her concern evident in her voice.

"Come on Christie. It's no big deal. It's not like I'm a depressive personality or something like that. I just don't laugh much, that's all. Don't try to read more into it than there is." Putting his arm around her shoulder, he gave her a loving squeeze and as he did so added, "besides, who knows what can happen now that I know you. There may be all kinds of laughter in my future."

Looking at him askance as she helped spread out the blanket on the sand, she couldn't help thinking that Lisa's one warning to her concerning Quint was about his essentially serious outlook on life—an attitude which had been a part of him from childhood. Don't be naïve enough to think that you can change him, she had warned Christie, because it wasn't going to happen. The one thing that did make Christie a little uncomfortable was when Lisa revealed that a number of people on Quint's father's side had suffered from what was quaintly referred to as melancholia. Lisa had said that it wouldn't be at all surprising if Quint had inherited that tendency from his father.

Shaking her head to rid her mind of such heavy thoughts, Christie reflected on how much she had to be thankful for. Although Quint hadn't verbalized his feelings to her, it was obvious that he was deeply attracted to her—enough so to break off with Cally—and more importantly, to reveal the depth of his emotional involvement in a number of subtle but important ways.

"Why are you so quiet?" Quint said, rolling over on one side, and propping himself up on his elbow.

Christie looked over at his beautifully proportioned body with open admiration, once again struck by how his natural strength and agility were clearly evident in even the most casual of movements, such as when he had just rolled over to speak to her. He really was a perfect physical specimen she thought, remembering Lisa's often repeated comment about how all her friends used to literally drool over him when they would come to visit her.

"To be honest, I'm still wondering when I'll see you laugh again with such abandon as you did back in the room and I'm also curious what it is in your background—your upbringing—that makes you so serious."

Quint reached over, took her hand gently in his and pressed it to his lips. "Christie don't worry about it. All right? I promise you that you're not ever going to regret —," he paused for a minute, then continued, "becoming a part of my life. Just don't expect to accomplish miracles overnight, O.K? Anyway, I'm going in for a quick swim; want to join me?"

Christie shook her head. "I think I'll stay here and get a little more sun. Besides, if I get my hair wet now, it's going to be a major project to get it in presentable shape for dinner."

As Quint leaned over and gave her a quick kiss before rising to his feet, he said: "You know what—I don't think it's possible for you to be anything less than presentable."

As she watched him stride effortlessly across the beach to the water, Christie's mind began unconsciously shifting into a sensual mode. She pictured them again, together in the shower, as she idly traced patterns in the sand, lifting up small handfuls and letting it trickle between her fingers. Admittedly, it was disconcerting at times to find herself so pre-occupied with the prospect of making love to him. In fact, her physical desire for him over the past several days had been so strong that she could think of little else.

Her mother would probably be appalled if she knew how sexually aggressive Christie could be with Quint; for that matter, anyone else who knew her, or thought they knew her, would most likely also be surprised at this hidden side to her. But it didn't really matter what anyone else knew or didn't know. What was important was knowing that Quint had been— would be—the only recipient of this gift. She had not only hoarded all her love for this man, but also all of her sexual energy, everything that she had to give of herself was going to be his and his alone.

She rolled over onto her stomach and propped herself up on her elbows, her chin cupped in her palms. Quint was swimming laps back and forth between the dock and a finger pier where the glass bottom boats were tied up, his strokes strong and smooth as he cleaved the water with a fluid, effortless motion. As Christie watched him with increasing fascination, curious as to when he would show some signs of tiring, she wondered if he ever did anything that wasn't purposeful, that had no particular goal. It would be interesting to watch him over the next forty-eight hours to see if, in fact, he was capable of truly relaxing, of doing something just to do it, with no particular point to it.

A few minutes later he was wading through the shallow water and walking back up the beach with the same energetic stride that he displayed before his swim.

"Aren't you even a little tired after such a strenuous work-out?"

He shrugged. "A little, which goes to show that my life style of late has been more draining than I thought."

Christie looked at him with a slightly disbelieving look on her face as they shook the sand off the blanket and moved it back up the beach out of reach of the incoming tide. "Well, you may have noticed a difference, but certainly no casual observer would have. You looked to me like someone who was trying out for the Olympics and had a good chance of making it!"

Quint grinned appreciatively. "Thanks for the compliment. I did some competitive swimming in college but that was a long time ago. I do feel as though I'm actually in better shape now than I was then. Of course, realistically speaking, it's probably all in my head."

Christie smiled reflectively as she said: "That's where it all begins anyway, for so many things. If you believe it, you can make it true. Or rather, it becomes true."

Quint gave her a skeptical grin, "The power of positive thinking and all that, huh."

"Absolutely. There have been a number of occasions when I've seen what a difference a little confidence can make—or, unfortunately, the absence of a little confidence."

"Maybe. But all the confidence in the world can't make up for a lack of preparation or training."

"True, but all that preparation and training by itself isn't going to be sufficient if the necessary confidence is missing," Christie countered.

"I suppose," Quint said in partial surrender, amused and impressed once again by Christie's persistence in pushing for acceptance of her point of view.

"By the way, not to change the subject, but since we have to walk right past the office on our way back to the room let's be sure and stop to see if we need to make reservations for the use of the snorkeling equipment or the ride in the glass bottom boat."

"Okay."

An hour or so later, as they were walking away from the registration office, Quint casually mentioned that Christie seemed pretty interested in the old photographs on the wall.

"Yes, I was surprised to see that there was a P-51 wing stationed around here during the war. I assumed that they were used exclusively in Europe.

"What do you know about P-51s?" Quint asked, making no effort to mask the tone of disdain in his voice.

Christie looked over at him quickly, somewhat surprised, but mainly annoyed by his tone.

"Probably a lot more than you think I do. And is there some reason that I'm not supposed to know about such things?"

"Well," he said, hedging a little, "frankly, yes. For one thing, you're an English teacher; it's not your area of expertise and for another thing you're a . . . ," he paused briefly, a part of his mind now warning him that he might be flirting with trouble.

"A what," she said, an edge creeping into her tone, "a woman? Is that what you were going to say? In another words, I'm not supposed to know about things like this because I'm a woman?"

Quint shrugged and hesitated again, but not quite long enough to realize that he was already in the middle of a minefield and that one mis-step could be his undoing. "Well, that wasn't exactly what I was going to say, but it is a little surprising that a woman . . . ." his voice abruptly trailed off as he realized that he had probably just taken the fatal step.

Especially when she suddenly stopped in the middle of the path, turned around, and standing with her hands on her hips, said in a voice that was ominously soft, "suppose I told you I knew about the P-51 because my father was a member of the original design team."

Quint shrugged. "There were all kinds of people involved in the design of that plane and even if your stepfather was one of them it's highly unlikely that you'd know much of anything about it. After all, Christie" he said a touch of impatience in his voice, "you were only about four years old at the time."

In addition to his chauvinism Christie knew that Quint could be condescending at times as well. Her voice took on the tone of an unfriendly interrogator who knew that a suspect was about to walk unwittingly into a trap from which there was no escape. "I suppose you're familiar with the big names in the aviation field—the men who have made major contributions to aircraft design and development over the years.

He shrugged. "Most of them, anyway."

"Do you know the name of the engineer who did the original research on the laminar flow wing?"

Even as Quint gave her a scornful look for asking something which any freshman engineering student would be embarrassed not to know, another part of his mind was registering astonishment that she should be familiar with such a technical term. "Of course, any self-respecting engineering student is familiar with the work of Richard John Whitman. He's also the one who discovered the area rule. There was an abrupt pause as he suddenly stopped in mid-sentence, his mouth opening wide in astonishment. "Wait a minute you mean that's who your stepfather is?"

"Yes."

"My God, Christie!" He had a dazed look on his face as if he had just awakened from a deep sleep. "Of course I see it now. How could I have been so stupid as to miss something so obvious," as he hit his forehead with his clenched fist.

"I'll tell you how," Christie said, the pent-up feelings of frustration now fueling her anger. "Because you were jealous; you didn't want to hear anything about someone who might be more successful than you were. Especially since you're obviously frustrated at not being able work in your field anymore," she added.

"Come on Christie that's not true, I'm not jealous—"

"—Don't interrupt me, I'm not through yet! I simply don't believe you. There were several instances when I made reference to my stepfather's engineering background and you deliberately ignored it. You know what," she said, thumping his bare chest with her finger for emphasis, "I see what your problem is now: behind that façade of confidence is just another insecure male. You're like every other successful man: tough on the outside but filled on the inside with many of the same insecurities and hang-ups that the rest of us are. The fact is, Quint Brewster," she continued, "I'm furious with you! Don't you ever think that you can patronize me like that again! I may not have the technical knowledge you do, but after all that time I spent with my father, it's safe to assume that I have a lot more than the typical layman's knowledge of the field. In fact," she said over her shoulder, as she turned and stalked off, "I probably know more about his research than you ever will!"

By the time Quint caught up with her back at the room, Christie had grabbed some clothes from her dresser and marched into the bathroom, slamming and locking the door behind her. Quint sat down tiredly on the edge of the bed and slumped forward with his forearms resting on the tops of his thighs while he rubbed the bridge of his nose between his fingers absentmindedly. His thoughts kept swinging back and forth between admiration for Christie's spunk, frustration that he had once again antagonized her, and amazement that she should turn out to be the daughter of a man who had been a hero to him ever since he could remember.

About fifteen minutes after the shower had stopped running, Christie emerged from the bathroom fully dressed, her hair wrapped up in a towel. She was wearing a sleeveless summer dress that clung suggestively to her lush figure.

"You decided to wash your hair after all," Quint said as he got his clothes together and started towards the bathroom, hoping to defuse the situation by his innocuous comment. Christie's only response was an imperceptible nod of her head as she sat down in front of the mirror and began applying her make-up.

"Are you still willing to go to dinner with me?" Quint said meekly.

She looked over at him, the fire in her eyes only slightly dampened. "Yes, but mainly because I'm starving and there's nowhere else to go and eat. And I certainly have no intention of sitting in the room while you get to go and feed your face."

As he reached for the doorknob, he turned to her and said, "I'm truly sorry Christie. I hope you'll forgive me," then closed the door softly behind him. After a quick shower, he slipped on a pair of light tan slacks and was pulling a short-sleeved blue polo shirt over his head as he stepped back out into the room. Christie was eyeing herself critically in the mirror, having just completed brushing her hair and adding the final touches to her make-up. After a minute or two, she turned to him and said in a somewhat concil-iatory voice: "I've decided to accept your apology with the hope that we can salvage something of this weekend, but I'm really concerned about this atti-tude of yours towards women who display even the slightest independence of thought—or who demonstrate knowledge in an area that you happen to think belongs solely in the male province. It doesn't make me think very highly of your taste in woman. And it would be a serious problem if you think you can bring that attitude into our relationship."

Quint put his hands on her shoulders and said, "Look, Christie, I really am sorry I reacted that way."

She shook her head in disgust as she glanced around the room for her purse. "Men and their damned fragile egos."

"Now you're beginning to sound like Lisa," Quint said, as he held the door open for her. "She was always pleased when something came along which would serve as a forcible reminder that I wasn't that much different from everyone else."

"And do you believe that?"

"What? That I'm not that much different from anyone else?"

"Yes."

"Well I always felt like I should, but my oversized ego kept whispering another message in my ear," he responded, laughing and ducking as she took a playful swing at him.

"You're impossible," Christie said, as they started walking over towards the dining hall. Looking up at him with a hint of a smile on her face she added, "And what you just revealed about yourself is probably the least surprising piece of news I've heard since I arrived on Okinawa." Before Quint could think of an appropriate rejoinder, she continued, "Furthermore, I know I'm probably going to regret saying this, but I don't think that I'd want you to act any differently."

Quint glanced over at her and said in response: "That's because it will give you an opportunity to deflate my ego every now and then like you did the night I drove you home from the cocktail party." She matched his grin with one of her own as they walked arm in arm into the dining area, oblivious to the looks they received from the other people who were already seated there.

XVIII

As they left the dining room an hour or so later and stepped out into the early evening shadows, Christie turned to Quint and said, "That was a delicious meal, Quint, although I have to admit that there were a couple of items which I was a little leery about trying."

He looked down at her and smiled: "Let me guess. The escargot."

"That's one thing."

"I don't have any idea what the second one would be."

"The squid."

"Oh yeah, that. You should have gone with the muscles. They were delicious."

"Actually, the escargot were quite tasty once I got past my initial revulsion at the idea of eating a snail. Anyway, what shall we do now?"

"How about a long, slow, romantic walk along the beach?"

"I don't know," she said playfully, "I could probably handle it but I'm not sure that you could."

"What do you mean?" Quint said, puzzled at her comment.

"What I mean," she said, giving him a playful shove, "is that I don't think you can stand to be unfocused for that long."

"What are you talking about? What do you mean 'unfocused'?"

"Meaning doing something that has no specific purpose to it."

"For Pete sakes, Christie do you think I'm that bad—that I can't relax for even a little while?"

"I just assume you're likely to become bored unless you're doing something."

"Come on, Christie give me a break. I don't always have to be busy—at least not physically, anyway. Now mentally, that's a different matter. But there's no way I'm going to be bored in the company of a beautiful, oftentimes unpredictable, woman like you!"

"So you think I'm unpredictable, do you," Christie said, thoughtfully.

Quint grinned broadly, "No question about it. Every time I think I have you pegged, you do something—or say something—that sends me right back to the drawing board again."

"Is that good—or bad—or neither?"

"Umm. . . Let's just say it keeps things interesting."

She mulled that over for a minute and decided that it was probably better that he thought of her in that vein than in various other unflattering ways. "I'd like to change into something more casual before we take our walk. Is that all right?"

"Sure."

When they got back to their room Quint flopped down in a white rattan chair and put his feet up on the edge of the bed. "Do you mind if I watch you change?"

"No," Christie said, then added teasingly, "Is that one of your hobbies?'

"What?"

"Watching women change."

"Only pretty women. In fact, they have to be exceptionally pretty."

"And I suppose there have been a lot of those," she said, matter-of-factly.

"No, not really. Less than half a dozen I'd say."

"Well. I'm honored to be in such select company."

Christie felt just a little self-conscious as she pulled the dress over her head and walked over to the closet in her bra and panties to get a hanger. Of course, she realized her concerns didn't make a whole lot of sense in view of the fact that he had unclothed her a couple of weeks earlier in her bedroom. Looking past her reflected image she could see him coolly studying her behind partially-lidded eyes. As his gaze moved down her figure, his mouth suddenly curved into a smile.

"What's so funny?'

"Promise you won't get mad at me," he said, trying unsuccessfully to wipe the smile off his face.

"I promise," she said, cautiously.

"What do you call it when the panties ride up the umm . . . ." pausing as he looked for a delicate way of putting it.

"The crack of my fanny?" she said, as she unhurriedly pulled the edge of her panties down, surprised at how she had flip-flopped in just seconds and now felt totally unself-conscious in his presence, " I call it a wedgie; I don't know what anyone else calls it."

"Well, whatever it's called, it's one of the most delightfully sensuous views one can have of a woman's behind. In fact, it's a heck of a turn-on; It makes me want to reach out and . . . and just grab it!" he said, his mouth twisted into a wry grin.

"Well you can grab all you want later on," she said as she pulled on a pair of white jean shorts, "but right now I want to go for that romantic walk."

"Oh, all right," Quint said, the mischievous tone in his voice clearly indicating that he wouldn't forget that promise.

Christie tossed her bra onto the bed and slowly pulled on a white T-shirt stopping momentarily when the shirt was just above her breasts. Quint wrenched his eyes away from the sight, grabbed a dry bathing suit and made a quick trip to the bathroom to change. When he came back out a couple of minutes later, Christie had slipped on a pair of flip-flops.

"Why aren't you wearing your bra?"

"It's a lot more comfortable to go without. Besides, it's one less thing to take off if we end up taking a swim."

"Okay. Let's head out."

"Do I need to bring anything along?"

"Why don't you bring the beach towel in case we find a place to sit. . . or something."

"Hmm. I like the sound of that suggestion," she said, "what are the prospects of finding a spot where there's no chance of being disturbed?"

"Very good to excellent around this place, I'd say. Especially since most of the people here this weekend seem to be young couples with small children."

As they walked along the lighted path towards the beach, Quint turned to Christie and asked, somewhat cautiously, "Can I ask you to tell me a little of what it was like to grow up as Dick Whitman's daughter?"

She looked up at him with a pensive look and said in response. "It would take a few hours to tell you in any detail, but I can summarize it in a few sentences. . My stepfather wanted more than anything to have a son who would follow in his footsteps. When my half-brother was born, I think it was the happiest moment of his life. When they discovered shortly afterwards that he was mildly retarded, I think it was the saddest moment of his life."

"You have a retarded half-brother?"

"Yes. But he's really quite functional and absolutely a delightful person."

"But not functional enough for your stepfather."

"No, I'm afraid not. Although Dad treated him very well and loved him as much as he was capable of loving someone like that, it was such a profound disappointment that he never really got over it."

"And that's how you became the heir apparent."

"Yes. My stepfather was aware all along that I had a bent towards literature and history, but since I was considered a gifted child, he thought that he could simply redirect my interests into math and engineering."

"Sounds to me like we both would have been better off if there had been a mix-up at birth and you had ended up with my father and vice versa.

"Since I'm ten years younger than you just how was that supposed to happen?"

He grinned. "Beats me! Anyway, how did he go about redirecting your interests? I'm almost afraid to ask you what form that took."

"Oh I didn't mean to suggest anything negative. He started taking me to work, which meant mainly on the weekends and holidays when I wasn't in school and when it wouldn't be an annoyance to his colleagues. And I went everywhere with him—from his office to the wind tunnel to the machine shops to the test fields. I've probably spent more time at Edwards Air Force Base than any other civilian."

"But what would you do there?"

"Oh, when I was really little I'd just bring along my coloring books and dolls—you know things like that. As I got older, he'd begin to explain things to me, in as non-technical terms as possible, of course.

"I imagine I was the only teenager in the country to have a complete collection of autographs of the pilots assigned to the X-15 program."

"You must have been the envy of every teenage boy in your school!"

"You bet. They were beside themselves that a girl—a girl no less!—should be fortunate enough to have a unique collection like that—as well as have access to such exciting people and places," Christie said, smiling at the memory. "They tried to trade me all kinds of things in exchange for those autographs. Then one of them finally resorted to a less ethical way of getting hold of them."

"What did he do?"

"When I was junior in high school I gave a talk on the X-15 program to my science class. I made the mistake of bringing in the autographs and using them as an exhibit. They were protected by plastic slipcovers in a ring binder but when I left the room to go the bathroom someone took them. And apparently no one saw it happen—or so they claimed anyway."

"Did you get them back?"

"Yes. My Dad went to the school and raised holy hell. Luckily the parents of the boy who took the autographs discovered them hidden in his bedroom. There had been a lot of publicity about it including a short article in the local newspaper so they knew right away who they belonged to. They made him return them to me and personally apologize for his actions —in front of the whole class, no less."

"Did he do it—in front of the class, I mean?"

"Yes. And I felt badly for him. I thought his parents were being unnecessarily harsh in making him do that. Needless to say that was the last time that I ever brought my autographs to school. Around that time my stepfather began to pressure me in a gentle but persistent way to consider engineering as a career."

"How long did that go on?"

"It went on for about a year. That's when he gave up and realized that I was as stubborn in my own way as he was in his. Gradually we managed to establish an amicable kind of arrangement in which I would continue to be his main confidant and supporter but would be allowed to follow my own interests. Actually, I did take a minor in math and did a lot of reading in the field so I could be on the same wavelength as he was."

"Wow. You really were pretty accommodating."

"Yes. Perhaps too much so, because it also caused another problem."

"Let me guess. Your mother became jealous of you."

She looked up at him with a new measure of respect. "You're pretty perceptive."

"You mean for a man?"

"Sorry," she said, "it's just that an insight like that would slide right by most men."

"But I'm not like other men—most of the time anyway," he said, smiling disarmingly.

"That's true—for the most part," she admitted. "Anyway, you were right about the jealousy thing. Unfortunately, that managed to drive a further wedge between us.

"How old were you when your father first started taking you along on these outings?"

"Young. Around nine—or maybe I was already ten. I really don't remember any more," she said, grabbing suddenly for Quint's arm as she tripped over an exposed root.

"You okay?"

"Yes. I guess I should spend less time talking and more time paying attention to where we're going.

"Here's the beach. The walking should be easier from here on."

"Good."

As they began walking along the beach, Christie was struck once again by the subtle but well- nigh irresistible feeling of tranquility, of serenity, of well-being that a tropical evening could evoke in her. Most visitors from the temperate climates would no doubt be quick to acknowledge the romantic spell which the tropics cast over all but the most insensitive souls. But did they feel the deeper emotions that such places always aroused in Christie. Somehow she doubted it. For her, places such as this represented something far greater, far more meaningful than simply a vacation spot, a break from the mundane quality of day-to day life. They warmed her heart, nourished her soul, and made her feel more alive than she had ever felt before.

"I think I'll go barefoot. The less I have to wear, the better I like it. In fact, when I'm all alone on those isolated beaches in the Caribbean, I don't wear anything."

"So you're a real nudist at heart, huh?"

Christie nodded. "I just can't get enough of the tropical warmth. I love to feel it soaking through my skin and seeping down inside me."

"Okinawa isn't technically a tropical island."

"I realize that, but ever since I arrived here I've had the same special feeling that I experienced when I was in the Caribbean. It warms my soul as well as my body and gives me a feeling of hope. Do you understand what I'm saying?"

"No, not really. Why do you think it gives you a feeling of hope?"

"I'm not sure, Quint. It's as though there's something waiting for me in a place like this."

"You mean, like a spiritual awakening?"

Christie shrugged. "Something like that maybe. I have to admit, it does make me feel closer to God."

"This is the second time you've shown me your religious side."

"My father's sister was a strong Christian and since she lived just a couple of blocks away from us during my childhood I saw a lot of her. So Aunt Sarah had a lot of influence on my spiritual growth."

"Well, I've got to admit that's not an experience I've ever had. Both my mother and father were nominal Christians and had nothing much to say about my spiritual growth. But my father's brother—my Uncle Bill—was a big help to me during my freshman year in college," Quint admitted.

"How so?"

"I was struggling with the meaning of life after taking an introductory philosophy course with this atheistic assistant professor who took great pleasure in running roughshod over the belief systems of college freshman. He told us that belief in God was completely unsupportable in the scientific world in which we lived. He also said that Christianity was simply a crutch for those people who didn't have the guts to face up to the fact that we were all alone in the universe. That it was up to us to create a world in which everyone would live together in peace and harmony and where there would be no poverty but all people would share equally in the goods and services needed to live a comfortable and fulfilling life. But that, of course, was after the capitalist system was overthrown.

"Anyway, I had lengthy talks about my doubts with my uncle over Christmas vacation and spring break. Uncle Bill was one of the Brewster boys who had toed the line and taken up one of the acceptable vocations. He became a protestant minister after attending Andover Newton Seminary.

"Did he help you?"

"Yep. He told me to pay no attention to that atheistic crap and Marxist drivel. He countered many of my professor's claims with well-reasoned arguments that made a lot of sense to me."

"So where are you at in your faith?" Christie asked.

"Well, I believe in God—if that's what you're asking—but I don't go to church very often."

"You're no different than a lot of other Christians, Quint."

"Yeah, I guess not. Aren't we usually lumped together under the heading 'Christmas Christians'?"

"That's about it," Christie said grinning at him. "Christmas and Easter Christians. Anyway, isn't this a magnificent night!" she said waving her hand at the scene which lay before them.

Although no words were exchanged, Christie sensed that Quint was not immune to the beauty of the scene which lay before them either. A full moon overhead created a landscape of sharp contrasts, bleaching the distant sand dunes a brilliant white and causing them to stand out in stark relief against the dark hills of the Motobu Peninsula. As far as the eye could see, long gentle swells rolled landward, their crests glinting like molten silver in the moonlight. Nearer to the beach, the water was luminous from the phosphorescent glow of innumerable tiny sea organisms. As they continued their walk, tall irregular columns of coral rose before them, standing like sentinels at intermittent intervals along the shore and reminding Christie of miniature versions of the sea stacks that were found along the Oregon coast.

They were now approaching a point where the beach curved sharply to the left and as they walked around the bend they came upon a group of coral columns that made an almost perfect half circle with the open side facing the water.

"What a perfect place to stop," Christie said enthusiastically. "our own private little oasis!"

"Looks like a good spot all right," Quint acknowledged.

After spreading out the blanket on the sand, Quint leaned back on his elbows while Christie lay with her head resting on his lap. For several minutes they lay still, neither moving nor speaking, not wanting to break the spell with the sound of their voices. The scents that wafted to them on the night air in combination with the soft sound of the water lapping on the beach had an almost hypnotic effect on Christie. She was gradually slipping into a dream-like state that bordered on the ecstatic, when her thoughts were abruptly brought back to earth by Quint's voice: "Have you ever come close to getting married?"

Christie was still lying on her back with her head in Quint's lap. She had both hands across her chest and had been idly studying the bright white orb of the moon while they had been talking. She wondered if it was really possible that there would be Americans walking on its surface by the end of the decade. How strange. That definitely would dispel some of her more romantic notions associated with the moon. To know that men were up there contaminating another of the heavenly bodies.

She suddenly realized that Quint had asked her a question. "Have I what?"

"I asked if you've ever come close to marrying anyone."

Christie got up slowly into a sitting position and sat cross-legged facing the water. As she mulled over Quint's question, she idly scooped up handfuls of sand and piled them in a mound in front of her legs. "Twice. No—technically only once. To a fellow Peace Corps staff member whom I met in Somalia. But there was another guy a couple of years before that whom I was absolutely mad about. He was one of my college instructors. In fact, he was the one I took the aerodynamics course with."

"What happened?"

"Neither one of them worked out. That's all."

"Do you mind telling me why?"

Christie slowly let out a deep sigh, then after scattering the mound of sand with the back of her hand, turned around to face Quint. "I met Rob when we were both assigned to Somalia after finishing the Peace Corps training program. He and I got along famously while we were serving together there but when we got back to the states and tried to make it work, it wouldn't. Something was missing which had been present when we were in Somalia.

"Maybe it was the day-to-day sharing of a common experience. I don't know. What I do know was that he was a very different person there. In Somalia, he had been adventuresome, intellectually stimulating, interested in everything around him. He was not only fun to be around but he energized you. Everyone felt that way about him. But all that disappeared once he got back to the states. Maybe he was depressed over the prospect of having to work at a nine-to-five job for the rest of his life. Not that that was his only option, of course. Anyway, I lived with him for about six months and then one morning I woke up and knew that it was time to end it. So I did. I packed my things and an hour or so later I left. I haven't seen or heard from him since.

"That was Rob.

"My first great love—as a grown woman, anyway—was Kent Wheeler, a teacher with whom I fell madly in love during my junior year in college. Kent was a rising young assistant professor in the math department at MIT at the time. He was the one who taught that aerodynamics course which I took.

The first day of the fall semester I walked into class and as soon as I laid eyes on him I lost it. It turned out the feeling was mutual. The chemistry between us was so palpable that I was worried that other people would pick up on it. They may have, but nobody ever said anything. We started dating after the second class of the semester. I would have gone out with him if he asked me after the first class but he had some kind of faculty meeting he had to attend."

"So what happened to him?"

"I discovered—quite by accident—that he was married."

"How did you find that out?"

"I found a framed picture of his wife in the living room of his apartment."

"Why did he leave it out where you could see it?"

"He never had me over to his apartment."

"You lost me. I thought you just said something about being in his apartment?"

"I did. On his birthday I decided I would surprise him by baking a special cake and bringing it over to his apartment while he was in class."

"You knew where he lived then."

"Yes, and I also knew where he hid a key to his apartment. I overheard him mention it once to one of his close friends. So I went over there that afternoon, found the key, let myself in, and put the cake on the coffee table where he'd see it as soon as he came in. As I turned to go I saw the picture. I couldn't miss it because it was a framed 8x11 sitting on the corner table next to his recliner. The message written across the bottom of the picture was very loving to say the least. And lying open, face up on the table, was a birthday telegram from his wife.

"So what did you do with the cake—sprinkle some arsenic on it?"

Christie looked over at him and grinned. "Nope. I did something almost as satisfying and a lot less drastic."

"What was that?"

"I took his picture out of my wallet and tore it up into little pieces which I stuck upright in the cake for decorations. Then I took the ring he gave me and pushed it as far down into the middle of the cake as I could reach, using a letter opener that was lying on the table. The last thing I did was to tear off a sheet from a legal pad and write a brief message on it which I placed next to the cake."

"What did the note say?"

"Something to the effect that I was sorry his wife wasn't there to enjoy a piece of his birthday cake but that I wouldn't want her to be the one to choke on the ring in the middle of it."

"Wow! You're no one to mess around with—that's for sure."

"Why do you say that? Did you think at one point that I was?"

"No. Not me!" Quint said, as he rolled over on his side and propped his head up with his upraised arm. "I started taking you seriously from the day I picked you up at Kadena. "So what happened after that? You were still in his class at that point weren't you?"

Christie nodded. "There were about three weeks left in the semester. Needless to say, it made things a little bit uncomfortable for both of us. But especially for him."

"Didn't he try to apologize?"

"Sure. At first he tried to get me to stop and talk to him after class. When that didn't work, he'd leave hand-written messages in my mailbox at school and even stick them under the windshield wipers on my car. They all said the same thing: he pleaded for a chance to explain himself. Just one chance, that's all he wanted, he said."

"But you didn't give him that chance." It was a statement, not a question.

"Absolutely not!" Christie said, rather vehemently. "He was a liar and a cheat—and he was married to boot! That's all there was to it."

"What kind of a grade did you get in the course?"

"An A minus. Exactly what I deserved."

"Well, at least he didn't strike back at you through your grade."

"It's a damn good thing he didn't. I would have taken it to the Provost—or even higher—if he had tried to pull that on me."

"And you never spoke to him again?"

"No," she said, staring absentmindedly at the distant horizon. After a brief pause, she continued, "I should have realized there was something fishy about the whole relationship a lot sooner; I missed out on a couple of obvious clues."

"Such as?"

"Well, he spent a lot of time sailing so he had a good tan. One time when I was holding his hand I noticed that there was a band of white skin on his ring finger where there was no tan. I don't know why I didn't think of its significance at the time. Obviously, he'd been wearing a wedding band all summer but then took it off right around the time he met me. That was one thing. Another thing that should have aroused my suspicions was the fact that he would never take me to his apartment. We used his friends' apartments, my apartment, occasionally motel rooms—everything but his place."

"What was his excuse for not using his own apartment?"

"He claimed that he had a friend from out of town who stayed at his place on a fairly regular basis but who often arrived unannounced. He also said that his landlady was pretty old fashioned and wouldn't approve of such carryings-on."

Quint shook his head in disbelief. "You talk about me being naïve!"

"You're right. It was pretty stupid of me," Christie acknowledged. After a brief pause she continued. "Actually, I did see him once more that semester. It was just before Christmas break and he had his wife with him."

"How can you be sure it was his wife?"

"It was her all right. I recognized her from the picture in his living room. But the picture didn't begin to do her justice."

"How so?"

"She was an absolute knockout!" A moment later Christie stood up slowly and stretched. As she did so she said, "I swear: I don't think I'll ever understand men. And you know what? I'm not so sure that it's worth all the effort to try and figure them out."

Quint wasn't quite sure that he wanted to try and respond to that comment. It was probably better to leave it alone. Instead, he said "how about going for a swim now?"

Christie hesitated. Now that the moment had arrived, she was more than a little nervous at the thought of swimming at night in unknown waters. "I don't know," she said cautiously, "is there anything in the water that could be dangerous?"

"You mean other than me?" Quint said with a smirk on his face.

Christie put her hands on her hips and gave him one of those looks that needed no words to convey its message.

"There shouldn't be—not around here anyway."

"How about sharks?"

He shook his head. "There aren't supposed to be any sharks in Okinawan waters."

Christie gave him a skeptical look.

"Scouts honor," he said, holding up his hand.

Christie stared at the water for several seconds then she started to unbutton her shorts, but part way through the process suddenly stopped. Christie had come to Okuma with Quint in spite of persisting reservations about the possibility of building a viable relationship with him. But each time he had touched her, no matter how innocently, bullets of liquid fire shot with the speed of light through her body.

"Come on, Christie don't chicken out on me now that we've gotten this far," Quint said.

The next few minutes were almost comical in tone, as each of them, a little self-conscious about undressing in public, tried to be the first to get their clothes off and into the water. Christie had less to take off than Quint because of changing back into shorts and a T-shirt before leaving the room. So his main impression of her was a slightly blurred vision of golden skin, soft flesh, and a stunningly curvaceous body before it disappeared briefly beneath the water in a shallow dove. By the time she surfaced and shook the water from her eyes, a few quick strokes had brought Quint to within reach of her. Half standing, half floating, they faced each other a few feet apart at first, but the sensual feeling of the sea in combination with the scent-laden night air proved irresistibly arousing, amplifying the intensity of the desire which had been simmering just beneath the surface ever since they had arrived at Okuma.

Taking a couple of steps forward, Quint bent his head down to the hollow at the base of her throat, feeling the increased tempo of her pulse as he massaged the soft flesh with his mouth, then moved down to the deep cleft between her breasts where he proceeded to nuzzle her with increasing ardor. His hands grasped her firmly by the hips and in the natural buoyancy of the water a gentle turn brought the firm pink nipple of her right breast over to his mouth where it grazed his lips. Christie moaned softly and leaned her head back while pushing her breast firmly against his mouth. Flames of desire seared both their minds and bodies. Quint's mouth opened and his tongue traced a circular path around her areola, gradually edging closer and closer to her nipple. Taking the full pink orb of her nipple in his mouth, he gently sucked at it, then closed his mouth over the soft mound of her breast while flicking his tongue back and forth across the swollen globe. Christie's moans took on a new urgency as she twisted the other way, hungrily seeking the same erotic treatment for her other nipple. Running her hands with increasing agitation through his hair, she abruptly twisted his face up to her's, crushing her open mouth against his, while pressing her body against the surging warmth of his manhood. Both hearts pounded out an erratic rhythm in unison, as the flames of desire spread throughout their bodies, ready to engulf them in a pyric explosion of sexual ecstasy. Taking her hand in his, he guided her down to the throbbing focal point of his being. She took him in her hands and began rubbing the tip among the folds of her femininity, moving in a circular motion that sent shock waves of electricity coursing through their bodies. Her head was tilted back and her mouth wide open as she stared unseeing up at the star-smudged night sky. "Quint, oh Quint." Christie called out his name in convulsive breaths, as her tormented groans cried out for the orgy of ecstatic release.

Somewhere, someone was speaking. Who? Why? Gradually, the sound of distant voices carrying across the water pushed against her mind until they penetrated her consciousness, breaking the spell and forcibly wrenching her back to their immediate surroundings. She pushed away from him and looked quickly over her shoulders. "Someone's coming!" she blurted out, a sudden sound of panic in her voice.

"Dammit, Christie, those people are nowhere near us," Quint muttered in frustration.

"But they're coming this way! We've got to get out of here before they see us."

Quint shook his head in disgust, "there's no need to be in such a rush," he added, but Christie was already wading quickly back to the beach. Quint deliberately took his time, arriving at the blanket after Christie had already pulled on her clothes and was sitting on the beach with her arms wrapped around her legs, her forehead resting on her knees. The voices they had heard just minutes before had already faded in the distance.

Quint by now was furious. He knew he probably would regret it, but there was no way he could hold his temper in check. "Now what the hell was that all about?" He deliberately stood in front of her, letting the night air partially dry his muscular body before he began slowly putting his clothes back on. "You know that was totally unnecessary, don't you?" he said, his voice thick with sarcasm. Then in a moment of spite he added, "If that had been Cally she wouldn't have cared if there were a dozen people on the beach watching us—and they all had binoculars!"

Christie looked up at him and spoke for the first time since he had gotten back to the blanket, her voice reflecting a mixture of anger and disgust, "Well then maybe you should have stayed with her."

"Maybe I should have," he said, the anger still holding him captive. "Here are the keys to the room," dropping them at her feet. "I'm going to take a walk—a long walk so I can try and cool off. In more ways than one, I might add." As he started to walk away he said over his shoulder, "if you turn around and follow your nose you'll get back to the room without any problem."

She stood up abruptly, shook out the blanket, and said in a flash of anger, "I'm not stupid, Quint; I think I can manage to find my way back along a half mile long stretch of sand." With that she turned and strode off angrily in the opposite direction.

—⟶⟵—

When Quint returned to their room forty-five minutes or so later, Christie was in bed facing towards the wall. The light in the bathroom was still on, however, and the door had been left ajar. Although she hadn't said anything, it was unnatural for someone who was asleep to be that quiet and that still. So she was obviously still awake. Should he say something or shouldn't he? What could he say? Maybe he should wait until morning. By then, she might be more approachable.

As he toweled dry following a quick shower to rinse off the salt and the sand, his thoughts kept coming back to the same conclusion: that someone or something had stacked the cards against them. Fate. The universe. The gods. Call it whatever you want. Somebody—or something—was doing a pretty good job of sabotaging his relationship with Christie. Or maybe he should say his attempt to establish a relationship with Christie. But even as that thought formed in his mind he was inclined to dismiss it as pure nonsense. His engineer's training made it extremely difficult for him to maintain the fiction that there was some unnamed entity that was the cause of all their conflict. Logic, in fact, clearly suggested that the problem originated much closer to home. But who was more to blame: him? Christie? Or were they both contributing to the situation?

Christie was, if nothing else, definitely unpredictable and therefore hard to read. However, it seemed clear that she was attracted to him. It was also apparent that there were depths of sensuality to her that he had only just begun to tap. On the other hand, there were those times when she came across as extremely reserved and shy. Plus, she had been far more nervous in the water than the occasion warranted.

Quint rubbed his chin idly and stared at his reflection in the mirror. He needed to shave but decided to postpone it until morning. There was no sense in bothering with it now since there wasn't anyone to appreciate it. Moments later, as he put the toothpaste back in his travel kit and reached for a cup of mouthwash, Quint had to admit that, if he was really honest with himself, he hadn't the faintest idea what to do next. Shaking his head in frustration, he slipped on a clean pair of boxer shorts and a T-shirt, turned out the bathroom light and walked back into the other room. Just as he sat down on the edge of the bed, the shrill jangle of the phone shattered the silence of the room.

"What the devil . . . ," he said. Snatching it up quickly from its base he answered tiredly, "Major Brewster."

"Quint, its Rick. Sorry to bother you but the old man asked me to call you."

"What for?" he answered, trying hard to smother the irritation in his voice.

"There's been another C-130 accident down south and he wants you to head up the investigation team."

"Why does it have to be me? There are plenty of other pilots who can handle it. Besides, it isn't even my turn yet."

"I know all that. So does Col. Crane. It's just that this is a special case."

"What do you mean by that?"

"The pilot was Senator Cranston's son, Jack Cranston."

"So?"

"It's just that he wants everything to go smoothly without any hitches of any kind. He thinks you're the guy who will insure that it happens according to script."

"Is there any reason to think that pilot error is going to be a factor in the investigation?"

"No, not that I'm aware of."

"Well then, I don't see why the old man needs me to oversee this particular one."

"It will make him feel better—just in case there is some kind of hitch—knowing you're in charge."

Quint said, to no one in particular, "I've got to get out of this life and go back to a civilian existence where I'm not at somebody's beck and call 24 hours a day, seven days a week."

The line was silent as Rick had no response to his last comment.

"O.K. I'll start home first thing in the morning. I should be back at Naha by late morning. Is there anything leaving around that time?"

"The old man has got one on standby; it will be waiting for you."

"All right," he answered his voice thick with a combination of fatigue and resignation.

"Good night."

He put down the receiver and glanced at Christie who had rolled over and was looking at him with a questioning look, trying to make sense of his half of the conversation.

"Who was that? Is there something wrong?"

"No. Yes. Well, not really. It was just Rick informing me that I've been assigned to another accident investigation board, so we're going to have to head back first thing in the morning."

"Isn't that a bit unusual—to call someone back like that from a weekend trip? Especially since you were planning on going down to Vietnam on Monday, anyway."

"Yes. But Col. Crane apparently feels it's important I get down there as quickly as possible."

"Sounds like you're the indispensable man."

He gave her a hard look, but she had said it matter-of-factly, with no trace of sarcasm in her voice. "No one's indispensable. Christie.

"Anyway, I owe you an apology. Comparing you to Cally is like comparing . . . ," he paused momentarily, groping for an appropriate analogy, "Actually, there is no comparison."

"I don't want your apology, Quint. What I want to know is the truth about your feelings for Cally. The main thing that bothers me about that comment you made is it makes me wonder if you really have let go of her."

Quint walked over and knelt down next to Christie. Taking her hands in his, he looked up at her. "Look, I promise you that I'm through with Cally. It's over. Period! All right?"

She nodded.

"Change of subject. I have a confession to make."

"About what?"

"Well," he said, hesitantly, "I more or less committed you to teach a remedial writing class to a group of my NCOs."

"You what?"

"No don't go jumping all over me until you give me a chance to explain."

"I wasn't going to. You just startled me, that's all."

"Here's what happened. I told you that I had to meet with Sergeant Ferris to discuss the issue of his writing skills. If I could get you to teach a short course—say once a week for six weeks—to Sergeant Ferris and my other senior NCOs—you would be helping them out, which helps me out, and at the same time you'll get to know Sergeant Ferris; or more importantly, let him get to know you. That way, not only would you have an opportunity to impress upon him the importance of good writing, you might also manage to convert him from an adversary to an admirer of yours. Especially after he gets a look at you! Anyway, it seemed like a much more subtle approach—one that had a better chance of working—than having me confront him about something so personal and take the chance of antagonizing him and maybe making things worse. Of course, I realize that you may not be too keen about taking on something like this in light of your recent phone conversation with him. It's entirely up to you, Christie."

He paused for a minute while she digested his plan, then breathed a sigh of relief when she looked up at him and said, "Okay, I'll do it."

"We have to be on the road by 7:00 or 7:30 at the latest if I'm going to get back by noon.

I'm pretty sure, though, that the dining hall opens around 6:30, so we can grab a quick bite to eat before we go. Is that all right with you?"

"Yes."

Lying there in the darkness, Quint thought again how frustrating it was that the evening turned out as it did. They should be lying in each other's arms, completely spent after an evening of passionate love-making, instead of being emotionally drained for other reasons.

His last thought before he drifted off was of an image of Christie many months pregnant, carrying their first child. Although he never knew it, he fell asleep with a smile on his face for the first time in months.

XIX

As Christie was letting herself into Quint's house several days later, she wondered if she was about to encounter another typical example of bachelor living quarters. But as she dropped her bag on the rattan couch and took a quick look around, it seemed apparent that Quint was the exception to the rule. She wasn't entirely surprised to discover that. On several occasions Christie had noted his tendency towards compulsive neatness.

Stepping back to get a better perspective on the layout of the living room, she nearly tripped over Sam. Apparently he had been sleeping in one of the bedrooms and had wandered out to see who had invaded his space. Christie reached down, picked him up, and cradled him in her arms.

"Hey Sam! I've been looking forward to meeting you," she said as she stroked him under the chin."

Sitting down on the couch she held him on her chest so that his face was only a few inches from hers and she started scratching the back of his head.

"You like that don't you," she said softly, as he closed his eyes and began to purr.

"Wow! You've got some purring apparatus there, old guy," she said, continuing to stroke him absentmindedly while taking in the details of Quint's living room.

The layout of his house was almost exactly like the house she shared with Sally. The main difference was the floor-to-ceiling picture windows that looked out on the East China Sea. A nice touch. She wondered if the house came that way or whether Quint had been responsible for the change.

But the furnishings, not surprisingly, were Spartan. A few pieces of the ubiquitous rattan furniture were scattered round the room. There was a credenza against the wall that separated the living room from the kitchen and no drapes or curtains on the windows. Overall, the place felt like nobody really lived there. Someone may have slept there and perhaps eaten an occasional meal, but it wasn't used for much more than that. In fact, the only warmth in the room came from a scattering of prints and original paintings. They had apparently been purchased during Quint's travels throughout Southeast Asia and, to Christie's unpracticed eye, looked to be superior examples of oriental art.

Another thing that struck her was the almost complete absence of any knickknacks, souvenirs, or decorative pieces. An empty vase sat on one end of the credenza; a pylon-mounted model of a C-130 on the other end. That was it. But Christie actually liked that quality in a man. She had always harbored certain suspicions about single men who were into knickknacks.

The only other things in sight were three neat stacks of magazines on the rattan coffee table. One of them was an aviation magazine. The other two were hydrology journals. When she leaned forward to pick up a copy, Sam let out a low growl which in cat language presumably meant he was not happy at being disturbed. After a few seconds, he stood up on her lap and stretched, apparently having decided the introductions had been completed.

Christie had always wondered what went on in a cat's mind. In the recesses of that tiny brain, was there an awareness that his master was gone. Probably not. All that mattered was there was someone around who would provide food, water, a reasonable amount of attention, and change his kitty litter. *I mustn't forget to do that every few days,* she thought. As Christie watched Sam walk slowly towards the kitchen, she decided that Quint was right about the cat. The way Sam moved suggested he had seen more than his share of rough times.

Christie was still sitting there a few minutes later, feeling a little lazy, when there was a light knock at the front door. It was Quint's neighbor, Mrs. Nakamura.

After introducing herself, and discovering that Christie would be staying for a few days to take care of Sam, she invited Christie to dinner.

"I'd be delighted to join you for dinner."

"Excellent."

When Christie slipped her sandals off and placed them on the tatami mat at the entrance to the Nakamura's that evening, Mrs. Nakamura and her husband exchanged subtle looks of satisfaction. Christie appeared to be exceptionally sensitive for a westerner. Of course, neither could have had any inkling of how thorough a briefing on Okinawan customs Christie had received that afternoon.

Shortly after receiving the invitation, Christie had called and interrogated Mariko Anderson, the school librarian and an Okinawan native who had studied in the United States and was married to an American serviceman.

Also, only about an hour before she was due at the Nakamura's for dinner, Christie had joined Marge Magnuson and two of her Okinawan friends for coffee at the A and W Restaurant near Fort Buckner.

Since Christie was mainly concerned with following the correct etiquette at the dinner table, that was the topic on which she quizzed her companions most closely. A number of their suggestions related to things she would have instinctively avoided anyway. So when she was informed that lipstick was a no-no because it might damage the delicate artwork on the dinnerware, and that perfume tended to mask the distinctive odors of the Okinawan dishes it was a non-issue from her standpoint. Christie generally used minimal make-up anyway, unless attending an official function or going out for the evening. Also, since she rarely wore any jewelry except for a simple pendant and chain, there was no need to worry about rings chipping her hosts' cups and dishes. After all the discussion, Marge ventured the opinion that the area in which one was most likely to commit a major faux pas would be in the use of chopsticks. There seemed to be an endless list of "do's" and "don'ts" when it came to their usage.

As Mrs. Nakamura was welcoming Christie into their living room that evening, Christie was struck by how tastefully it was decorated. She had already concluded that the Nakamuras were much better off than most Okinawan families. For one thing, the typical Okinawan family would be in no position to own a western style house. But there were other clues as well. The tatami mats that covered the floor were embroidered with a heavy gold stitching along the perimeter. Another difference between the Nakamura house and the ones that she and Quint lived in, was the wood paneling on the walls of the living room and dining area. The Nakamuras' walls were paneled with a rich, tropical wood, probably teak, which created a much greater sense of warmth than the plaster walls that were common to houses on the island. In addition, Christie recognized the folding screen, which served to separate the dining area from the living area, as an exquisite example of Bingata art. She had learned through her reading that Bingata was a textile coloring technique that was unique to Okinawa and had nearly become a lost art as a result of the turmoil and destruction of the war years. The most obvious example of the Nakamura's affluence, however, was reflected in the paintings and wall hangings. Even though her exposure to the world of Okinawan art was limited, it didn't take an expert to recognize the work of Seikichi Tamanaha. A professor at the University of the Ryukyus, Tamanaha's work had gained an international following.

Of course, there were certain features which were common to all Okinawan households and had no bearing on their degree of affluence. In one corner of the living room, flower arrangements, small sculptures and miscellaneous art objects were on display in a small decorative alcove. Also, there was the ubiquitous family shrine, which included the memorial tablets, cups for wine and tea, and a small box that usually held the family genealogy and valuable heirlooms.

While Mrs. Nakamura went into the kitchen to finish preparing the food, Mr. Nakamura moved the screen back and led Christie into the dining area. As her host was indicating where Christie should sit, his two daughters filed in from another part of the house and sat down next to each other on the side of the table adjacent to Christie. They looked about seven years of age and were obviously identical twins. The page boy haircuts and matching clothes served to reinforce Christie's impression. They were good looking children, with the same finely chiseled bone structure as their father. When Christie greeted them, they smiled shyly but otherwise sat quietly throughout the entire meal.

The meal consisted of a clear soup, rice, and champuru, a stir-fry made of somen noodles, tofu, seasonal vegetables, and tuna. Christie soon discovered that champuru virtually held the status of an Okinawan national dish. For dessert, there was an aesthetically pleasing arrangement of fresh fruit.

All the food was placed on the table at the same time on individual meal trays. Once that was done, Mrs. Nakamura sat down next to Christie. With everyone seated, Christie knew they could now commence eating.

Mrs. Nakamura spoke in her faultless English. "Major Brewster informed us that you came here to do some research for a doctoral thesis."

"Yes. I'm especially interested in the role that woman play in Okinawan society."

Mrs. Nakamura nodded slowly while taking a sip of tea. "If you are interested, I will be happy to give you a brief overview of a typical woman's status here on Okinawa."

"Thank you. I would very much like to hear about it."

"I suppose it might be nice to start out on a positive note. So I will begin by pointing out that the women of Okinawa are a lot more independent than their counterparts on the Japanese mainland."

"Why is that?"

"There is no question in my mind that the single biggest reason for this difference is the impact of the war on Okinawan customs and traditions."

"I doubt if an American could imagine how tumultuous those times must have been," Christie said.

"No, I don't think anyone can imagine something so traumatizing unless they had actually been through it," Mrs. Nakamura said, politely. "The impact on one's psyche is unbelievable. Especially for a child. I was fifteen at the time, so I had a clearer understanding of what was going on. On the other hand, I also had complete responsibility for the care of my three siblings since both my parents had been killed during the initial bombings." She shook her head to clear away the painful memories that had briefly enveloped her mind.

"Tell me about the specific changes the war brought about and the impact it had on Okinawan women," said Christie.

"Some of the credit must go to the Americans, of course," Mrs. Nakamura responded. "During the occupation, women got the right to vote and made progress on many other fronts as well, thanks to the enlightened administration of General MacArthur on the mainland. Also, since many of the Okinawan men died in the battle, to a large degree the effort needed to rebuild Okinawa in the immediate post-war period fell on the shoulders of the women. Many of them were forced to become the breadwinners of the family through necessity. And that fact sheds light on some of the major differences between the situation of the mainland Japanese women and the Okinawan women."

"What do you mean?"

"It is much easier for an Okinawan woman to get a job because the Okinawan economy is overwhelmingly a service economy. There are plenty of jobs available for women, especially on the American bases. Also, one doesn't have to travel that far, because the populated part of the island is concentrated in such a small geographic area. In Japan, people have to travel great distances by train to get to their jobs. And child care on the mainland is an expensive proposition. Here on Okinawa, we have large supportive families who are willing to step in and help out. However, unfortunately, there's also a negative factor that serves to reinforce the presence of women in the work force."

"Which is?"

"Salaries are much lower here than on the mainland. It really is not possible to support a family on a single salary."

Christie was already wishing she had asked Mrs. Nakamura for approval to tape their conversation. Hopefully, she could remember most of what was said tonight. Especially, if she made notes as soon as she got back to Quint's house.

While Christie was deciding what to ask about next, she complimented Mrs. Nakamura on the flavor of the champuru.

"Have you ever had it before?"

"No. I'm struck, however, by the complexity of the flavors. It's a very interesting and a very tasty dish. What are the ingredients, if you don't mind my asking?"

"There are as many versions of champuru as there are Okinawan cooks," Mrs. Nakamura said. "That's a slight exaggeration, but only a slight one. Tofu is one of the most common forms of the dish. But bean sprouts, eggplant, goya, and many other vegetables, can also serve as the primary ingredient. I suppose it would be correct to say this is an eggplant champuru that we are eating tonight, but it also contains bean sprouts, and goya. But not too much goya," Mrs. Nakamura added, winking at her children.

"What's goya?"

"It's a vegetable. Actually, a member of the gourd family. Okinawan adults have developed a virtual addiction for goya champuru. But it's definitely an acquired taste. Probably similar to what you Americans would say about foods like olives and caviar.

"Most Okinawan children find it much too bitter for their taste. Unfortunately for them, it has considerable nutritional value, so I use it a lot." She smiled at the twins who were vehemently nodding their heads in response to her comment. "But I do add eggs to the dish to make it more palatable for the children.

"But to continue our discussion about Okinawan women, there are many deeply embedded cultural factors," said Mrs. Nakamura, "which make it difficult to achieve any real progress in gaining rights for women."

"But don't you think that's pretty much a universal problem?" Christie asked, as she focused on picking up the pork and vegetables instead of spearing it. Piercing the food, she recalled, was a definite no-no.

"Yes. But here on Okinawa it is much worse than in the states. Frankly, we have so many instances where males receive preferential treatment that I hardly know where to begin. For instance, there's *totome*."

"Totome?" Christie repeated, being careful to pronounce the word as her host had.

"Yes. That's the tradition whereby the first born male in the family is the one who gets to inherit everything—the parent's money, property, and, of course, the *ihai*—those are the mortuary tablets on which the names of the deceased members of the family are engraved."

That was one tradition which Christie couldn't see losing any sleep over. Why anyone would want to be the keeper of a mortuary tablet was beyond her understanding. But, of course, she kept her thoughts to herself.

Mrs. Nakamura continued. "Since the first born male knows this is going to happen, typically, it tends to make the eldest Okinawan male arrogant, spoiled, and lazy."

Christie stole a quick look at Mr. Nakamura to see how he was reacting to this. As far as Christie could determine, he seemed completely unaffected by his wife's harsh criticism of Okinawan men.

Almost as if Mrs. Nakamura had read Christie's thoughts, she added, "My husband is very different from the typical male. Not only is he far better educated than the majority of Okinawan men, but he is one of the hardest working men I've ever known, from any cultural background. That's one of the many reasons I married him," she added, smiling lovingly at her husband, who looked up from his meal and nodded appreciatively at her.

"There's an expression on the island, *danson john.* Roughly translated it means 'men are raised up and extolled, women are put down and treated as inferior.' It starts at birth and continues to the grave," she said, a trace of bitterness in her voice.

"How is that the case?" Christie asked as she placed her chopsticks on their rest and reached for her cup of tea.

"I remember when my mother was pregnant with my youngest sister. The women who lived in the neighborhood were determined that she should have a boy and they were quite vocal about it. I can still hear their shrill voices as I walked by with my mother. They kept repeating 'have a boy' over and over like some kind of sacred litany. "I remember asking my mother, 'Why do they want you to have a boy? I'd rather have a sister.' But the women were honestly worried about the fact that my parents might not have a son to pass on the *ihai* to."

"Did they have a son?"

"No. But not for lack of trying. There are four girls in my family," she said. "There were two more, but one lived only a few days, and the other died when she was only a year old. I am just thankful that the four surviving ones made it safely through the war."

"So who inherited the *ihai* in your family?"

"I did. And that's about all I inherited. There never was any money and the property they owned was confiscated by the U. S. government. Admittedly, we do get a fairly generous monthly rental income from the U.S., but I'm not sure that makes up for not having it available to use as we see fit."

Mrs. Nakamura went on to lodge another complaint associated with males, which was the Okinawan burial customs. "If a woman marries, she is considered part of her husband's family. So when she dies her remains are placed in his family's tomb. But if she's unfortunate enough not to marry, then she has no place to be buried when she dies. One solution is for her family to make a small grave next to the family tomb. But I feel that's hardly fair. It's almost like being treated as an outcast." She paused momentarily to pass a dish to her husband.

"I find this fascinating," said Christie, "although at the same time very disturbing. It just confirms my feeling that women are discriminated against in virtually all societies, no matter how much the societies may differ in other respects. But I was also under the impression that there were areas in which Okinawan women hold the upper hand over men. Is that true, or have I been misled?"

"No, you have not been misled. There are local exceptions to the general rule. In Itoman for instance, a fishing village south of Naha, the women have traditionally controlled the finances in the family, making all the financial decisions. This grew out of necessity. It wasn't something that the men of the town voluntarily relinquished. Because the men were often away for long periods of time on extended fishing voyages, it fell to the woman to handle the family finances. Therefore, it became common practice to record property in the wife's name, and the inheritance was passed down through the daughters rather than the sons. But this is, as I said, an exception to the typical situation here on Okinawa and throughout the Orient."

"I read somewhere that the divorce rate on Okinawa is the highest in Japan. Is that true, and if so, what does that say about the women of Okinawa and their view of marriage?" Christie asked as she finished the last of the champuru, waiting for the rest of the family to finish before turning her attention to the fruit dish.

"Yes, it's true that we have the highest divorce rate of any of the prefectures. But do not assume it means that Okinawan women take their marriage vows less than seriously. That is not at all the case. However, those figures reflect yet another difference between the attitude of the mainland women and the Okinawan women. In Japan, women do not typically hold jobs. They don't need to, but, of course, this makes them financially dependent on their husbands. In turn, they are more likely to stay in a bad marriage. They really don't have any other options. But here on Okinawa, women are more independent and I believe much stronger. Okinawan women will tolerate a bad marriage for only so long, and after that they say *sayonara!*" Mrs. Nakamura waved her hand and smiled broadly as she summarily dismissed some imaginary husband who had refused to toe the line.

"It's also true that if you go to a marriage counselor on the mainland you're going to be told to stay in the marriage and work at it for the sake of the children. What a lot of nonsense! If an Okinawan counselor said that, the Okinawan woman would laugh in his face. But they don't say that. They say, 'Go ahead. Get a divorce. It's not the end of the world!'

"Furthermore, on Okinawa there's much less of a stigma associated with having a child out of wedlock than on the mainland."

As she ate her dessert, Christie decided to broach the subject of her father as soon as everyone was finished with dessert. After finishing the last of her fruit dish, Christie poured some green tea into her empty rice bowl. She dipped the tips of her chopsticks in the tea and wiped them off with a paper napkin. Then she began to tell her hosts about her quest for information about her father's stay on Okinawa. As she spoke, she noticed that Mr. Nakamura was watching his wife very closely, as if he was trying to read her thoughts. But Christie felt it was more than just that. There was a look of expectancy on his face. It was almost as if he knew that his wife had information which might be helpful to Christie and was trying to decide when she was going to come forth with it. After Christie finished speaking, she looked with anticipation at Mrs. Nakamura.

Mrs. Nakamura took a last sip of her tea and slowly placed the cup back on the saucer. Then she turned to Christie and spoke. "There were quite a number of military people who helped out in the refugee camps. And they performed a very great service to the Okinawan people. But there isn't any one individual in particular who stands out in my mind. Do you have a picture of him taken back at that time?"

"No, I don't have any pictures," Christie said, "although my aunt might have a picture taken when he was younger. Before I left the states I called and asked my cousin Amy if she would look through the old family photo albums. Amy wrote back and said that so far she hadn't found anything but would continue to search."

Mrs. Nakamura said "there is a woman that might possibly have some information about your father. But I emphasize the word possibly, Miss

Atherton. I will be seeing a mutual friend in the next few days and I will broach the subject to her. Hopefully, she will speak to this woman about it. But please do not get your hopes up."

Christie thanked her warmly and said that any help she could provide would be greatly appreciated. It seemed apparent that it was time to excuse herself and head home. Part of the reason was that, from a practical standpoint, it was probably also about time for the Nakamuras to get the twins ready for bed.

After putting her sandals back on by the door, Christie turned to face her hosts. *"Domo arigato gozaimasu,"* she said, thanking them and bowing to both of them. Christie would liked to have said something more than that, but was not yet comfortable enough with the language. Her hosts returned the bow and said, *"Do itashi-mashite."*

As she left the Nakamura's yard and walked back into Quint's yard Christie had to try hard to keep from getting her hopes up.

Once in the house Christie headed straight for the kitchen and pulled a can of beer from the refrigerator and then headed back to the living room and flopped down on the couch. Moments later Sam jumped up on the couch and settled down next to her. She stroked his back idly while sipping her beer. "Well, Sam, it looks like you and I might be riding out a typhoon together. Presumably, you've been through them before. Any sage words of advice for a newcomer to the experience?"

Sam looked up at her, yawned widely, and then put his head down on his paws and closed his eyes.

After finishing the beer, Christie decided it was so comfortable laying there that she would put off correcting her school papers. They could wait until the following day.

It was nearly midnight when Christie awoke with a start to find herself still on the couch with Sam, both of them in exactly the same position they'd been in when she first laid down. She hated it when that happened, falling asleep fully clothed before her regular bedtime. It took a real effort to force herself to get up off the couch, wash up, brush her teeth, and get into bed. By the time she finally headed for the bedroom, she was wide awake. And another hour passed before she finally fell back to sleep.

In the meantime, typhoon Cora was acting like a typical typhoon, changing speed and direction for no discernible reason. It was now aimed directly at Okinawa and was moving towards the island at twice the speed recorded earlier that day. The next morning Christie heard that it was certain to hit Okinawa, probably by the end of the week.

By Thursday night it seemed clear that typhoon Cora would be making landfall sometime the following afternoon. The Superintendent's Office decided to err on the side of safety by closing the schools and sending the children home an hour early on Friday. Shortly afterwards the teachers and staff were encouraged to leave. That left time to run a few errands before the typhoon's winds would be felt on the island.

Christie delayed her departure from school until 1630 hours when there was already a stiff breeze blowing. After a brief stop at the Base Exchange, she took the shortcut behind the Exchange to the Commissary. Moments later she was pushing a cart up and down the aisles, grabbing an occasional item from the shelves. Turning a corner while looking back over her shoulder led to a near collision with a carriage full of groceries being pushed by a burly senior NCO. Before she even had time to utter a quick apology, she heard a voice behind her.

"Hi, Miss Atherton!"

It was Keith Ferris which led Christie to conclude that the guy frowning at her must be his father, Chief Master Sergeant Ferris. "*Uh-oh,*" she thought. *With two strikes against me, I don't want to collect a third one.*

"Hi, Keith. It looks like a lot of people had the same idea. Get to the commissary before the typhoon gets to Okinawa."

"Yes ma'am. There are a lot of other things I'd rather be doing, but my mother isn't feeling too well, so we sort of volunteered to run out and pick up a few things. Hey, let me introduce you to my father."

Turning back to the NCO, whose frown was gradually replaced by an expression of mild astonishment as he realized who Christie was, Keith said, "Dad, this is my English teacher, Miss. Atherton. You know, the one I've raved about so much."

"Miss Atherton," he said, as he nodded and shook her hand. "Between Major Brewster and my son I've heard quite a bit about you. And now that I've met you I understand why English is one of my son's favorite subjects. If I had a teacher that looked like you when I was in school, English might have been one of my favorite subjects, too."

Although Christie knew his comment was intended as a compliment, she found such remarks irritating and demeaning because of the emphasis on looks over brains. However, this conversation was off to a much better start than their previous one. She assumed that Quint must have carried out some promotional effort on her behalf spite of his annoyance with her. And since that was the case, Christie decided to begin laying the groundwork for a changed outlook right then and there.

"Did Keith tell you that Major Brewster and I are old friends?" she asked.

"Yes ma'am, he did. And so did the Major himself."

"Actually, I've known him since I was in high school."

"Is that so? Well, I don't mind telling you that Major Brewster is one of the finest officers I've known in my eighteen years in the service."

"You know, Sergeant Ferris, you might be surprised to learn that Keith and Major Brewster share some things in common, in spite of their age difference."

"Really? And what might that be?" His tone reflected an equal mixture of gratification and skepticism.

"Well, they are both highly analytical and very capable when it comes to putting their thoughts down in writing. And those qualities, along with the ability to speak comfortably in public, have proven to be two of the strongest predictors of success in today's world." Christie glanced at Keith and then back at Sergeant Ferris. "You can be very proud of Keith. He has some real gifts and, most importantly, he's doing whatever is necessary to nurture them."

"That's really good to hear, because I keep reminding him of how important it is to do well in all of his school subjects."

Christie wasn't sure that she was ready to swallow that particular assertion, but at least she had taken the opportunity to plant another small seed.

"Well, I don't want to hold you up," Christie said. "I'm glad that I had the chance to meet you, Sergeant Ferris. I find that things usually go better when I meet the parents in person. Basing one's impression on a single phone conversation can sometimes lead to misunderstandings," she added.

"I think I understand your point," he said, touching the brim of his service cap.

With that, Christie smiled. "Goodbye, Sergeant Ferris. Goodbye, Keith."

"Bye, Miss Atherton. Don't get caught outside in the typhoon!"

"I'll try not to," Christie said, as she headed for the next aisle.

A couple of hours later, Christie emerged from the shower just as a strong gust of wind rattled the shutters. It was a clear hint of what lay in store for the island over the next several hours. With typhoon Cora tracking in a north-northeasterly direction at a steady fifteen to twenty miles an hour, it wouldn't be long before the winds reached a point where walking would be difficult, if not impossible, and loose objects would be transformed into deadly projectiles. Even as the thought crossed her mind, an object of indeterminate nature and origin slammed into the shutters with a dull thud.

Christie slipped on a pair of old jeans and one of Quint's sweat shirts and went into the living room. Just then the direct line to the base lit up, indicating an incoming call. She walked quickly over to the couch and picked up the receiver.

"Hello."

"Hi, Christie. It's Rick."

"Hi, Rick! I didn't expect to be hearing from you. Does this mean you're on duty during the typhoon?"

"Yep. It's my turn to man the Operations Desk."

"Is Sandy nervous about going through this thing alone?"

"Nah. There's not much that makes her nervous. She'll be fine. She's got the kids to keep her company. Plus she can call me as often as she wants. How about you? Are you feeling a little nervous about facing this thing by yourself?"

"A little, I suppose."

"Well, I'm giving you the same option I gave Sandy. Call me anytime you want, as often as you want. I'm a man of many talents, Christie. I can sing you a lullaby or recite some soothing verse to calm you down."

"Thanks, Rick. I appreciate the offer. "You're a good friend. I can see why Quint values your friendship so much."

"I can assure you that I've never sung a lullaby to Quint, Christie."

Christie chuckled. "I didn't think you had. But I'm sure you've been a sympathetic listener as he tries to decide what to do now that he's been permanently grounded."

"I like to think so. But seriously, Christie, if there's a problem don't hesitate to call me. For any reason. You're not going to be interrupting anything important. Once all the preparations are done, this is about the most boring job there is. All I'll be doing is sitting around for the next twelve hours or so watching the phone, hoping that some minor crisis will pop up so that the time will pass a little faster. Phone calls from friends will be a welcome break from the monotony."

"Okay, Rick. I promise to call if I need a little pep talk. Catch you later."

"Bye, Christie."

At Sally's suggestion, Christie had turned on the radio to the Armed Forces network. While she was talking to Rick, she had heard the announcer mention that the winds were now blowing steadily at around twenty-five miles an hour with occasional higher gusts. Clearly, it was no longer a good idea to be outside.

Christie had been sitting on the couch for several minutes with the phone in her lap when she realized someone was knocking at the door. Between the softness of the knock and the noise of the wind, it took some time for it to register. She walked quickly across the room and reached for the door knob, wondering who it could be.

"Hi, Mrs. Nakamura! What can I do for you?" Christie asked, as she opened the door and ushered the tiny Asian woman into the living room.

"I'm very sorry to bother you, but I was wondering if I might use your phone. I tried to call my husband's office to make sure he is on his way home, but my phone is not working."

"Of course. Please have a seat. The phone is on the floor next to the couch."

A few minutes later, Christie came from the kitchen to the living room and Mrs. Nakamura was placing the receiver back down on its base.

"I spoke to the office secretary. She said she's the last one there and everyone else left about a half an hour ago."

"How long does it take your husband to get home from the office?"

"Fifteen or twenty minutes on a normal day."

"But it might take him longer under these conditions."

"Perhaps. I am sure he is very frustrated because he's unable to reach me. He is very thoughtful and does not like me to worry unnecessarily."

"Didn't I see your car in the driveway earlier?"

"Yes, you did. My husband left the car for me to use today, so he was depending on his boss to drive him home."

"Will his boss drive him down to the house?"

"No. He will probably drop him off at the entrance to the housing complex."

"Why would he drop him off at the gate on a day like this?"

For a moment Mrs. Nakamura looked like she wasn't going to answer Christie's question. But after several seconds she said, "My husband's boss is not an especially thoughtful person. He does not like to go out of his way to help someone. Besides," she added, in an attempt to present him in a better light, "it really isn't that far to walk."

"It must be around a half a mile from the gate to this part of the housing complex."

"Yes," Mrs. Nakamura acknowledged, obviously uncomfortable discussing it with Christie.

"With the wind gusting, it could be a hazardous walk," Christie said, trying to avoid being overly critical.

Mrs. Nakamura replied, "We have had so much rain lately that the potholes are even worse than usual. And Mr. Hirata has a very fancy Cadillac which could be damaged if he drove down to the house."

"Is Mr. Nakamura's boss an Okinawan?"

"Yes. His immediate supervisor is."

Now Christie understood why Mrs. Nakamura had been so careful to avoid making harsh comments about her husband's boss. Obviously, she felt uncomfortable criticizing a fellow Okinawan in front of a Westerner.

"On a day like this, you'd think they'd close the office early so people would have plenty of time to get home."

"Mr. Hirata's military superior probably told everyone they were free to leave early but Mr. Hirata expects his immediate subordinates, the department supervisors, to stay until the very last minute."

After Mrs. Nakamura left, Christie stood in the living room trying to decide what to do next when the phone rang. It was Rick calling again.

"Hi, Rick, now what's up?"

"I was talking to Quint a little while ago, and he asked if I'd relay a message to you. He said it was a lot easier for me to call you than for him to try to get through to the house."

"What's the message?"

"He wanted you to know that there was extra food and kitty litter for Sam out in the cabinet in the laundry room."

"Yes. I already discovered it. Is that all he wanted?"

"That's all he said. But I'm pretty good at reading between the lines, especially when it comes to my friends. I have a hunch he's worried about you staying there alone during a typhoon. I told him I'd already talked to you and that you sounded like you were doing fine. I also told him what I told you, that you could call me anytime you wanted."

Christie was about to hang up when she decided to tell Rick about Mrs. Nakamura's visit.

"Maybe her husband took the foot path that goes along the bottom of the ravine to get back to his house," Rick said. "Did you know there's a path there?"

"Yes, I noticed it the night of the party. But I had no idea where it led to."

"It connects with the main road into the housing complex up by the gate house."

"But you've never walked it yourself."

"No, but Quint has used it on occasion. That's how I know it connects to the main road."

"What's the path like?"

"It's just a narrow foot path used by Okinawans going fishing or taking a shortcut to the ball field."

"What makes you think that Mr. Nakamura would use the trail?"

"I'm not sure if he would. But since it cuts through a narrow ravine behind his home, there'd be some protection from the wind for part of the way."

While Rick was talking, Christie was doing some thinking. Suppose Mr. Nakamura had decided to take that route home and was injured in the process. Someone should go down there and check to make sure that wasn't the case. But who?

"Do you think he'd really go that way? Isn't there a good chance of running into a Habu (poisonous snake) down there?" asked Christie.

Although Rick couldn't have known the reason for her question, she had indirectly acknowledged one of her most persistent fears since coming to Okinawa. Her mind had populated the dense tropical undergrowth with every imaginable form of repulsive creature including the Habu as well as other species of venomous snakes, poisonous spiders, rodents, slugs, and assorted other types of disgusting creatures. The idea of having to venture into that mess with darkness rapidly approaching while contending with typhoon-driven wind and rain was a profoundly unsettling prospect.

"I seriously doubt it," said Rick. "No snake with half a brain is going to be outside on a day like today. They're going to be holed up in their caves or wherever else they hang out."

"Are you sure about that?"

"No. But it seems like a logical deduction. Don't you think?"

"I don't know!" she said, trying to keep the growing anxiety from showing in her voice.

"How do you know snakes feel the same way about storms as we do? Maybe they enjoy getting out in this kind of weather."

"I doubt it, Christie. Animals' instincts kick in when they're threatened by anything in their environment. So forget about the snakes. Your neighbor's biggest problem is going to be managing to get safely over the section of the path that goes along the edge of the cove. There's a narrow section of the trail that passes over an outcropping of coral. It's right on the edge of the cove. The footing is bound to be treacherous, because it will be slippery from all the rain. And to make matters worse, by now the surf might be breaking over that part of the trail."

"Well, the more you tell me, the less likely it seems that he would come that way. I better let you go. You've probably got things to do now that the typhoon is almost on top of us."

Christie was anxious to get off the phone before Rick's suspicions were aroused. If he had any idea that she was considering going down there, he would surely try to talk her out of it. Her next thought was to call Mrs. Nakamura to ask if she thought her husband would use the path, but then Christie remembered that their phone was out of order. Christie decided there was no time to waste. The wind sounded as though it had increased since Mrs. Nakamura's visit. It was time to get going before it grew any worse.

Christie went into the guest bedroom and put on an old pair of sneakers she had brought with her. Then she got an old yellow rain slicker that had been hanging behind the door in the laundry room. Hopefully it would provide some protection from flying objects. And it might help if the winds got any worse and she was forced to crawl along portions of the path. A pair of goggles would have been useful in keeping the wind-driven rain out of her eyes, but she hadn't seen anything like that in the house. A quick search of Quint's bedroom uncovered an old baseball cap. If she jammed it down on her head, the brim might help to serve the same purpose.

Moments later, Christie stood by the front door taking a final inventory. Was there anything else that would prove useful? Gloves, of course. If she did have to crawl at any point, gloves would keep her hands from becoming lacerated by the coral. Coral cuts were not only painful but were slow to heal. She found a pair of work gloves under the kitchen sink. After surveying the room one last time, Christie turned around and carefully opened the front door.

Stepping out of the sheltered wooden alcove that protected the front door from wind and rain, she crouched down and scurried across the yard to the cinderblock wall. Then she made her way to the corner of the yard where the trail ended. Once there, she rose up into a half crouch and rolled over the top of the wall, landing on her back on the other side.

Lying on her side, Christie edged her way safely to the bottom of the hill. Then she crawled about a half dozen yards on her hands and knees to the point where the path crossed the coral outcropping at the edge of the cove.

She lay there studying the situation, conscious of the fact that she'd been silently arguing the pros and cons of crossing the coral ledge that Rick had warned her about. *Okay, I know that this is not the same kind of situation I faced that winter evening back at Long Pond. Even though I'm already soaked to the skin, the temperature is probably in the seventies. And my foot was stuck underwater then and I couldn't get it free. That's not the case now. On the other hand, the water had only been four or five feet deep where I broke through the ice instead of six to eight feet like it is in this inlet. And I didn't have to deal with near gale force winds. And there is no Quint Brewster waiting in the wings. But what can go wrong? Well . . . I could slip on the wet coral and break my neck; or I could be knocked off my feet by the wind and washed into the cove and drown; or I could . . .Stop it! Stop it right now! I've got to get moving. Someone's life may depend on it.'*

Feeling a little better after the verbal self-flagellation, Christie rose gingerly to her feet and stepped out onto the coral ledge. Although the surf was washing over the coral it was only a few inches deep. That was one good thing. And the fact that the wind was coming in off the cove was also a help since it would tend to push her away from the water.

Standing up and bracing her left hand against the vertical face of the ledge to keep from being pushed off her feet, Christie began to make her way carefully across the coral ledge. The water, splashing against her legs, felt warm, although the rest of her body was beginning to feel chilled from exposure to the typhoon winds.

She was about two-thirds of the way across and beginning to feel optimistic about making it the rest of the way when she momentarily lost her footing and fell to her knees next to the lip of the coral ledge. Moving forward again in a half crouch, she made it safely to solid ground and soon passed into the ravine where there was protection from the wind, although the cataracts of rain continued to hamper her ability to see very far. From that point on, Christie made fairly good progress along the path. It took less than ten minutes to reach the point where the path came out to the main road.

Now what? She stood there for a minute trying to decide what to do next. A sudden thought struck her. If Mr. Nakamura had taken this path home, it was highly unlikely he would follow it all the way to the end. If he did so, he, too, would have to negotiate the treacherous passage across the coral ledge. Surely, he would realize it was unnecessarily risky to try, which meant there must be another branch of the path that he could use to get up to his house.

Moving slowly, Christie retraced her footsteps. Brushing the water out of her eyes she tried to pierce the increasing gloom while focusing her attention on the right side of the path. And just before reaching the beginning of the ravine she noticed a small break in the undergrowth. It wasn't surprising she had missed it while heading up the path as a large fern blocked the view from that angle.

Christie turned into the opening and took a few tentative steps before wondering if she had been mistaken. Despite her apprehensions, she continued to push her way deeper into the underbrush, thinking the path might widen again a little further in. But after another fifteen or twenty feet even the barest traces of a path had disappeared.

Then she heard another sound that was not the wind. It sounded like someone calling for help in a pain-wracked voice. Christie crouched down and began moving to the left, which seemed to be the direction from which the sound was coming. She parted the palm fronds and discovered Mr. Nakamura lying half buried in the thick shrubbery. Glancing up at the slanting face of the rocky crag rising above them, she guessed that he had been making his way up there when he lost his footing and half fell and half slid to the base of the cliff.

She knelt down beside him and pushed aside the fronds that were covering his face. "Mr. Nakamura. Mr. Nakamura. It's Christie Atherton. Can you hear me?"

Mr. Nakamura moaned again, and his eyelids fluttered but remained closed. Christie bent down closer to him and repeated her words. "Nakamura-san! Can you hear me?"

Mr. Nakamura slowly opened both eyes, and after a few seconds he focused on Christie's face. At first she wasn't sure if he recognized her.

"Miss Atherton, what you doing here?" His voice was very weak.

"Can you tell me where you're injured?"

"My ankle," he said slowly, moaning again, as he tried to push himself up into a sitting position. "Much pain there. Think maybe ankle is broken."

"Don't try to sit up. I need to know if you are injured anywhere else. How about your head? Did you hit your head when you fell?" Even as she was asking the question, Christie was running her hand lightly over the surface of his head, searching by feel for any lacerations or bruises.

"Don't think any injuries to head."

"That's good," Christie said, with a genuine sense of relief. If there had been any serious head trauma or bleeding, she would have had no idea what to do. It occurred to her as she knelt beside him that the thick underbrush had cushioned his fall and prevented him from sustaining any critical injuries.

Now, how am I going to manage to get him—us—out of this mess?

Mr. Nakamura was propped up on his elbows, looking at Christie, with a frown on his face.

Noticing his expression, Christie asked, "What's wrong?"

"Did wife ask you look for me?" he said, in a perturbed tone.

"No. She didn't."

"You tell truth?"

"Yes, I am."

She was going to have to carry him. There was no other choice. Christie guessed he weighed barely a hundred pounds which meant she outweighed him by more than thirty pounds. Plus she had a lot of upper body strength for a female.

When she told Mr. Nakamura what she planned to do, he began to object vociferously, insisting she go back inside before it was too late to do so.

Christie contended with equal force that she was not about to leave him down there. After helping him stand on his uninjured leg she instructed him to lie over her shoulder so she could carry him back up to the house. As she began retracing her route with the added weight she was careful to step in the exact spots she used when entering the underbrush.

Hopefully, if there had been anything there to be concerned about, it—or they—would have been frightened away. When Christie made it back to the main trail, she realized that she was shaking. And it wasn't just from the added exertion.

The trip back across the coral ledge was more hazardous than before, because it was now under a half a foot of water. Christie used a sliding motion to feel her way across the ledge, since she could no longer see where she was going. In spite of the worsening conditions and the added weight, she made it to the other side without any mishaps. Just as she reached the other side, a piece of wood whipped through the air by the gale force wind delivered a glancing blow to the side of her head. She managed to remain upright, staggered forward and began climbing the hill.

The return trip back up the hill was considerably more challenging as there was no protection now from the wind. The added weight of Mr. Nakamura made her top-heavy so it was more difficult to maintain her balance. Moments later, just as they reached the top of the slope, a piece of metal strapping from the 2nd Logistical Command storage yard caromed off the wall only inches from her head.

By the time Christie made her way across both yards and up to the Nakamura's front door, she was ready to collapse. It was doubtful if it would have been possible for her to carry her neighbor any further. When Mrs. Nakamura opened the door, a look of horror crossed her face. But Christie quickly blurted out, "It's only his ankle." Mrs. Nakamura led Christie into the living room. Together, they placed Mr. Nakamura gently on the couch. And after hugging her husband, she looked questioningly at his rescuer. Christie briefly described where she had found him. Before she could offer any explanation about why she happened to be down in the ravine, the twins arrived on the scene from their bedroom and they began to cry when they saw that their father was in pain. He promptly took them in his arms, calling them by their names, and reassured them that he was going to be okay. After the twins had calmed down, their mother ushered them back into their bedroom. And by the time she returned, Christie had removed his shoes and elevated his injured leg so that it was higher than his head.

Christie told Mrs. Nakamura they would need a doctor and possibly an x-ray to determine whether Mr. Nakamura was suffering from a bad sprain or whether he had one or more breaks in his ankle. And Christie suggested they put ice on the ankle at intervals for about twenty minutes.

When it was time for Christie to leave, Mr. Nakamura called out to her. He wanted to express his profound thanks. Mrs. Nakamura stepped back into the living room and told him that he could thank Christie after the typhoon had passed.

Christie crawled on her hands and knees back to Quint's house until she reached the protection of the alcove. At that point, she was able to stand up again. When she got inside, she shed the filthy, wet clothes and deposited them on the floor in the laundry room. Then she headed for the bathroom and a hot shower.

Christie savored the feeling of being warm and clean again. And a corner of her mind was beginning to acknowledge a rather surprising fact: she sensed that she had gained the upper hand over certain irrational fears. Not that they had been completely conquered, but she felt they would never again loom quite so large in her mind.

Several minutes later, Christie turned off the shower with some reluctance, and after toweling dry and slipping into a bathrobe, went out into the living room to tackle the pile of essays on the coffee table.

An hour or so later, the winds had dropped off dramatically, the rain had become a light drizzle, and there were breaks in the cloud cover. But Christie knew it was only a temporary lull while the eye of the storm passed over them. In the meantime, she was going to go to bed and sleep soundly for the next eight hours. The typhoon could rage all it wanted to, but it wouldn't bother her in the least. She had met it on its own territory, and on its own terms, and she had come out the victor. *More or less anyway,* she thought, gingerly rubbing the bump on the side of her head.

When Quint awoke at Cam Ranh Bay the following morning, it was to the accompaniment of a pounding headache and the realization that he wanted out of there by mid-afternoon at the latest. Between meetings he was able to determine that the first C-130 flight back to Naha was departing around 1400, which he quickly calculated would get him back into Naha by 2100 hours at the latest. Although far from ideal, it was highly likely that he would be able to sleep all the way back what with only getting about four hours the previous night. There was no question that he intended to be on that plane providing he could get the meetings out of the way by late morning and start digging into the maintenance records immediately afterwards.

By 1300, Quint felt that he had a realistic shot at catching the flight that afternoon. In fact, the records review had gone better than expected. His first important clue surfaced in mid-morning when he was about half way through his examination of records from planes that had suffered heavy structural damage during their flights into unimproved army strips such as those found in the northern highlands and the delta. Two things struck him: they had all recently returned from major maintenance back in the states. Most significantly, they all had been to the same repair facility in Ohio. He thumbed rapidly through a stack of records looking for those planes that had been back at that particular repair facility in the past several months. In virtually all cases, the same planes had been in for major field maintenance repairs at Naha within a relatively short time span following their trip back from the depot. It looked increasingly like the problem's roots could be traced back to quality control problems with the depot-level maintenance performed by civilian contractors back in the states. Col. Crane, he was certain, would find this to be a most interesting bit of news. It clearly indicated that the training deficiencies were taking more of the blame than they should have. Not that they were without fault, because clearly there was a need for improvement in that area. But this information at least allowed for a more balanced picture of the whole situation.

If he could only get rid of the damned headache. But unfortunately it seemed impervious to even the strongest medication that the flight surgeon's office could prescribe.

Quint spent the noon hour in a concentrated burst of activity during which he managed to put together a package that included several pages of analysis along with photocopies of sample records which would corroborate his findings. Stuffing them into his briefcase, he grabbed his flight bag right after a hurried lunch and hitched a ride out to the C-130 which already had three of its four engines running at full rpms and was just turning over number four.

Less than ten minutes later they were off the ground and climbing out over the ships anchored in the harbor. As Quint settled on top of a stack of mail his only concern was how Christie was weathering the typhoon. After he grabbed a few hours of sleep, he'd give her a call.

Unfortunately they didn't leave Cam Ranh Bay in time to beat the typhoon to Okinawa. They had to divert to the Philippines. About two-thirds of the way there they encountered strong winds as their flight path took them into the outer edges of the typhoon. Piloting the aircraft was such a fatiguing business that the two pilots were delighted when Quint offered to take over the controls and give them a short respite from the ongoing battle simply to maintain straight and level flight. Total flight time to Clark Air Base was approximately five hours. The flight back to Okinawa the following morning only took around three hours.

XX

When Christie awoke on Saturday morning she thought it was still the middle of the night. Then she glanced at the clock and saw it was almost nine o'clock in the morning. The shutters were still closed to protect the windows from the typhoon winds. Quickly slipping on her last clean pair of old jeans and lightweight cotton blouse, she started the coffee maker and then went outside to open the shutters.

It was a beautiful, early fall morning, which, on Okinawa, simply meant that the temperature and humidity were both at a relatively comfortable level. The sky was clear and cloudless and the sun glittering on the water reminded her of a field of diamonds. The air smelled fresh and pure. During the time she had lived on the East coast of the U. S. she had noticed that the air was typically swept clean of all its pollutants after a Nor'easter or hurricane passed through the region. Now, for a brief period, she enjoyed that sweet, newly-minted scent, which must have been the way it was back at the beginning of creation.

Christie went in and poured herself a cup of coffee, and then went outside with Sam in tow. Leaning against the house, she sipped her coffee while idly surveying the scene of her adventure the previous afternoon. In full daylight, with no typhoon to mar the peacefulness of the setting, the area beneath the cliff looked relatively innocuous. If she had been walking down there today, traversing the coral ledge by the edge of the cove wouldn't have given her a second's pause. Even the profusion of vines, ferns, and other plants that flourished in the ravine looked picturesque and pleasing, rather than menacing and forbidding, in their myriad shades of green.

After several minutes, Christie decided it was time to go in and do some laundry and then tackle the pile of essays on the dining room table. She came back into the kitchen from the laundry room and heard a knock on the front door. Upon opening the door, she found several men jabbering in Japanese. One who spoke English introduced himself and another man with camera in hand as a reporter and photographer, respectively, from the English language daily newspaper The *Okinawan Morning Star.* Interpreting for the others, he identified them as reporters and photographers for the Okinawan Japanese language papers, the *Okinawa Taimusu* and *Ryukyu Shimpo.*

"What can I do for you?"

"Answer a few questions and allow us to take a few pictures."

"Whatever for?"

"Because, Miss Atherton, you are a heroine."

"I don't understand."

"Rescuing your Okinawan neighbor makes you a heroine."

"I certainly don't see myself that way."

"Well, your neighbors do and so will the rest of the world after they read about what you have done."

"Is that why you're here? Did Mrs. Nakamura contact you?"

"Of course, Miss Atherton. What you have done is very newsworthy. To repeat myself, you are a true heroine."

"I disagree, Mr. Roberts. I'm sure there are many people who would do the same thing under similar circumstances."

"You are either very naïve or hold too high an opinion of your fellow man. There are very few Okinawans who would risk their lives as you did to go out and look for a neighbor. And it would be even more unlikely that a westerner would take such a risk. When the military hands out a medal, the citation that accompanies it states how the act reflects great credit upon the individual and upon the branch of the service of which they are a member. So, Miss Atherton, at a time when relations between the United States and Okinawa are under a severe strain, your act shows the citizens of Okinawa that Americans can be a genuine blessing to this small island country. This is a wonderful news story and you can be sure it will receive wide coverage and not just on Okinawa."

After submitting to interviews by English-speaking reporters from the Okinawan newspapers, Christie was asked by the photographers to stand next to the wall pointing down to the trail over which she had carried Mr. Nakamura. They also took a photograph of her holding the piece of metal strapping that had narrowly missed her head.

By noon, Christie was beginning to realize that her actions had caused quite a stir. She received several calls for phone interviews from the United States. A short while after the last call Quint showed up. He told her that she took an enormous risk but that he was very proud of her.

"You mean you're not going to chew me out for what I did?"

"I admit that I thought about it, but all things considered, it didn't seem appropriate or necessary considering you're unlikely to be in a situation calling for a repeat performance. How is Mr. Nakamura, by the way?"

"His ankle is severely sprained, but there are no broken bones."

"Have you visited him yet today?"

"Yes, I saw him this morning after he returned from the doctors."

"What did he have to say?"

"He kept repeating how fortunate he was that I was staying at your house while you were away."

"He's right, Christie, because the chances are pretty slim that anyone else staying there would have felt the same obligation that you did."

Mrs. Nakamura visited Christie while she and Quint were chatting in the front yard and handed her a slip of paper with the name and address of the woman who might have some knowledge about Christie's father.

"Nobuko Yamada, Yomitan," Christie said, sounding out the words tentatively. "What makes you think this woman would be willing to speak to me?"

"I explained to the mutual friend that you were a good person and a true friend of the Okinawan people. I also told her you are suffering much anguish over the absence of reliable information about your father's fate." Mrs. Nakamura looked slightly embarrassed, apologizing to Christie if she had inadvertently exaggerated Christie's feelings about her father. Then she continued, "I asked her to see if Yamada-san would be willing to meet with you and pass on any information she might have about your father. Yamada-san agreed and said next Thursday afternoon would be the best time for her."

Christie nodded, but her mind was elsewhere. Her thoughts had drifted back to a time long ago when an eight-year-old girl stood on the front porch of a small suburban house and waved goodbye to her beloved father, aware that he would be gone for a long time but having no idea it would be forever. Christie abruptly shook her head to clear away the memories and turned her attention back to Mrs. Nakamura.

"I don't know what to say. You must be aware of how much your gesture means to me. Even if it leads nowhere, I truly thank you."

Before leaving, Mrs. Nakamura said to Christie "You are a most extraordinary young woman, Miss Atherton. I have never met anyone from any country who has impressed me as much as you have." Looking at Quint she added, "It is clear that my husband and I owe Major Brewster our deepest thanks for asking you to watch his house. It has been an honor to get to know you while you have been here, and we will never forget what you have done for us." With that she bowed again and left to return to her home.

As Christie watched her return to their yard, she realized that the news about her father had triggered a strange mixture of elation and apprehension.

"You look worried," Quint said.

It didn't take Christie long to reach a tentative conclusion regarding the source of the apprehension. There was a real possibility of obtaining information about her father that might undermine her idealized image of him—an image which she had carefully nurtured over the past dozen years.

She nodded. "I have to admit Quint, I am. Suppose my father turns out to be something other than what I imagined him to be?"

But then after some reflection Christie dismissed her concerns. She couldn't picture her father doing anything that would cast a shadow on her memory of him. She was anxious to meet Ms. Yamada, however, and regretted having to wait several days before their meeting. But Quint agreed to go with her to Yomitan village to provide emotional support.

Quint picked up Christie at the close of school on Thursday, and they were soon winding their way along the coast heading in the direction of the Zanpa Peninsula. Before they left, Mrs. Nakamura had called Christie to say that Ms. Yamada lived in the small village of Takashino, a short distance north and east of Yomitan Village. Quint had looked at the map and decided to follow Highway One north to the village of Kina and then turn east on Route 12. He guessed that it would take less than a half hour to get to Takashino.

They drove in silence for minutes until Quint passed a slow-moving Okinawan truck and then turned to Christie and said, "We'll be coming into the village in a few minutes. Sure you want to go through with this?"

"I need to do so—for my own piece of mind."

"Okay. Do you have directions to this woman's house?"

"Not exactly. But it's on the outskirts of the village. The west side. Mrs. Nakamura said the road through the village was dirt and was quite narrow, so it might be better to park and walk to Ms. Yamada's house. The village is small and it should take less than ten minutes to get to her house."

Quint pulled off to the side of the road and parked the car, and they began making their way through the village. The road was even narrower than they had anticipated. Sections of it were bordered by stone walls and it looked like the smallest of Okinawan cars could barely squeak through.

Takashino was known as a nucleated village. There were houses on both sides of the road rather than being dispersed throughout the countryside. Although it was primarily a farming village, the fields were outside of the village proper. The houses were separated by stone walls and rows of Ryukyuan pines, which served as a windbreak in addition to providing privacy.

Most of the houses seemed typical of the poorer areas of the island: wood sided with thatched roofs. A few had more modern construction with red tile roofs that were common throughout the island. But no matter how primitive the house, two objects were always present: the Shi-Shi lion and television antennae.

Ms. Yamada's house was larger than most of the others. As they approached it, Christie caught a glimpse of a small garden in the back and behind that a grass-covered hill that rose to a fairly steep slope and ended abruptly at the edge of a forested area.

Ms. Yamada met them at the door. Although her greeting was friendly, Christie sensed a certain reserve in her manner, perhaps because they were strangers and westerners, or perhaps because of the reason for their visit.

They were ushered into a large room that could be sub-divided into two or three smaller rooms through the use of wood or paper partitions. Each corner of the room had the ubiquitous alcoves, one dedicated to ancestors and the second to other deities the family paid homage to. There were at least two more rooms in the back half of the house. One was probably the sleeping quarters, the other the kitchen. The partition separating the front room from the kitchen was open, so Christie could see into the room, but it was too dark to distinguish anything.

Ms. Yamada invited them to join her around a low table while tea was brewing. Christie knew they would not discuss the reason for their visit until the tea had been served and there had been a certain amount of light conversation. To Asians the western penchant for getting right to the point was rude. So Christie dutifully bowed to custom, and after a brief explanation about Quint's presence, proceeded to ask Ms. Yamada a series of non-personal questions about life in the village. Christie was particularly interested in the changes in the village life since the war and whether her host viewed these changes as good or bad. Ms. Yamada had studied English and worked for many years in the office of a local Baptist church, so her English was nearly as good as Mrs. Nakamura's.

Christie's sensitivity to the Okinawan culture, which had impressed the Nakamuras, gradually resulted in Ms. Yamada becoming more relaxed, and the mood of their conversation became less formal and reserved.

"I have been told that you came to Okinawa seeking information about your father."

Christie nodded, unable to trust her voice at that moment.

"Did you bring a picture of him with you today?"

Christie reached in her purse, pulled out the old black and white photo her cousin had mailed to her, and silently handed it to Ms. Yamada.

After glancing at it, she looked up and for several seconds stared unseeing out the window. Then looked down at it again and studied it.

Christie was transfixed. During that minute of silence, which seemed to go on forever, Quint reached over and covered her hand with his.

Ms. Yamada slowly handed the picture back to Christie. "Yes . . . That is the man who often stayed with us," she said solemnly.

In answer to Ms. Yamada's questions Christie told her about her father' gradual decline and subsequent death. But Christie couldn't get herself to admit that he seemed to be pining for the life he left behind on Okinawa. After Christie got her emotions back under control, she asked Ms. Yamada what she could tell her about her father.

"Your father was a very good man, and he was deeply committed to helping the Okinawan people recover from the war. I believe that, in some ways, he suffered almost as much as we did. That is how closely he identified with our people and our situation."

"Can you tell me any details about what he was doing here?" asked Christie.

"You knew, of course, that your father was providing medical support at a refugee camp a few miles south of here, close to Kadena base?"

Christie nodded.

"My sister, a nurse, was also helping out there. They became good friends, and as the months passed and the situation began to improve, they had time to do things other than provide constant care to the people who were staying there."

"What do you mean?"

"On weekends, they would often come here to the village to relax and seek physical and spiritual renewal. The three of us got along very well. My elderly parents were still living at the time, and they, too, felt the same bond with your father. Although food was scarce and things were still in a state of upheaval, in many respects, it was a time of special blessing for us all."

"And during this time did my father ever speak of his life back in the States?" Christie asked, not without a certain amount of trepidation.

"Of course," Ms. Yamada replied. "He spoke of you often, and he was looking forward to the time when he would see you again."

"Did anyone from the military come to your village looking for him?"

Ms. Yamada shook her head. "No. Never."

Christie gave Quint a quick look. He shrugged but said nothing.

The opening into the kitchen was in Christie's line of vision. While they were talking to Ms. Yamada Christie thought she saw something moving in the shadows, but the lighting was so poor she couldn't be sure. And there was no sound to indicate there was anyone else in the house. Christie's extreme sensitivity to her surroundings sometimes bordered on a sixth sense. At one point, she sensed that someone was listening at the kitchen door. For a moment, she thought she could hear quiet breathing. But Christie decided she must be mistaken, since she knew Ms. Yamada's parents were both dead and her host had not mentioned that anyone else was living there.

"Your father and my sister would often sit up on the hillside behind the house. The peace and comfort they enjoyed here was very different from the noise and chaos of the refugee camp.

By now Christie's eyes were watering in spite of her determination to keep her emotions under control. Quint still had his arm around her shoulders. He handed her some Kleenex that he brought with him.

"Come with me," Ms. Yamada said, as she got up from the table and led them outside and around to the back of the house. In the back of the garden facing the hillside, there was a small stone bench.

"There," she said, pointing to the crest of the hill, "that is where they often sat—for hours at a time."

"Would it be all right if I walked up there and visited the area for a few minutes?"

Ms. Yamada shook her head. "I do not advise it. Ever since the grass has been allowed to grow tall, it has become a place for the Habu to roam."

Even in the midst of her sadness, Christie could see the irony of the situation. She had waded into thick underbrush several days earlier and suffered no harm as a consequence. Yet today, wanting to visit one of her father's favorite spots, she was warned against walking through a field of tall grass in broad daylight. But, admittedly, she might not be as fortunate this time.

Christie turned to Ms. Yamada and asked permission to sit alone on the stone bench for a short while. Ms. Yamada agreed as she felt it would be an opportunity for Christie to commune with the spirit of her father. Although strongly influenced by her contact with Baptist missionaries, Ms. Yamada still believed that the spirit of the departed hovered around the place where they had spent their happiest times. Before going back into the house to prepare dinner Ms. Yamada told Christie to stay as long as she wanted. Christie looked over at Quint and asked him to wait for her out at the front of the house.

"I won't be long."

Christie sat down on the bench and closed her eyes. The only sounds to be heard were the laughter of children in the distance and the hum of a few insects. The late afternoon sun was warm on her face but it only touched the surface of her skin. On any other day, she would have reveled in the quiet beauty of the garden and the scent of the flowers, but not this day. She tried sitting quietly for a few minutes longer, harboring the vague hope that she might be able to conjure up some sense of her father's presence, since this was where he had spent a great deal of time. But nothing happened. The only thing she felt was a great emptiness inside.

Christie rose slowly to her feet and prepared to leave. Impulsively, she turned and blew a kiss in the direction of the distant hillside. "I love you, Daddy, and I'll miss you as long as I live." As she walked quickly back towards the front of the house, she couldn't remember whether she had spoken the words out loud or merely said them in her mind, and the tears began to flow. By the time she reached the front of the house where Quint was waiting, she was sobbing. He took her into his arms and held her tightly for a few minutes, speaking words of comfort into her ear while gently stroking her hair with one hand. After a while, they turned away and walked slowly back down the road towards the car. He kept his arm around her protectively until they got back to the car.

Neither of them was aware that Ms. Yamada was standing in the doorway watching them until they were out of sight.

Quint and Christie were only a few minutes out of Takashino when she turned and asked him for his thoughts on the situation.

"Do you really want to know what I think?" he asked.

"Yes, of course."

"All Ms. Yamada provided was some very basic information about your father."

"So I'm not supposed to be satisfied then?"

"Let's just say I have a distinct feeling that she knew more than she was telling you."

"What other type of information could she have provided?"

Quint shrugged. "Like the small details of your father's everyday existence. The kind of things that would breathe life into your image of him. Things that would make him seem more real to you."

"I see what you mean. I never thought to ask her about those things."

"Well, that's not surprising considering that the conversation was so emotionally loaded for you."

"The other thing I didn't think of asking for was a small memento, something he had owned or something that was meaningful to him. But after twenty years there probably wasn't anything like that to offer me anyway."

"Perhaps you can ask Mrs. Nakamura to arrange another meeting for you and Ms. Yamada. Maybe Ms. Yamada does have something she can give you. If not, she might provide a little more insight into what your father was like when he was here on Okinawa. Even if it was a long time ago, she's got to remember some things about him."

Christie nodded but said nothing for a few minutes. She was mulling over the possibility that Ms. Yamada may not have been entirely forthright, that she may have been hiding something. When she posed the question to Quint, he said, "Are you suggesting she's hiding some dark secret that would change the way you view your father?"

"No. I don't think so. At least I hope not."

"Well, what then?"

"I don't know, Quint. I guess maybe my imagination has been working overtime. For instance, there were a couple of points during our conversation when I felt like there may have been someone else in the house."

"What made you think that?"

Christie explained that she suspected that someone was moving in the shadows of the kitchen and at one point actually thought she heard someone breathing.

Quint shook his head. "I didn't see or hear anything to indicate someone else was there. Besides, who could it be? Her parents are long since dead and I got the impression that her sister is no longer around. And if she was still in the area she probably would have wanted to be there to participate in the conversation."

"Maybe her sister has something to hide."

"For Pete sakes, Christie. Let it go! You're beginning to sound a little paranoid. And that's not like you."

XXI

A week after Christie visited Ms. Yamada, Sally attended a professional workshop followed by a luncheon at the Fort Buckner Officer's
Club. She returned to the house around mid-afternoon to find Christie
stretched out on the couch with a damp towel covering her eyes, a George
Shearing album playing quietly in the background, and three empty beer
bottles lined up neatly on the floor between the coffee table and the couch.

Sally stood in the middle of the room trying to decide if she was
sleeping, when Christie lifted one corner of the towel and looked over at
her.

"Hi," Sally said, as she put her book bag down on the footstool and
perched on the arm of a rattan easy chair.

"Hi yourself."

"What's up? Are you feeling okay?"

Christie slowly removed the towel from her eyes and, holding it
between her thumb and forefinger, dropped it onto the floor. After massaging her forehead with the fingers of each hand for a few seconds, she
struggled to a sitting position, and propped herself up against the end of

the couch with her feet tucked under her. Only then did she respond to Sally's question.

"Not particularly."

"What's wrong?"

"Tension headache. That's all. But it's a beaut all right. Long time since I had one like this."

"Downing three bottles of beer isn't going to help your headache, Christie."

"I suppose not," she said, glancing idly around the room.

"What's bothering you?"

"It's all there in that telegram I got from my stepfather," Christie said, waving her hand in the general direction of a paper lying face down on the coffee table.

"Telegram?" Sally said as she got up and walked over to the coffee table. She picked up the message, then looked inquiringly at Christie.

Christie nodded her head up and down slowly. "Go ahead and read it. It affects you almost as much as it does me."

Sally gave her a hard look before reading the message silently to herself. CHRISTIE: REGRET TO REPORT YOUR MOTHER HAD FAIRLY SERIOUS STROKE LATE SATURDAY STOP AFFECTED ONE WHOLE SIDE OF BODY INCLUDING SPEECH STOP ALTHOUGH SHE HAS TROUBLE FORMING WORDS SHE APPEARS TO BE MENTALLY AWARE FOR THE MOST PART STOP WHEN SHE DOES TALK ITS TO ASK FOR YOU STOP ITS CLEAR SHE REALLY MISSES YOU AND NEEDS YOU STOP HATE TO DO THIS TO YOU BUT CAN YOU COME HOME ON FAMILY LEAVE STOP THERE IS NO NEED TO DROP EVERYTHING AND TAKE THE NEXT FLIGHT OUT OF NAHA STOP YOUR MOTHER'S CONDITION IS STABLE STOP LOVE DAD STOP PLEASE CALL ME WHEN YOU GET THIS MESSAGE STOP CAN BE ANY TIME OF DAY.

"Wow! Just what you want to hear. After being on the island for only two months you're looking at another eleven thousand mile trip." Sally dropped the telegram back down on the table and flopped down in a chair across from Christie. Neither spoke for a minute or so. Christie picked up a throw pillow and wrapped her arms around it. "Yep. Just what I need."

"So when did you get the telegram?"

"Just before lunch. Spoiled a good lunch, too."

"Have you talked to Joe Magnuson yet?"

Christie nodded. "I called him."

"What was his reaction?"

Christie hesitated for a moment before answering her question. "He said he thought he could cover my absence for a while with substitute teachers but if it looked as if I was going to be gone for longer than a month it would be best if I submitted my resignation."

Sally was silent for several seconds after that announcement. "He's really bending over backwards to help you out, isn't he?" she finally said.

"Yes. That's for certain," Christie said, as she leaned forward and placed the empty cup on the coffee table. "He's been very helpful during my first several weeks here."

"Have you told Quint yet?"

"No, he wasn't in his office."

A few minutes later, when Christie got up and started walking unsteadily in the direction of the kitchen, Sally cleared her throat a couple times.

Christie stopped in mid-stride and looked over at her. "What?"

"Where are you headed?"

"I need another beer."

"Don't you suppose four beers before dinner are a little much?"

Christie looked longingly in the direction of the refrigerator, then shrugged, turned around and went back and dropped down on the couch. "Okay . . . I suppose you're right."

"Why don't I make you a cup of coffee, Christie?"

"No. Don't like coffee in the afternoon. Just in the morning to start the day," Christie said haltingly.

"I'm going to make you some anyway. You need to sober up. It makes me really nervous to see you this way."

"Why?"

"Because you're supposed to be above all this."

"Above all this? You mean . . . You mean I'm not allowed to act like everyone else and take out my frustrations with a good old fashioned buzz?"

"No, you're not. It's beneath you. It's not dignified!" Sally blurted out, the agitation showing in her voice. "Look, Christie, I'm going to make that coffee, and you're going to drink some. And that's an order," she said, trying to sound stern. "Okay?"

Christie shook her head slowly from side to side. "You shouldn't do that, you know."

"Do what? Order you to drink a cup of coffee?"

"No, no, no, no. I wasn't talking about that. What I mean is that you shouldn't order someone to do something and then turn around a second later and ask them in a wimpy voice if it's okay."

"All right. I take back the wimpy part. You need to sober up, and that's that."

"V-e-r-y good," Christie said, nodding her head approvingly. "That's much better. I'll bet you can get to be a pretty tough cookie with some practice, and me to urge you along, of course," she added, as she flopped back down on the couch. "I sure wish this headache would just go away and leave me alone."

"You just stay here. I'll be back with the coffee in a shake."

"I— I didn't know a coffee milk shake was supposed to help you get rid of a buzz."

"That's not what I said. What I said was . . . oh, never mind! I'll be right back."

"Fine. I fully expect to be here when you come back. Right here," she said, patting the cushion in an exaggerated fashion with one hand.

"Good," Sally said, rolling her eyes and shaking her head as she walked out to the kitchen. Looking back over her shoulder, she added, "By the way, Christie, this was a lot more than a simple buzz. And you know that as well as I do."

—⟶⟵—

Christie made a wry face as she took a last sip of coffee before setting the empty cup down on the end table next to where she was sitting. "Lord, how can anything that smells and tastes so good first thing in the morning taste so yucky later in the day?"

"I don't have any idea. It doesn't make any sense to me," Sally said. "How do you feel now?"

"Physically not much better. Maybe even a little worse. But the fog in my brain seems to have lifted, so I'm seeing things a little more clearly now."

"That's a relief. I really don't like to see you like that," Sally said with feeling.

"Sorry. I'll try and be a good girl from now on."

"Why don't you go and take a quick shower while I figure out what we're going to have for dinner."

Christie nodded and plodded down the hallway to her bedroom while Sally headed into the kitchen.

A short while later, Sally stuck her head into Christie's bedroom and announced there were two Okinawan women at the door who wanted to know if Christie was home.

"Who?" she replied.

"A couple of Okinawan women."

"Did they give their names?"

"I didn't ask them."

"Did you ask them in?" Christie said.

"Of course. They seemed quite nervous about coming in—the older one especially—but I told them you were here and I'd get you. By the way, I have to make a quick run to the commissary. I have something special in mind for dinner, but there are a few things that I need."

"All right," Christie said, as she followed Sally down the hallway and into the living room.

"Ms. Yamada!" Christie exclaimed, "What brings you here?"

"A guilty conscience, Miss Atherton."

Ms. Yamada's cryptic response didn't immediately register, as Christie's attention was immediately drawn to the young Okinawan woman standing next to her. She was probably about twenty, tall and shapely with shoulder-length shiny black hair and really quite beautiful. Although there was something vaguely familiar about her, Christie didn't think she had ever seen her before. She would certainly have remembered someone that striking.

Noticing the direction of Christie's gaze, Ms. Yamada glanced nervously at her companion and said, "This is my . . . a relative of mine. Her name is Miyako."

Christie was uncertain whether to bow or hold out her hand but the young woman didn't hesitate. She held out her hand and said in perfect English, "It is a pleasure to meet you, Miss Atherton."

Again, Christie was struck by a strange feeling of familiarity. Was it possible that she had met her and for some reason didn't recall the occasion? Once again, she dismissed the notion. Perhaps she had seen someone in a magazine who looked like her. This young woman was attractive enough to be a model. *That must be it!* she thought. Satisfied that she had stumbled on the correct explanation, Christie turned her attention back to Ms. Yamada.

"Did I hear you correctly, Ms. Yamada? Did you say something about having a guilty conscience?" Christie asked as she motioned for them to take a seat on the couch.

"Yes, Miss Atherton, that is correct."

"Why is that?"

"There are two reasons. First of all I neglected to give you a keepsake that will be a constant reminder of your father," she said while handing Christie one of her father's dog tags.

Christie glanced down at the information stamped on the dog tag: her father's last name, first and middle initial and blood type. How appropriate she thought: blood type O, the universal donor. But, of course, he wouldn't have been eligible to be a donor because of the malaria and TB.

"What else do you have to tell me?" Christie asked.

Ms. Yamada bowed her head. "Something that may cause you some distress, I am afraid to say," she quietly acknowledged.

"Is it something bad? Something that would make me ashamed of my father?"

"I cannot say for sure, but I hope that is not the case."

Christie sat expectantly, waiting patiently for her guest to shed some light on her enigmatic reply. In the meantime, she noticed that Miyako was staring at her. In fact, although she was trying not to be obvious about it, Christie sensed that the young woman had been staring at her ever since Christie walked into the living room from her bedroom. Not casually, but with an intensity and, with what Christie would almost describe as an air of expectancy. It was a look that one might direct at someone they had not yet met, but whom they had heard about. Christie smiled warmly at her and noted her features more carefully. As she did so, a sudden thought struck her. Although Miyako was clearly Okinawan there was something about her that suggested another ethnic background. *Miyako must be of mixed blood. That would explain her unusual beauty.* Christie remembered the stunning beauty of Caribbean women with mixed ancestry.

Ms. Yamada, after clearing her throat a few times, began to speak, "Do you remember me telling you that I had a sister?"

"Yes. You said she was a nurse who had worked with my father at the refugee camps. I meant to ask what had become of her, but as you know, I was quite upset by the end of our meeting, so forgot to bring it up."

"She moved to Brazil shortly after your father returned to the states."

"Does she still live there?"

"No, she died many years ago."

"I see," Christie said, thoughtfully. "I'm sorry to hear that." Then, as an afterthought, she added, "I would like to have had the opportunity to meet her and talk to her about my father. She must have gotten to know him quite well since they worked together every day."

"Yes, they were very close—very close indeed," Ms. Yamada repeated softly.

Christie was beginning to feel like the one person among a group of people who was ignorant of some important piece of information that everyone else was privy to. She sensed there was more than one level of meaning to Ms. Yamada's comments. Her mind moved back and forth over everything that had been said during the past several minutes. It hovered over the last comment, and then, on a sudden hunch, settled on it.

"Just how close a relationship did my father and your sister have?"

Her guest said nothing for several seconds. She sat unmoving, looking down at her hands. Christie had a distinct feeling that she was wrestling with something that caused her anxiety.

Ms. Yamada finally looked up and met Christie's gaze. "They had fallen in love, Miss. Atherton."

Christie glanced quickly at Miyako and back to Ms. Yamada. For a moment she could think of nothing to say. Various thoughts tumbled around in haphazard fashion. The overriding picture in Christie's mind was of a man being pulled in two opposing directions. His choices were to stay with a woman who reciprocated his love, one who he would probably never be free to marry, or return to a destructive marriage in order to reclaim his young daughter.

Paul Atherton had been a profoundly moral human being. In addition, he was an exceptionally gentle and sensitive man, the type of man who would find such a dilemma impossible to resolve and intolerably burdensome. Christie thought she understood now what had killed him. It was neither the diseases he suffered from nor the strain from the long hours at the refugee camp.

"I am very sorry it turned out the way it did, sorry for your sister, sorry for my father, sorry for me. But I am glad he found happiness with a woman who would love him as he deserved to be loved." *But did she really feel that way? Was she being honest with Ms. Yamada and, more importantly, with herself?*

No one spoke for a few minutes. Christie suddenly wished that these two people would leave so she could be alone with her thoughts and memories, but she didn't want to appear to be rushing them out the door. One last question occurred to her, although she suspected she already knew the answer to it. "Why did your sister move to Brazil? To try and get away from the source of all that emotional pain?"

"That was one reason," Ms. Yamada said, nodding her head. "But there was another reason she needed to leave."

"Oh? And what was that?" Christie asked.

"She was carrying a baby inside her."

"A baby?" Christie repeated, her tone reflecting a mixture of surprise and confusion at this latest revelation. She was about to say 'who's baby?' when her mind made a sudden intuitive leap, and in less time than it takes for one to snap their fingers, the various pieces of the puzzle suddenly fell into place.

She looked over at Miyako with widening eyes. A baby, she thought. A baby who would now be an individual in their early twenties. And the young woman who sat across from her was not only the right age, but reflected the genetic features of two different races. No wonder Miyako had looked so familiar to her. Miyako was her father's daughter. Miyako was . . . Christie's half-sister!

My sister. I have a sister! Her mind momentarily reeled at this latest discovery. As her eyes began watering, she could see through slightly blurred vision that Miyako's were, also. A moment later, her sister came over, sat down next to her, and took Christie's right hand in both of hers. Miyako's voice trembled as she spoke.

"From the time I first realized I had a sister in a faraway land, I wanted nothing more than to meet her and get to know her. Now that we have found each other, I pray that my gods and your Christian God will never separate us again. Do you think that it's all right for me to ask for such a thing or am I being selfish?"

"I think," Christie said, softly, through tear-filled eyes, "that both your gods and my God are very pleased that we have found each other. And I also believe there is someone even more pleased. Someone who is looking down from heaven at this very moment, filled with joy that his prayers have been answered."

Miyako looked up at her sister with shinning eyes. Christie wrapped her arms around her younger sister, and they sat like that for a few minutes, savoring the closeness, while Ms. Yamada sat across from them, wiping her eyes with a handkerchief she had brought along in anticipation of such a moment.

During the next few weeks Christie had to fight feelings of resentment that arose in her mind from time to time, but she quickly quashed them as she realized how unfair it was to her new sister as well as to the memory of her father.

The week before she left for the states Christie took her younger sister shopping. She loved buying clothes for Miyako. They ate at local restaurants and went for a long walk at Moon Beach and Onna Point. One afternoon they took a picnic lunch to Manza Moh, the grass covered plateau on a high bluff overlooking the East China Sea where she and Quint had stopped on their way to Nago. The following afternoon Miyako took Christie on a sightseeing tour of historic ruins in the vicinity of Naha city. Much of the time they simply sat and held hands . . . and laughed . . . and talked . . . and cried. Christie felt like they were like two lovers who had been apart through no fault of their own and had twenty years of experiences to share with one another. On the other hand, since they were sisters and not lovers, there was no need to worry about whether they were saying the right things and making the right impression on each other.

XXII

Office of the Commander of the Corps of Army Engineers, Okinawa District

"I understand your graduate degree is in civil engineering, is that correct Major Brewster?" Colonel Reynolds asked, skipping any preliminary comments and getting right to the main point of the meeting.

"Yes, sir. I have a Masters. But no doctorate as of yet."

"I've been told that your area of concentration was water resource development and management. Is that information also accurate?"

"It is, sir."

"Well, here's the situation, Brewster. Back in 1958, a plan for an Integrated Island-wide Water System was generated and given a stamp of approval by the American Military Command and the U. S. Civil Administration. The Ryukyuan Domestic Water Corporation was the agency created to implement the provisions of the plan. A number of water development projects have been initiated since the establishment of the IIWS including the construction of the Zukeyama dam back in '61. Unfortunately, those efforts amounted to little more than a drop in the bucket—no pun intended. After a few years it became apparent that a Comprehensive Master Plan was needed to identify the actions required to meet the rapidly increasing demands being made upon the available water resources.

"Now, the Okinawa Office of the Corps of Army Engineers has been charged with the responsibility of determining what can be done to alleviate the situation. We're going to be working closely with a couple of professors—one from the Hydrology department of Shibara Institue of Technology and one from the University of the Ryukyus. Unfortunately, our own water resources specialist transferred back to the states several months ago to take an academic post at the University of Arizona, so we don't have anyone currently on staff who can work with the local specialists. My question is this: would you be willing to help out?"

"Yes Sir. I'd be glad to."

"Excellent. Colonel Crane told me that your business at Wing should be wrapped up during the next several days so you would be available to start working with us by the beginning of the following week."

"Yes sir," Quint said, as he stood up, saluted, and turned to leave.

"Just one more thing, Major."

"Sir?"

"I'm very sorry that an unfortunate encounter with a bulldozer has put an end to your flying career. But you may very well have an opportunity with this next assignment to make a more far-reaching contribution than you could possibly make during the course of a lifetime of flying."

"Yes Sir. I'll try and remember that."

Later that day Quint was sitting at the bar at the Naha O Club discussing the news with Rick.

Rick patted his friend on the shoulder. "I always thought you had too much going for you to spend a good chunk of your life in the air. And you always struck me as the type of person that wouldn't be satisfied unless you went on to do research in your field."

Quint nodded. "I have to admit, at times I regretted not going on to do my dissertation."

"So now you're thinking about doing that. Well, good luck my friend. Better you than me." Rick grimaced. "An advanced degree is not exactly my cup of tea. It's bad enough that I have to spend a lot of time reading and interpreting new regs for the old man. There's no way I'd want to be back on the academic scene again. "By the way, I hear that Christie's heading back to the states because her mom is sick. Is that true?"

"Yeah, it is."

"How long will she be gone?"

"Beats me. Several weeks at least."

"That's tough—for both of you."

"Yep. That's for sure."

"I've got to go," Rick said, glancing down at his watch, "Colonel Crane asked me to show the new deputy commander around the base."

"Okay. See you later."

A few days later Quint drove Christie around while she carried out all the necessary errands before leaving the island. After a light lunch they returned to his house and collapsed on his couch in front of the air conditioner.

Christie opened her eyes after a short nap and looked around. Where was she? What place could this be? Then she remembered. She turned her head and looked up at Quint. He was looking down at her with a soft smile on his lips. "Did you take a nap, too?" she asked.

"Uh-uh."

"How long did I sleep for?"

He glanced down at his watch. "About an hour, maybe a little more."

"What time is it, anyway?"

"A little after three."

"Is there something that I can get you?" Quint asked her.

"I am a little thirsty," she admitted, "but don't get up—not just yet, anyway. It's so special to be lying here with you. I don't want to break the spell because I don't know how soon we'll be doing this again."

"I feel the same way," he said, as he shifted into a more comfortable position.

Christie looked over at him, "You're not bored?"

"No. How could I be bored lying on a couch with a beautiful woman in my arms?"

"It's just that you're so active. I thought maybe you'd be getting impatient to get up and start doing something."

"Nope. Anyway, now that you've had some time to digest the fact that you actually have a sister what are your feelings? Good, bad or indifferent?"

"Not indifferent, that's for sure."

"Do you resent her?"

"No, not any more. I have to admit I did at first because I would stew about whether my father would have favored her over me if he had remained on the island. Especially since he had found a woman who could love and appreciate him the way he deserved. But my feelings about Miyako changed pretty quickly. We've spent a lot of time together over the past few weeks."

"That's good because I remember how emotional you got on the beach at Okuma saying how much you had always wanted a younger sister."

"And now I have one!"

"Yep. And she's some doll all right!

"Does that mean I should be jealous?"

"No way."

Quint gently took Christie's cheeks in his hands and smothered her face with kisses. "My beautiful Christie, I know I'm no knight in shining armor but I do promise to try to be everything you could want in a man. I've wanted to tell you before how I really felt about you, but didn't have the guts to do so. I never imagined I could love anyone as much as I do you."

"Quint, those are the words I've been waiting to hear from your lips," she said, flinging her arms around his neck. As their mouths eagerly sought out each other, she shrugged off the bathrobe and tossed it on the floor. Quint rose to a sitting position, then picked her up and carried her into the bedroom. No sooner had he deposited her on the bed than she rose to a kneeling position and began helping him unzip his jeans. When she had worked them down the length of his body, she bent over and used both her tongue and mouth to draw deep moans of ecstasy from Quint's lips. When he could stand it no longer he reached down and gently pushed her back onto the bed, lowering himself on to her. Starting in the hollow of her throat, his lips traced a skin-scorching path down the deep valley between her breasts then gradually began circling the outside of the mounds, climbing towards their crested peaks. Christie moaned with delight as he took the swollen orbs in his mouth, alternately kneading them with his mouth and licking them with his tongue. She gently pushed down on his shoulders, encouraging him in his exploration of her body. Sliding down to her navel, he paused there to nuzzle her briefly before moving on, gradually edging closer to the seat of her femininity.

His day old whiskers caressed her skin like finely graded sandpaper as he buried his face in her thick soft down. Each time Christie felt as though she had reached the ultimate erotic peak, Quint's loving pushed her to yet another dizzying height. When he lowered his mouth to the haven of her womanhood, using his tongue in ways that she had never experienced before, she felt as though he was literally draining her very essence into his mouth, and that nothing would be left of her but an empty shell. But even as she approached the pinnacle of ecstasy, the point beyond which there would be no chance of turning back, of stopping the mad plunge into the turbulent maelstrom of that final shattering moment, Christie still had enough self-control to pull back briefly from the abyss.

Knowing that this was not the way she wanted it to end—not this time—she rolled over and straddled him. Leaning over him with her hands on either side of his head, she looked down at him with an erotic glaze in her eyes as she pushed down against him, taking his fullness inside her. As he thrust upward in response to her downward motion, the rhythmic rocking of her body, simultaneously up and down as well as back and forth, brought her breasts in a swinging, pendulous path that was tantalizingly close to his mouth. In his mounting ardor, he flicked at them as they went by, trying to capture the firm buds as they swung back and forth in an erotic arc just above his mouth. Unable to restrain himself any longer, he reached up with both hands and pushed the mounds together until the marble-hard nipples touched. Taking them into his mouth as one, he began to suck on them with frenzied pleasure.

That was all that Christie needed. She felt herself pushed her over the edge into a dimension where time ceased to exist and sensation replaced thought. Engulfed by a series of explosive waves, she felt for a few numbing seconds that she was drowning in a floodtide of ecstatic sensations from which she would never surface—or would want to surface. Quint, sensing her on the verge of ecstatic fulfillment, allowed himself to follow her over the edge into the bottomless abyss where pure sensation ruled and thought was fragmented and spun off into nothingness. As they both yielded to the liquid fire that threatened to consume them, her cry of release melded with his guttural moans in an erotic duet that frightened Sam and sent him scampering into the kitchen.

Later, when their breathing had finally returned to normal, she looked up from the cradle of his arms and said, "There's still an issue that we need to talk about."

"What issue do you mean?" Quint asked, while he casually stroked her hair with his free hand.

"Come on, Quint, you know what it is."

"Who wants to think about things like issues right now? But I'll tell you what I will talk about," he said, the whimsical tone in his voice making it clear that he was in no mood to start a serious conversation, "let's discuss how many times we can make love during the next eight hours. Which means, of course, that being of an analytic bent, I'll want to apply the scientific method in order to test our assumptions. Repeating such an experiment several times could be somewhat taxing, but then it's all in the interest of advancing our scientific knowledge. What do you say? Are you game for such an effort?"

"Quint, will you please be serious for a minute," Christie said, partially amused and partially exasperated by his silliness.

"But I am being serious. What could be more serious than pushing back the frontiers of science. Of opening yet another door of human knowledge. Why, we may even want to write up the results in the New England Journal of Applied Medicine!"

"The article I have in mind to write would be more appropriate for the Journal of Conflict Resolution," Christie said, interrupting him. "And you're the one who provided most of the material for it. Come on, Quint, admit it: If you hadn't been so damn chauvinistic we wouldn't have any issue to deal with."

"O.K. All right. I give up," he said, reluctantly pulling his jeans back on, "but would you please put my bathrobe back on or do something to cover that luscious body of yours. If you expect me to have a serious conversation, you're going to have to dress for the occasion. I mean, how do you expect anyone to concentrate with a nude goddess reclining next to them."

"I'm flattered, but I see your point, so I'll do as you requested," she said, reaching for his bathrobe as she followed him out into the kitchen.

"How about some leftover coffee?"

"Sure," she said, while rubbing up against him suggestively, "that way I'll be sure and be awake for the next round."

"Next round of what—arguing or lovemaking?"

"Whichever," Christie said teasingly.

"Now who's not being serious," Quint said, frowning down at her as he poured each of them a cup of coffee. "Anyway," he continued, sitting down across from her at the kitchen table, "as far as I can see, there are only a couple of issues that really impact our relationship. With regard to the main one, namely, your contention that I have been more than a little chauvinistic on certain occasions in our relationship to date, I stand guilty as charged. Accordingly, I promise to turn over a new leaf in that area of my life."

"Don't make a promise, Quint, unless it's something you're really going to be able to keep. Choosing to make such a decision is one thing," she said slowly, the underlying doubt evident in her tone, "but can you abide by it, that's the question? From what I've seen so far, it might just be something that's easier said than done."

"Look, I know what I'm committing to and I promise to honor that commitment."

"So you understand," she said, looking him directly in the eyes, "that we either have a fifty-fifty relationship or we have no relationship at all? Furthermore, I expect to see an entirely different attitude when it comes to the Okinawans."

"Yes ma'am," he said, solemnly, reaching across the table and giving her hand a quick squeeze. "I give you my word."

"All right. I do want to believe you, Quint."

"But there's another issue I have to face, Christie. And you know what it is."

"Your career."

"Right. Should I stay in or should I get out. I've been on the horns of a dilemma for months now as to which way I should go." His finger idly traced a path along the parquet pattern on the tabletop as he continued speaking. "I really think that I'd be better off if I resigned my commission and tried to get back into the hydrology field. But I really would like to hear what you think I should do." He glanced over at her, waiting for an answer.

She looked up at him with a quizzical expression on her face. "That's easy to answer. Do whatever you want. I mean it. I think you should do whatever is going to make you happiest—and be truly fulfilling!"

He stared at her for a minute. "You really mean that?"

"Of course I do. Whatever it is you do, I know you'll be a success at it. Besides, I'm not about to try and tell you what to do with your life, after all the complaining I've done about how everyone else tried to direct my life."

"You're the best, my Christie. I can't believe there's another woman like you anywhere in the world. Not for me, anyway!"

She wrinkled her nose at him. "I like to think that's the case."

"So what can I do for you?"

"Stop talking and start making love to me again," she said as she shrugged out of the bathrobe and wrapped her arms around his neck. "Right now!"

ACKNOWLEDGMENTS

I am grateful to Patty Clauser, an old friend, who scrutinized an early draft of my novel, chapter by chapter, with an editor's eye, the end result, of which, was a considerable improvement in plot and character development.

My thanks also to Noel Higgins and Sue Canavan who are professional editors and who were kind enough to review a later version of the novel and who also contributed to the overall quality of the manuscript.

Finally, my special thanks to Mary Dattilo, a published novelist in her own right, and a former editor, who made suggestions that significantly improved the storyline. Among her recommendations were to add some steamy passages to the novel to give it a more modern flavor.

AUTHOR BIO

Welles Brandriff is a native of Connecticut, a graduate of the University of Connecticut, and has an MBA from the University of New Haven. He served for seven years as a USAF officer during the 1960s, the last three years of which were on Okinawa as an Aircraft Maintenance officer. His first novel, *Born to Soar,* was about the WASP pilots of World War II. In his second novel, *A Secret in the Shadows,* he draws upon his experiences on Okinawa and Vietnam. Quint Brewster, the hero of his novel, is based loosely on himself and his role as a maintenance officer for a Wing of C-130s on Naha Air Base on Okinawa.

30983048R00169

Made in the USA
Charleston, SC
01 July 2014